D0803406

3 1232 00110 8424

Cautionary Tales

Cautionary Tales

Chelsea Quinn Yarbro

DOUBLEDAY & COMPANY, INC.
GARDEN CITY, NEW YORK 1978

Acknowledgments

"Everything that Begins with an 'M'" Copyright © David Gerrold 1972; appeared in *Generation*, Dell Books.

"Frog Pond" Copyright © Universal Publishing & Distributing Co., *Galaxy* Magazine, March 1971.

"Un Bel Di" Copyright © Thomas N. Scortia and Chelsea Quinn Yarbro 1973; appeared in *Two Views of Wonder*, edited by Thomas N. Scortia and Chelsea Quinn Yarbro, Ballantine Books.

"Lammas Night" Copyright © Cedric Clute, Jr., and Nicholas Lewin 1976; appeared in *Sleight of Crime* edited by Cedric Clute, Jr., and Nicholas Lewin, Henry Regnery Publisher.

"Into My Own" Copyright © Chelsea Quinn Yarbro 1975; *Planet #1 Tomorrow Today* edited by George Zebrowski, Unity Press, Santa Cruz, California.

"Disturb Not My Slumbering Fair" Copyright © Chelsea Quinn Yarbro 1978.

"The Meaning of the Word" Copyright © Universal Publishing & Distributing Co., 1973; *If* Magazine.

"The Generalissimo's Butterfly" Copyright © Chelsea Quinn Yarbro 1977; appeared in *Dark Sins, Dark Dreams* edited by Barry N. Malzberg and Bill Pronzini, Doubleday & Co., Inc.

"Allies" Copyright © Chelsea Quinn Yarbro 1977; appeared in *Chrysalis* edited by Roy Torgeson, Zebra Books.

"Dead in Irons" Copyright © Chelsea Quinn Yarbro 1976; appeared in *Faster than Light* edited by Jack Dann and George Zebrowski, Harper & Row, 1976.

"Swan Song" Copyright © Chelsea Quinn Yarbro 1978.

"The Fellini Beggar" Copyright © Chelsea Quinn Yarbro 1975; appeared in *Beyond Time* edited by Sandra Ley, Pocket Books.

Library of Congress Cataloging in Publication Data
Yarbro, Chelsea Quinn, 1942–
Cautionary tales.
CONTENTS: Everything that begins with an "M".—Frog pond.—Un bel di.—Lammas night.—Into my own. [etc.]
I. Title.
PZ4.Y25Cau   [PS3575.A7]   813'.5'4
ISBN: 0-385-13145-3
Library of Congress Catalog Card Number 78-3265

1.95

*for all those perspicacious
editors
who bought the stories
in the first place*

Contents

Introduction to
Quinn Yarbro's Stories

It seems to be the fashion, when introducing Quinn Yarbro, to exclaim over the fact that these stories with fangs and claws issue from a young person of gentle and beguiling aspect. One editor went so far as to call her "cuddly." Now it seems to me that we must have passed the stage of assuming that the view of a writer's outside bears some necessary resemblance to the fires burning within. So I am not going into what a darling, dauntless person Quinn is, nor even into the extraordinary life she marshals. I am going into the stories, and they are not—repeat, not—cuddly.

Another thing they are not: If you are looking for the jolly engineering dilemmas of plastic space jocks on the Aldebaran mail run, look elsewhere. You will indeed find a spaceship here, but what goes on among the all-too-real crew of "Dead in Irons" is harsh human shame, a story of innocence compelled to participate in ghastly deeds, able at the end only to strike one lost blow of vengeance. Deftly touched behind the grind of pain is a convincing extrapolation of the star civilization that bore it.

On the other hand, and just to surprise you, Yarbro has given here what is the only merry, even charming tale of After the Holocaust that I can recall: "Frog Pond." And for still another facet, view the curdlingly mundane problems besetting a lady ghoul attempting to gain access to the city morgue, in "Disturb Not My Slumbering Fair." (It should be noted that Yarbro does a brisk business in vampires in another of her many lines of work.)

But for pure alien beauty, remarkably seen through alien eyes, UN BEL DI is quite unforgettable, even apart from the cruelty that is perpetrated there.

Indeed, none of Yarbro's worlds are like any other, although all share the quality of being implied with telling detail rather than panoramically explained. "Into My Own" takes place almost entirely inside an aging playwright in a hospital bed, trying to resign himself to giving up his soul to an organic computer. Conversely, "The Generalissimo's Butterfly" cynically sketches in the whole of a social revolution, pivoting around the scientist who made it possible. The scenario is close to home; it bears chillingly on our own hopes. And as for "Everything that Begins with an 'M' "—well, perhaps it is time to say something about two unifying themes that run through the stories.

The first, which shows up most brilliantly in the fine "Fellini Beggar," is a vision we might call the jewel shining in the rubbish heap: the self-sufficiency of its glory, the magic mystery of beauty and love surviving, however doomed, against all odds. "The Meaning of the Word" conveys this strongly; dying, the hero glories in his long-sought jewel of knowledge. Hers is a morality beyond moralistic reward; the essential goodness of many of her chief characters shows this quality of shining in the charnel house, their very existence its own statement.

As though to make wry fun of this very special vision, the author has taken liberties with it. In "Everything that Begins with an 'M'," the jewel—literally in a rubbish heap—is given a mocking social history and turns out to be—well, read it for yourself.

The second theme, or rather, stylistic sense, of Yarbro's stories has to derive from her talents in opera and music. You will find here many grand scenes, one-on-one confrontations that almost cry out to be sung. Her plots are often not of the ordinary "What happens next?" format, but instead are built around situations in which characters go through deeper and deeper changes, advancing, deceiving, retreating, reminiscing, hiding, bursting out in revelation. One can almost hear the contrapuntal arias, voice rising above voice, while the singers sweep out hieratic gestures. I defy anyone to read "The Fellini Beggar" without audible impressions of the beggar's last triumphant solo.

This is, in short, a rich book, no story like any other. It is in a sense a young book, too; with its great variety of tones and settings one has the feeling that the writer finds so many narrative possibilities unrolling in all directions that it is difficult to stay long with any one. But that is the reader's gain. Enjoy!

James Tiptree, Jr.
McLean,
Virginia

A Word of Caution

For the record, I was born 15 September 1942, in Berkeley, California. My father is Finn; my mother, Italian. I have one younger sister. My husband is Donald Simpson, whose artwork is on display in the Smithsonian Air and Space Museum, among other places. I write serious music as well as stories. I love my work.

My commentary, such as it is, on the stories in this collection come at the end of the story, where you may feel free to ignore it. To paraphrase one of my favorite poets, if the stories are any good, they don't need the commentaries, and if they aren't, the commentaries won't make them any better.

I'm very much indebted to James Tiptree, Jr., for her kind and thoughtful words, as well as her many, many years of stalwart friendship. Also, thanks are due to Sharon Jarvis and Pat LoBrutto, the editors at Doubleday who have worked on this collection with me.

Albany, California

August 1977

Cautionary Tales

EVERYTHING THAT BEGINS WITH AN "M"

Martin was quite mad. He sat by the sand pit with dust in his hair, murmuring a humless hum and rubbing against the wind. He was quite harmless. Have a look at him for yourself. See there? That nebulous man in the rags with the haunted face and the vacant eyes? The one with long bones in him. He pats himself, curls around his legs. That is Martin.

All manner of things have been thought of him. There are those in the town who claim that he was a prophet who had seen the future and it had driven him insane. The idea appeals to the poetry in them. There are also those who insist that he was possessed of a devil. A learned man from the Far Places believes that Martin's soul is on a journey. Whatever they say, it simply confirms his madness.

As is often the case, when someone is wholly unable to appreciate it, the unique comes and sits on his shoulders. Such was the way with Martin.

I do not know how it happened, nor from where the idea came, but there grew a rumor in the town that Martin had been a great man once, with great estates and much knowledge. As the rumor grew it acquired embellishments of a wonderful nature. It was said that he was in fact the true ruler of the land, that those unseen and mistrusted functionaries were impostors.

It began with a piece of paper which had blown down the wind and clung to Martin. As it happened, Martin was able to realize this, and he took the paper and spread it out before him on the ground.

Now, you must know that this sand pit was used to bury the ashes and wastes of the town, so there were often miscellaneous bits of charcoal or vegetable or dung readily available. On this day, as it was just turning to spring, there were a great many bits of wood ash and sharp sticks of charcoal close at hand.

Martin had often dangled his fingers in the sand, making idle swirls and feathery fronds with the tracery of them. But on this occasion he picked up a bit of charcoal and began to draw on the scrap of paper.

Also it happened on this particular day, the tax collector had come to the town, and was stopped at the inn while he went and gathered the payments from the townspeople. He had taken his payments from the poor first, and placed the humble bags of coins and grain in his room and gone to the parlor to have his midday meal. He was served by the landlord, and his meal was the best that might be offered. But the town was poor, the winter had been hard, and the roast was tough.

Do not think the tax collector a hard man. He did not demand better from the landlord, for he knew that what he had was the best. Although the townspeople gave him horns and a forked tail, he was a gentle man who did his job with more than a few qualms. He was kind to birds and dogs and children, and occasionally gave an apple to his horse. This man, then, this tax collector, did not begrudge the tough meat but went on chewing it, doing his best to wash it down with the local ale. While he was chewing and washing down, a largish lump of particularly leathery meat lodged itself in his throat, refusing to go either up or down.

At first the tax collector was mildly annoyed, and then he was anxious. He tried to cough, but it made him choke. His air was cut off badly when the chunk settled on his windpipe. He made an effort to call for help but there was none. He pounded the table with his fists, but he turned from ruddy to blush, and from there to livid. His eyes nearly pushed out of his face while he leaned first forward and then backward, but without result. With a thud that brought the landlord running from the kitchen, he and the chair fell to the floor. Alas, only the chair stood again.

The townspeople quickly heard of what they thought was their good fortune. And it was somehow remarked that at the time the tax collector had died in that most unusual, most unnatural, most arcane manner of death, Martin had been seen drawing something on a piece of paper in the sand pit.

This was taken up by a few who found it suited their preconception of poetic justice. But most refused to believe that Martin would actually draw anything.

At last several of the town worthies trudged out to the sand pit, and coming as near as their noses would allow, leaned over Martin to see if there was any truth to this drawing business.

They drew back, much amazed when they saw that he had indeed been drawing, but now the paper flapped listlessly in his uncaring fingers. One of the bolder and more skeptical finally pulled the paper from Martin's hand, and clutching his trophy, retreated to the waiting crowd.

On the paper, Martin had drawn what appeared to be an irregular pile of ellipses, one very large circle and a great scribble.

Aha! This was seized upon at once. It was the first coherent thing that Martin had produced, and two or three of the more important townsmen said as much.

On this note of pondering and speculation the worthies adjourned to the inn to discuss the disposition of the tax collector's body. There was an attempt, although not a very hearty one, to inter him in the local graveyard. But it was inevitable that he end up in the sand pit.

And there was some attempt at burying the tax collector, so that the riper smells would not disrupt the townspeople. His corpse was heaped with various garbages, and fresh sand was brought from the riverbank. After all, it was the least they could do.

Even with these precautions, there was bound to be some notice paid to the very strange situation of having Martin sighing his madness over the decomposing tax collector. It was a most fertile ground for rumor and conjecture.

There is a work that wearies the body and dulls the mind, that breeds superstition as fast as that body in the sand pit might breed maggots. It rots the intellect. And in towns where food is scarce and pleasure dear, it festers as surely as an open wound.

One afternoon some several days after the incident of the paper and the tax collector, when the slow wind was from a most inopportune quarter, a child came running into the square of the town, in tears that neared hysteria, claiming that she had seen Martin walking on the road dressed in silks and velvet. This was soon known to all, and much thought on.

In point of fact, the girl had seen Martin walking, but not on the road. He had risen to search out a better place to lie, where the wind was less fulsome. As to the silks and jewels, the velvets and ermine that had been attributed to him in ever more exaggerated terms, why, he had taken the tattered cloth from a dustman's bag in a moment of what might have been inspiration but was more probably chill.

Again the pilgrimage was made to the sand pit, where both Martin and the tax collector were in evidence to varying degrees. The towns-people stopped and regarded the scene. There was the madman with his halo of sand about him, and a tattered cloth. There in the pit was litter of every type, and part of a left hand with the index finger—more accurately what was left of an index finger—pointing at Martin.

When this was seen and appreciated, there was great unrest. Surely there was significance in it. There must be forces and powers at work here, great unseen creatures hovering over the place.

It did not occur to any of them that they were a small starving village, the last outpost on the edge of desolation, neglected by satrap and renegade alike. No one wondered that perhaps the powers that move the stars would be wholly uninterested in the vagaries of their sand pit.

They had their proof in Martin's paper; it assured them of their intimate association with the marvelous. From that time on, there was no peace for them, no quiet. And they plunged into it with relish.

A woman screamed in the night, claiming that Martin had come before her in a cape of gold with a crown in his hands. This was important, it was agreed, because it indicated that he did not have the position to which he was entitled.

Soon after, a dog who had been digging in the sand pit died in convulsive agony. By this time the whole village was aware that Martin was responsible. True, they could not agree as to whether he was protecting the tax collector's remains or authorizing some postmortem vengeance, but that was not the issue. There were mysteries here.

Then the great sturdy blacksmith came with the news that he had heard Martin mention cups in his rambling song. Cups and tea. The sage from the Far Lands who had come to the town on the edge of desolation to be as close to his home as he would ever be again remarked that he could not be sure, but perhaps there had been words of a sort in Martin's sleep, but that the questions were of a nature more profound than he could understand. When pressed, he reluctantly revealed a garbled statement on winged pigs, kings, and the boiling of great bodies of water.

One of the company, the worthy who served as town judge, stated he thought Martin was a mighty alchemist who had been trapped by the demon he had called up.

Again the wind bore to them whiffs of the sand pit. It was agreed then that, come tomorrow there would be a general inquiry into the portentous doings in the sand pit.

Sure enough, in the morning the townspeople met at the pit, the men in full regalia, the women as dressed as would ever be allowed.

Martin sat as he always had, on the sand, the filaments of his hair wrapped across his head, sliding into his distant eyes. There had been a sparse rain, and the shreds of cloth around him were still damp. He faced toward the center of the great mound, unblinking.

What caprice there is in chance. The sky pried open the clouds that scudded over the town long enough to let a trickle of sunlight through. For a matter of seconds there was light bright and true. It shone with a radiance that contrasted the squalor around the townspeople. The light fell on Martin alone. It lingered over him like a kiss, and then was gone, and the day was bleaker than before.

But, oh, the change that had occurred. There were those in the town that would swear to you today that there were jinns and angels in the light, that there were great wings whistling over the sand pit. One or two will admit that they did not actually see it for themselves, but know it to be true. And truth, after all, is what we agree it is.

There was a moment after the sunlight when nobody spoke, when the wind alone blended with the music Martin made. Then several rushed forward, throwing themselves down before the gentle vacant lunatic, sobbing, begging for a fulfillment that seemed so illusively near.

Slowly they all came forward, each bearing in his heart the yearning for something, anything, that would give him a sense of reason.

In the afternoon Martin was brought a cloak of the finest wool in the village. It was placed about his shoulders with great care and ceremony. And if he did not accept it, he did nothing that would be thought of as rejection.

See? The holy man is beyond such things. He is in the clouds communing with the wind. He is free of the earth. By that they mean that he was not filled with the toil they endured all the days they lived. In this they were quite right.

The next day he was reverently brought a crown. It was not much of a crown. Made of wood that had been painted with a paste of saffron, it was grotesque and sat before him like an ungainly crow's nest. Yet for a moment his eyes passed it and seemed to pause before continuing over the sand pit.

Realizing that Martin was a holy man, and not part of worldly things, all efforts to change his chosen living place were disregarded. It was recognized that he had gone beyond that need. But there were many housewives who would find a way to put a bit of braised meat in the bucket bound for the sand pit.

It was found that Martin would listen to any townsman about anything. He would sit with his crown in front of him, his eyes wandering, and hear whatever was said to him. If he remained unmoved, it was because he was a man more advanced, a man who had soared with angels. Most who went to the sand pit came away with bewilderment; a few garnered tranquillity.

Had the first visitor to the town been anyone but an officer come to investigate the disappearance of the tax collector, the fame of Martin might have spread. As it turned out, it was an officer, and the hand of the law came to rest heavily on the shoulder of the little town.

Goods were confiscated, money seized. The innkeeper was taken away to a murky doom. In some instances children joined Martin on the sand pit in their search for food, and tribulation was upon them.

So it was that Martin became neglected. He was still regarded as strangely powerful, but there were those who hinted that it was Martin who had brought on the disaster. These were balanced by those who claimed that it was the body of the tax collector who had brought the trouble. The latter were fully correct, but not for the reason they believed.

The demands of work closed in, taking its toll in the drudgery and boredom it brought to the townspeople. There was little time to contemplate the dancing of angels.

However, the dying flame managed a last flicker. It happened this way: While walking home, the blacksmith was passing the sand pit when he noticed that Martin was moving. This being unusual and certainly indicative of another change of order, he approached the pit hoping to observe the madman.

He was squatting in the dust, beating a pattern on it with what appeared to be a stick but proved to be a shinbone.

The blacksmith fled, eyes white all around the dilated pupil. He careened into town, arms flailing, to gasp out his story. This time only a few dared return to witness this most bizarre spectacle.

They stood a way off from the place, wondering, each knowing a terror indefinable, and then they too fled the place.

After that the sand pit was shunned. Even the old sage from the Far Lands did not go near it. Dark whispers hinted at things monstrous. Gradually it came to be believed that Martin had entered into a battle with demons so fierce that the sand pit had been imbued with the evil presences. All wept for the holy man, but none would go to him. It was known that he was of a higher order of things and would not be able to make use of their puny human strengths.

They seemed to be well borne out, for there came a day, a day of rare and crystalline sunshine, when the wind blew from purer places to clean the reek of sand pit and desolation from the town, when a few incautious souls went to the edge of that pit. There was no one there. Nothing remained of Martin but the woebegone crown that had been given to him in their confused turmoil of love. This was taken up and brought back to the town, where the worthies pondered it.

Finally it was decided that Martin had emerged from his fight triumphant and would be even now in the company of the good and blessed powers that had converged on the village.

Almost everyone was satisfied with that solution. It fit well into the scheme of things; it completed the adventure in noble unity. As for those few dissenters—those who had lost the feel for wonder, who insisted that Martin had either wandered away in the company of his madness and his song or starved to death—they were ignored.

Even to this day there are a few who insist that there is a special air over the abandoned sand pit, but there is only hearsay evidence to present, and I wouldn't believe a word of it.

about "Everything that Begins with an 'M' "

This is a very early story, written in my first professional year. David Gerrold bought it for his anthology *Generation*, and until now it has not been reprinted.

The title comes from *Alice in Wonderland*, specifically from the Dormouse's Tale during the Mad Tea Party. When I began to write the story, which I did in one sitting, I had only the title and the first line. Everything else burbled up from the unconscious.

In general I don't like to write that way. Usually I have a pretty solid idea what a story is and where it is going by the time I sit down to put it on paper. In the case of novels, I have outlines to guide me (from which I only occasionally depart). With shorter works I often have notes or a couple of pages of what I call sketches. Then I take the thing through two drafts and either it gells or it doesn't. In most cases, if it gets to the actual draft stage, it will gell.

But this little tale was different. It has certain Dunsanylike resonances, I think, and a touch of the psychic claustrophobia that boredom creates. And then again, maybe it doesn't.

FROG POND

No matter what Mr. Thompson said, it was a good day for frogging and fishing. The morning sun had that bright double halo that meant the whole day would be clear. I got up before Mom, took some old pie from where she hid it last night, grabbed my wading shoes and net and lit out for the creek. I had to leave real quiet. I'm not supposed to be going down to the creek any more. They say it's dangerous down there.

But the creek ain't dangerous if you know what you're doing. You just have to stay away from pink water spots and you're safe all the way.

I took the long way around the Baxter place. I think Pop was right about them; something's wrong there. Dr. Baxter ain't been at Town Meeting for a long time—Pop thinks that maybe some sick people moved in on the Baxters.

So I walked through the brambles on the edge of the woods where the new trees are growing. It was sunny and fine and the breeze came in nice and sweet from the north. No cities up that way, not for hundreds of miles.

Caught some crickets along the way, the big kind with the long wings. They make good bait for the stickery fish in the shallows. All I got to do is tangle them up in the net and put it down in the water. The stickery fish go right for 'em. Mr. Thompson, he says that it ain't safe to eat 'em, which just shows you how much he knows. I eat 'em all the time.

I headed right for Rotten Log Hollow. There's a nice big hole in there and a gravel bar and you can catch lots of frogs there if you're careful. They like to hide under that old broken pipe, under the foam. I got maybe a dozen there, last time out.

First I walked along the bank, looking down into the water to see what was there, you know. It was still and there wasn't a lot of foam piling up. There wasn't any fish either, so I sat down in the warm gravel, ate my pie, and pulled on my wading shoes. They've got high tops that Pop always tells me to pull all the way up, but I ain't bothered with that for years. Heck, a little water can't kill me.

After a little while I went into the water real cautious—careful not to scare the frogs. I worked my way out into midstream and started peering around for frogs. I had my net in my belt but I don't use it much—not for frogs.

So there I was in the creek, careful as could be, when all of a sudden this bunch of rocks and grass comes rolling down the bank and this city fellow comes down after it, trying to grab hold of bushes on the way. He hit the pipe and it stopped him, but he sure messed up the water.

A couple of minutes went by and he started to get up. He had a heck of a time doing it. He kept flailing his arms around and pulling himself back onto the pipe.

I was mad because he'd scared the frogs, so I yelled out, "Hey, mister, don't do that!"

Boy, did he look up fast. You'd of thought I was a C.D. man or something the way he snapped around. His eyes got wild and he shook all over. Before he could fall again I called out. "It's just me, mister, down in the creek."

He turned around, grabbing the pipe for balance. I waited till he'd steadied himself and then I said, "You're scaring the frogs."

"Scaring the frogs?" he yelled back, sounding like frogs were monsters.

"Yeah, I'm trying to catch some. Can you just sit there a minute?"

I could see he was thinking this over. Finally he sat back on the pipe like he was worn out and said real quiet, "Why not?" And he leaned his head back and closed his eyes.

I got three frogs while he was sleeping there. They were big and fat. I put a stick through their throats and let 'em dangle in the creek to keep fresh. I almost had the fourth one when the city guy woke up.

"Listen," he called to me. "Where am I?"

"Rotten Log Hollow."

"Where is that?"

I sure couldn't see the point in yelling all the time, so I told him to come closer and we could talk. "Talk makes less noise. Maybe I can still catch some frogs if we're just talking."

He hustled off the pipe and scrambled along the shore, splashing dirt and stones into the water.

"Hi," I said when he got closer.

"Hello." He was still awful nervous and had that funny white look around his eyes, sort of like turtle skin. "What's your name?"

He was really trying to be friendly and even if Mr. Thompson says in that spooly voice of his that there ain't any friendly strangers, well, this guy wasn't anything I couldn't handle.

"My name is Althea," I told him, polite like Mom tells me to be. "But mostly my friends call me Thorny. Who are you?"

"Uh—" He looked around then back. "Stan!—Stan—just call me Stan."

You could see that he was lying. He wasn't even good at it. So I said, sure, his name was Stan. Then I waited for him to say something.

"You like this place?" he asked.

"Yeah. I come here lots of times."

"You live around here, then?"

A dumb question. He was really all city. Maybe he thought we had subways out here in the country. He kept looking around like he expected a whole herd of people to come running out of the pipe.

"Yeah, I live at the Baxter place." It was a lie but he'd told me one—and besides, Pop said I wasn't to tell people where we live, just in case.

"Where's that?" He said it like he wasn't really interested, like he didn't give a damn where the Baxter place was. He just wanted to talk to someone. I pointed back toward the Baxter place and told him it was about a mile along the road.

"Do a lot of people live there, at the Baxter place?"

"Not too many. About six or seven. You planning on moving in, mister?"

He laughed at that. It was one of those high laughs that sounds like crying. My brother Davey cries like that a lot. It ain't right a six-year-old kid should cry like that. About this Stan—or whoever—I didn't know.

"What's funny, mister?" I would have gone and left him there, but I saw that he was standing almost in some green gunk that comes out of the pipe and washes on shore so I said to him a little louder, "And you better get away from there."

He stopped laughing. "From where? Why?"

Wow, he was nervous.

"From that." I pointed so he would not get panicked again. "That stuff is bad for you. It can give you burns if you're not used to it." That isn't quite right. Some people can't get used to it, but it never burned me, not even the first time. Mr. Thompson says that means selective mutations are adapting to the new demands of the environment. Mr. Thompson thinks that just because he's a geneticist he knows everything.

Stan leaped away from the green stuff like it was about to bite him.

"What is it?"

"I don't know. Just stuff that comes out of the pipe. When the Santa Rosa pumping station got blown up a couple of years back, this broke and started dripping that green stuff." I shrugged. "It won't hurt you if you don't touch it." Stan looked like he was going to start laughing again, so I said, real quick, "I bet you're from Santa Rosa, huh?"

"Santa Rosa? What makes you think that?" He sure got jumpy if you asked him anything.

"Nothing. Santa Rosa's the first big city south of here. I just figured you probably had to come from there. Or maybe Sonoma or Napa, but those ain't too likely."

"Why do you say that?" He was real close now and his hands were balling into fists.

"Simple," I said, trying to keep my eyes off his fists. He must have been sick or something, the way he kept tightening and loosening his fingers. "The big highway north is still open, but not the one between Sonoma and Santa Rosa."

He wobbled his head up and down at that. "Yes, yes of course. That would be why." He looked at me, letting his hands open up again. I was glad to see that. "Sorry, Thorny. I guess I'm jumpier than I thought."

"That's okay," I told him. I didn't want to set him off again.

So Stan stood back and watched me while I looked for frogs.

After a while he asked me, "Is there anyone needing some help on their farms around here? Anyone you know of?"

I said no.

"Maybe there's a school somewhere that needs a teacher. Unless I miss my guess I could teach a few things. You kids probably don't have too many good teachers."

What a spooly thing to say. "My Pop teaches at the high school. Maybe he could help you find work." We didn't need teachers, but if Stan knew about teaching, maybe one of the other towns could use him.

"Were you born around here?" Stan was looking around the hollow like anyone's having been born here was real special and unlikely.

"Nope. Over at Davis." That was where Pop had been doing the research into plant viruses, before he and the Baxters and the Thompsons and the Wainwrights and the Aumendsens and the Leventhals bought this place here.

"On a farm?"

"Sort of."

His voice sounded like being born on a farm was something great like saving the seaweed or maybe going back to the moon some day.

"I've always wanted to live in the country. Maybe now I can." He stumbled along the bank to the sandy spot opposite the gravel bar and sat down. Boy, he was really dumb.

"There's snakes there," I said, real gentle. Sure enough, up he shot, squealing like Mrs. Wainwright's pig.

"They won't hurt you. Just watch out for them. They only bite if you hurt 'em or scare 'em."

And with him jumping up and down I wasn't going to get any more frogs, that was for sure. So I decided to settle just for conversation.

"Is any place safe in this bank?" he asked.

"Sure," I said with a smile. "Right where you were sitting. Just keep an eye out for the snakes. They're about two feet long and sort of red. About the color of those pine needles." I pointed up the bank. "Like that."

"Dear God. How long have the pine needles been that way?"

I slogged over into the deep water. "About the last five, six years. The smog does it."

"Smog?" He gave me a real blank look. "There isn't any smog here."

"Can't see it or even smell it. Mr. Thompson says there's too much of it everywhere, so we can't tell it's there any more. But the trees know it. That's why they turn that color."

"But they'll die," he said. He sounded real upset.

"Maybe. Maybe they'll change."

"How can they? This is terrible."

"Well, the pines are holding up. Most of the redwoods south of the Navarro River died years ago. Lots of them are still standing," I explained, seeing him go blank again. "But they aren't alive any more. But the pines here, they haven't died yet and maybe they aren't going to." A real sharp shine was coming into his eyes and I knew I had said more than I should have. I tried to cover up as best as I could. "We learn about this in school. They say we'll have to find ways to handle all the trouble when we grow up. Mr. Thompson tells us about biology." That last part was true, at least.

"Biology. At your age."

That kind of talk can still make me mad. "Look, mister, I'm thirteen years old, and that's plenty old to know about biology. And chemistry, too. Just because this is a long way from Santa Rosa, don't think we can't read or like that."

I was really angry. I know I'm little, but, heck, lots of people are small now.

"I didn't mean anything. I was just surprised that you have such good schools here." Boy, that Stan really couldn't lie at all.

"What do they teach where you come from?" I knew that might make him jumpy again, but I wanted to get back at him for that.

"Nothing important. They teach history and language and art with no emphasis on survival. Why, when some of the students last semester requested that the administration include courses in things like forestry, basket making and plant grafting, they called out the C.D. and there was a riot. One of the C.D."— Stan licked his lips in an odd way—"was ambushed and left hanging from a lamppost by his heels."

"That's bad," I said. It was, too. That was the first time I found out how bad it had got in the cities. Stan was still smiling when he told me what had been done to the C.D. It wasn't nice to hear. He kept trying to make it better by calling it gelding. He said that the last time they did it was during the black-white trouble.

And that guy wanted to teach in our schools. He said that he knew what it was really like with people all over and could contribute to our system. I could see Pop's face getting real set and hard at what Stan was saying. But Stan insisted he thought that it was very important for people to understand "The System"—like it was a religious thing. You know? I was beginning to get scared.

"Thirteen is too old," he went on. "Do you have any brothers or sisters younger than yourself?"

I was pretty cautious about answering him. "Yes. I got two brothers. And one sister." I didn't tell him that Jamie was already doing research work or that Davey didn't do anything. Or that Lisa was getting ready to board in the next town so that we could keep the families from interbreeding too much.

"Older or younger."

"Mostly older." So I lied again. At least I was good at it. He didn't think to ask anything more about them.

"Too bad. We are going to have to change what's been happening. Martial law, searches without warrants, confiscations. It's terrible, Thorny, terrible."

He must have thought that living out here we didn't hear anything or see anything. He kept telling me how bad it was to have soldiers everywhere and how they were doing awful things. I knew about that and a lot of other things, too. And I knew about how there were gangs that killed people and robbed them—and murder clubs that just killed people for fun. Heck, Jules Leventhal used to be a clinical psychologist and he taught us a lot about the way mobs act and how too many people make problems for everybody.

"How are things north of here?" Stan was asking.

"Not too bad. Humboldt County is doing pretty good and there are more people around the Klamath River now." I sure didn't want a guy like him staying with us. I figured that maybe telling him about conditions up north might encourage him to move on. But he just looked tense and nodded, like that crazy preacher who wanted us all to die for God, a couple of years back. "Of course, that's redwood country, so they might have trouble there in a few years."

He looked at me real hard. "Thorny, do you think you could tell me how to get to Humboldt county?"

Dumb, dumb, I told you. All he had to do is keep going up old 101 and there it would be. That crazy guy hadn't even looked at a map. Or else he had and was trying to trap me, but I ain't easy to trap.

"You can keep going up the main highway," I said, talking real sincerelike. "But there might be C.D. men up ahead, you know, near Ukiah. Or Willits. The best way is to cut over to the coast and just follow it up."

There, I thought. That ought to get him; he was jumpy enough before.

"Yes, yes, that would work. And Eureka is a port—there would be the ocean for access—"

He went on like that for about five minutes. He wanted to launch some kind of attack against The System, to protect the People, but for another System. He kept talking about rights and saying how he knew what the People really wanted and he would change things so that they could have it. He said he knew what was best for them. Wow, I wish Mr. Leventhal could have heard him.

"And what about you? You should be in school, right?"

"Nope," I said. "We have school just two days in the week. The rest of the time is free."

I wondered if that much had been all right to tell. We weren't supposed to let out much about our school.

"But it's a waste, don't you see?" Stan crouched down on the bank, looking like a huge skinny rabbit squatting there. "This is the time when you must learn political philosophy. You should be learning about how society works. It's terribly important."

"I know how society works," I said.

Heck, all the kids who learned from Mr. Wainwright know about that. After all, one of the reasons the Wainwrights came along with the rest of us was that the politicians in Sacramento didn't like what he was teaching about the way *they* worked. And they were society.

"Not this society," he said in a real haughty way, like Mr. Thompson when he's crossed. "Society in the cities, in the population centers."

He was going on that way when I saw a couple of frogs moving on the bottom. I watched where they were going and then I reached down for them, holding my breath as my face hit the water. I dragged one of them out but the other got away.

"Spending your time catching frogs," Stan spat.

"Sure. They taste real good. Mom fixes 'em up with batter and fries 'em."

"You mean you eat them?" he squeaked, looking gray.

"Of course. They're meat ain't they?" I waded over to the other frogs on the stick and stuck the new one on, too. He wiggled and jerked for a bit and then stopped.

"But frogs? How can you eat frogs?"

"Easy." I didn't think he was going to get over it: that we eat frogs. Just to be sure, I reached over and grabbed the stick with the frogs on it. "See? This one"—I put my thumb on one's belly—"is the fattest. It'll taste real good."

"And do you really chase after them without seeing them?"

I turned around and looked at him. He was standing up on the other bank and the frightened look was back in his eye. "No. You got to see what you're after."

"But in that water—"

"Oh, I don't open my eyes like you do," I said, real casual-like. "I go after them with these." And I slid up the membranes.

Stan looked like he'd swallowed a salamander. "What was that?" he demanded, looking more scared than ever.

"Nictitating membranes—I was engineered for it," I said.

"Mutants," he gibbered. "Already!"

He started trying to back up the bank watching me like he thought I was a werewolf or something. He slipped and stumbled until he got to the top and then he ran away—I could hear him crashing through the brush making more noise than a herd of deer.

By the time he left, the whole hole was filled with leaves and sticks and rocks and I knew that there wouldn't be any more frogs or fish that day, so I took the frogs on the stick, got off my wading shoes, and started back for the house. I knew Mom would be mad but I was hoping that the frogs would help her get over it. I guessed I had to tell them about Stan. They didn't like people coming here.

They were real mad about it. The funny thing is that they were maddest about my having shown my eyes. But cripes, that was just one little flap of skin that Mr. Thompson got us to breed. Just one lousy bit of extra skin near the eye.

But to hear him tell it, you'd think he'd changed the whole world.

about "Frog Pond"

About a year ago I had the dubious pleasure of reading a paper about "Frog Pond" that had been published in a small, very academic magazine. It was full of comments on "developing parallel imagery" and the "equation of contaminated water with the contamination of the world" and so forth. The earnest young PhD. discussed at length the strange feeling of this far future setting. But "Frog Pond" takes place roughly around the year 2000, which is relatively near future. There was also a great deal of analysis in the paper about the ironic significance of the place names in the story. What irony? Get a map of California and you can find every location mentioned in the story. And please, no more papers.

Thorny grew up, in a later story and novel. She became Thea in *False Dawn.*

UN BEL DI

As his terrifying smile widened the Janif Undersecretary watched the procession of Papi wind its way up the far side of the valley. "They're like fine children, perfect children, every one of them." The Undersecretary licked his outer lips; it was a furtive darting movement. "So sad they aren't truly intelligent. If they were . . ." He broke off. If they were . . .

His companion almost put a hasty hand on the Undersecretary's auxiliary arm. "We are still in doubt about that here. We have not run many tests yet. They might have greater potential than we know." The Ambassador made a weak gesture of apology.

Undersecretary Navbe waved him away in an offended manner. "Certainly, certainly. Keep your ambassadorial pride. I myself look for signs of genius in my pets. You are free to do the same."

Instead of the accepted answer the Ambassador raised a primary arm slowly and remained rigidly silent. He then bowed with maddening propriety to the lengthening shadows.

The Undersecretary closed the screen, stepping back with a gesture of regret. It was a great pity that he had to be so very isolated. And the Ambassador was just as bad as the others of his status. He would be tolerant to absurdity of the locals, then become unyielding and moralistic with the others of his kind. Navbe had seen it often in his post and bitterly rued having to deal with such perversity.

But the Ambassador was speaking. ". . . for the Papi, in this instance. You will want to observe them while you are here, Undersecretary."

Privately the Janif Undersecretary thought this a lamentable state of affairs. "Of course. I look forward to it," he said.

"This is quite a unique place," continued the Ambassador, warming to his subject.

They all are, thought Navbe.

"We've found not only that the Papi have a highly developed social order, but that they surgically alter their young to fulfill specific cultural functions." Here the Ambassador hesitated.

"Oh?" Navbe managed the illusion of polite interest.

"Yes. They can make truly amazing changes. Each of the modifications has a definite place in the culture, although a couple are odd, dependent creatures."

"They can actually do this?" Navbe asked lazily.

"It appears so," answered the Ambassador cautiously.

"Before or after birth. How?" Under his meticulous exterior Navbe felt a deep elation. Perhaps his temporary exile would not be as terrible as he had feared it might be. There could be great solace here after a few special arrangements.

"I am sorry to say that we have not yet discovered their reproductive mechanism. They are probably ovoviviparous." He moved uncomfortably, knowing how far he had stepped beyond the bounds of allowable ceremony. It was also a blot to his record that he knew so little about the people he lived with.

At this Klin Navbe all but laughed. So there was a mystery, was there? That made for a challenge. And this sniveling diplomat had not found it out. "Probably?" He was scornful, but not so much as to discourage the Ambassador from talking. As all others of his status, Navbe despised the Representative status. Yet there was a chance that his host knew the reason for his temporary exile, and he dared not put himself in a compromising position with such a person.

"As I have told you, we cannot do the tests. We lack the full authorization to do so. I do not know how we shall function if we are not properly authorized."

"Precisely." What was this fool's familial name? Lesh? Yes, Ambassador Lesh. He wanted the authority to proceed with tests and Navbe could give him that authorization. Plans blossomed in his mind.

It was perhaps fortunate that the Meditation Bell rang the summons to the Third Cycle just then, it provided cover for the awkwardness between the two officials. Their Janif formality asserted itself, and they strode silently down the hall together.

When they had completed their ritual exercises, Navbe put Ambassador Lesh at his ease with that age-old question beloved of off-planet Janif officialdom: "How did you come to serve on Papill, Ambassador?" And he masked his boredom at the too-familiar tale of a diplomat's career.

In the long twilight the two Janif sat together on the terrace listening to the distant Night Song of the Papi. In the valley below Ambassador Lesh's estates the waning light shifted, slid, and was gone, and the soft white fogs followed the shadows to wrap the valley in sleep. On the ridges the tasseled, angular trees sighed in the wind, their hard thin leaves clicking endlessly above the fog.

"A beautiful place, Lesh, even with just the two stars. It is like a children's story." Navbe watched the valley's soft change, dreaming absently of violated children and the strange Papi, intense pleasure hidden in the formal set of his face. He had picked a flower and was stroking it with the extending sensors of his thumbs. "You are to be envied, Ambassador—to be surrounded by all this loveliness."

"I have thought so myself," said the Ambassador in an unbecoming burst of familiarity.

Navbe ignored the solecism. "And the Papi are such pretty people. So delicate. Not like those creatures on Tlala or Isnine. You have beauty here, and tractable natives."

The Ambassador, lulled by the Undersecretary's flow of remarkable condescensions and innocuous questions, was betrayed into elaborating on the Papi. "They are a gentle people. It is of great importance to them that they bring delight to their neighbors. It is unfortunate that they do not recognize the laxness of their social order, but their errors are charming. They have made almost a religion of their kindness. Over the years I have observed their spirit of self-sacrifice." He became aware of his blunder. "But it is nearly impossible to take advantage of them. They know their own order." His confusion led him to a further mistake and he showed his primary hands as he shifted position.

Irritated, Navbe wondered how many more insults he would have to endure at the hands of Ambassador Lesh. He savagely desired to humiliate his host, but he wanted information more so he forced himself to respond with calculated ease: "Certainly, to see the Papi is to want to protect them from abuse. They must be greatly in your debt."

"Not at all," Lesh said hastily, looking wretched.

Navbe flung back both pair of arms in his best offensive manner.

"You must not fear me, Ambassador Lesh. Surely you know the Judiciate would not have allowed me to come here if they had found any real basis to the scandal. But such talk, especially about High officials, is dangerous. I have willingly elected to leave Jan to come here in order to allow the tale to be forgotten."

The Ambassador twitched uncertainly. He had heard tales of the Undersecretary's strange perversions, but was loath to ask about them. Even to admit he had heard the rumors would be more shame than he would deliberately bring on himself.

"Come, come, you must not be afraid. You have heard something of me caught alone with the children of Sub-council Hariv. No, you needn't deny it. The grosser strata, disobeying every Janif law, have repeated the story, elaborating and embellishing it, if the versions I have heard are indicative. That I have been allowed to see the children is true, and I am fully aware of the honor done me in this, but how, in a High House, would I have obtained that access to the completely sequestered offspring of such an official? Only think of the obstacles and be reasonable." It had been difficult to get to them, but Navbe was well-aware that the task was not as difficult as the public had been led to believe.

The Ambassador knew about the guarding of High children, and he wavered. "They did speak of bribes and extortion . . ." It was a terrible breach of courtesy, even to mention it, but he was too deeply involved to deny his knowledge.

The Undersecretary bit out a laugh. "What man of Sub-council Hariv's stature would have such servants around him? He would never tolerate so low a status to enter his House. How do high status servants behave? Bribes are out of the question." That much, at least, was correct.

"I hadn't considered . . ."

Navbe remembered how very long it had taken for him to find his accomplice, one who shared his need to use the young bodies for cruel pleasure. How delicate the maneuvering had been, and how quickly the problem had been solved when he had discovered the night hand-servant to be addicted to Unjy. Then it had been easy. All the careful searching, the obtuse questioning, the days of painstaking effort had been worth it. He could recall the tearing of the flesh when his antlers touched it, the smell of the soft inner tissues when he fingered them . . .

"Yes, I had not thought of that. With such talk rife in the lower strata, the honor of high status servants would be impugned. It is no wonder you chose to disassociate yourself from such improper conduct."

"So you see," Navbe said expansively if vaguely.

The Ambassador was painfully relieved. He settled back in the soft cushions and offered the Undersecretary another dish of Merui. Navbe accepted it with a skilled blend of humility and contempt.

All the Papi that waited at the gates looked uniformly young to Navbe. They all had the serene, childlike faces and downy antlers that marked Janif children, made more attractive by huge violet eyes. Their clothes were a soft, clinging fabric that Navbe longed to fondle.

"We bring you the morning, you who are new among us," the Papi said in chorus. "We have come to welcome the new Janif visitor and to beg him to visit us in our houses."

The Ambassador stole a warning look at the Undersecretary, but Navbe was far too careful to be so carelessly trapped. "It will give me much honor to walk with you one sundown," he said with a slight bow in the proper ritual intonation.

The soft garments moved in the wind, and the Papi were outlined in their clothes, naked to Navbe. His thumb sensors stirred urgently. "It is close to the First Meal, and I wish you nourishment."

The Papi were obviously happy with him. They rustled among themselves, whispering in their chantlike speech.

Then a Papi, whom Ambassador Lesh had identified as the local leader, came forward with his offering of three finely wrought platters. Each was covered with squares of the fascinating cloth. "A gift for you," he said to the Janif with an acceptable show of respect. "It is our delight to bring these few things to you, in the hopes they might please you."

Navbe had studied this part of the ritual the night before, and was able to respond without noticeable hesitation. "Here are three rare things; but the light in the valley and the mist ensnared in a tree are rarer." He touched each of the platters without removing the cloths. "I will value the gifts as they are valued by the givers."

The Papi and Ambassador Lesh regarded him with approval, although Lesh's look was tinged with relief. "You will be welcome among us at any sundown," said the Papi spokesman. "I am known as Nara-Lim. This one is Tsu-Lim and this one is Ser-Tas." He did not introduce the others, to Navbe's delight. Apparently only the platter-bearers had that distinction. Navbe approved of that, the recognition of status. Ambassador Lesh had told him that Lim and Tas were thought to be titles, which revealed the extent to which he had deluded himself about the Papi's intelligence potential. Titles among those who lived as the Papi did would be ludicrous.

The platter-bearers put their offerings on the steps, then went ceremoniously to the rear of the group. Nara-Lim touched each of the platters and then he, too, went to the rear of the group.

"I am honored by Nara-Lim and his generous companions." And Navbe turned, walking slowly up the steps at the gateway.

Behind him, the gentle, fragile Papi waited until the gates were closed before they left the Ambassador's estates.

"That was well done," Lesh said, forgetting himself.

"I wish to make my stay as pleasant as possible." Navbe informed his host with a sarcastic laugh. As he spoke he was thinking of ways to obtain a Papi for his own use. Seeing those lovely animals at the gates that day had awakened his need again and had strengthened his resolve to have one. He knew that his position was an advantage but could not find the best means of using it.

"Make no doubt, Undersecretary; they will want you to visit them." Ambassador Lesh stopped at the terrace. "Will you take your meal now?"

"It is customary," Navbe said witheringly.

"Must this be with the Janif meats, or will the local ones do? We have the Janif available, but during the day I have tried to run this establishment on native foodstuffs . . ."

"Your economy is no doubt admired. Serve what you wish. If I am to go to their homes, I should learn what to expect." He saw Lesh's embarrassment and was pleased.

Nara-Lim looked expectantly at his guest, hesitating as he held the door to his house open to the Janif. "Undersecretary? What am I to have the pleasure of doing for you?" He bowed low.

Klin Navbe opened both sets of hands in obsequious display, hoping to disarm the Papi with this extraordinary courtesy. "I have come as a student, Nara-Lim. I desire to learn more of the life of your people." He knew that these natives were stupid and trusting. This approach would be the most likely to succeed. Any species of low technology that flattered itself with the illusion of intelligence was easy to convince of your interest.

"We are delighted." Nara-Lim opened the door wider.

"I wish also to thank you for the cloth, the stone work, and the herbs you presented to me. I am impressed."

"It is enough that you value them. If you enjoy our poor offerings, they are made rich."

Navbe moved closer. "You must tell me how to proceed, since your ways are not the ways of the Janif." Cynically Navbe watched the approval in the old Papi's eyes. These little people were incapable of understanding insults.

"Certainly. It will be an honor to this house." He stepped aside to let the Janif Undersecretary enter.

After a long and boring afternoon, Navbe was allowed to leave, promising to return when he could, thanking his host in the most effusive terms.

Then, when he stood in the door, he turned back, as if suddenly aware of a new question. "I have just thought . . . But it would be too great a favor. I must not ask it."

"What were you thinking of?" Nara-Lim asked eagerly, his wide Papi eyes alight, and his soft clothes quivering. "The Janif have not shown so much curiosity about us until now. We are certainly ready to fulfil any reasonable request."

With this encouragement Navbe put on a display of reluctance, sneering privately at the naiveté of the creatures. As if any Janif could be so concerned with Papi. "You told me of the . . . did you call them companions? . . . Yes? Companions."

"Yes?"

"They are adapted for the pleasure of the owner, is that not correct? Do I choose the words badly?" Navbe paused as if uncertain as to how to continue. "I thought that I might arrange to buy one, if that is the usual transaction . . . You see, I would then have one of you with me, to instruct me and tell me what I need to know of your world and your ways. I am right that the companion is always with its . . . master?"

Nara-Lim looked chagrined. "I should have suggested it to you. You must forgive my manners. It would naturally have been offered to you if I had thought your interest was so great."

Realizing that his boredom had shown, Navbe made a show of confusions. "I will confess that when I first asked you, it was idle speculation but your talk has shown me that Papill has much to offer those of us from Jan." It was the first honest statement he had made, and it pleased him to think that Nara-Lim would hear it as a compliment. Such foolish creatures deserved to be prostituted.

"Then I will arrange for a companion for you. Perhaps you will be kind enough to call here one day soon."

"In three days, then?" Here Navbe held his breath.

"Of course," was the answer as Nara-Lim bowed. "I will select a companion for you, one known for grace and docility and boasting much beauty." He paused, looking up to the sky. "There will be heavy mists tonight. You will want to return to the Ambassador's estates quickly. It is dangerous to be abroad in the mists. Even Papi have been lost quite hopelessly in them."

"Your concern flatters me," Navbe said, touching the homing device that would guide him unfailingly back to the estates. "I will leave you now."

"Your interest in Papill is a great honor to our people. Your companion will be here in three days." He kept his deep bow even as he closed the door against the approaching night.

As he strode back along the mountain path in the steadily thickening fog, Klin Navbe gloated to himself. Success was so easy with fools, and the Papi were certainly fools. They thought themselves possessed of tradition when all they had was a stagnated culture of decaying blood lines. What an opportunity this presented to him! It would be ridiculous to waste it.

Ambassador Lesh met him by the terrace. "You were out?" he asked shrilly. "Where were you?" In his fear he forgot to use Navbe's title.

"I went to see Nara-Lim. For what little concern it is of yours." He paused for this to sink in, then: "I will require room to accommodate a Papi servant. Nara-Lim is providing me with a companion."

"A companion," Lesh repeated blankly. He had a sudden picture of those most special Papi with Undersecretary Navbe and was afraid.

"It will arrive here in three days. I assume you can be ready."

Lesh's primary arms twitched. "I can." He thought for a moment. "We can move you and your companion into the Terrace House." Ordinarily such a thing would be unthinkable, but Lesh no longer wanted to be involved in the affairs of the Undersecretary any more than protocol made necessary.

"That should be satisfactory. I rely on you to arrange it for me in time for my companion's arrival." And with that he went past the Ambassador into the house, his robes hissing derisively.

The companion looked up at Navbe with huge, adoring eyes. It was specially dressed for the occasion, wrapped in innumerable layers of tissue-fine cloth. It regarded Navbe with awe and a little ill-concealed fear.

"This is most kind of you, Nara-Lim," Navbe said without looking at him. "I will treasure this, you may be sure." He reached out to touch the slender sprouting antlers. "Remarkable."

Nara-Lim looked pleased and murmured some words that Navbe didn't hear.

"Yes, I will certainly treasure this." Inwardly he was still reeling from the first sight of the companion. Of all the Papi he had seen, this was the most childlike; a small figure without any of the grosser features of most of the natives. He had been told that they were made so, but did not realize until now that the change would be so impressive. Formed like a Janif child, with limpid eyes and soft antlers that were downy to the touch. He would have to be careful at first, make no moves to reveal his intent.

"You are pleased, then. This is satisfactory?" Nara-Lim asked quietly.

"Are you pleased?" The companion asked with a becoming urgency.

"Yes. Yes, I am pleased." He dragged his eyes from the companion and turned to Nara-Lim. "You have done me great honor, and I am beholden."

The old Papi turned almost double. "It is we who are honored. No Janif has ever before been so generous of his interest, no Janif has even bothered to learn from us. You have been most kind."

"Really," he said. "What more is there for me to do? Are there rituals, or documents . . . ?"

"A brief ritual," Nara-Lim said diffidently. "It is to assure your care of your companion, since it is wholly dependent on you. They are made for one individual and may not be changed. We feel it is essential to have a ceremony to establish this."

"Commendable," Navbe said, hoping that the ritual would be short. He was anxious to return to the Terrace House. The companion would be his then, for whatever purposes he chose. His auxiliary arms drew his robes more closely about him so that the Papi could not see the agitation he was feeling.

"Then, if you will come this way?" Nara-Lim held open the door to the garden. "I arranged for the proper setting earlier. I hope this does not distress you. Ordinarily it would be for you to do, but I thought that you would forgive me this liberty."

"Your behavior is excellent, Nara-Lim." How he hated exchanging these useless formalities with this race of precocious animals. Only the promise that was held in the companion's body kept him reasonable and accepting of the ridiculous wishes of the Papi. "I am unfamiliar with your ways and find your tact most rewarding."

They went into the small garden where Nara-Lim had lit a number of ornamental fires in braziers. Then he threw scented water on the companion. He next gave each a plant to hold while he recited some unfamiliar words. When the plants had been burned in the braziers, it was over.

"Very pretty," Navbe remarked, thinking it all very stupid. The companion clung to his auxiliary arm.

"In five days there will be a ceremonial visit paid to you, as assurance that you are taking proper care of the companion. But you must not let this concern you. It is merely our way." He made an elaborate gesture to signify the perfunctory nature of the visit.

"I thank you for telling me." This was genuine thanks, for Navbe realized that he must be careful to leave no mark that might arouse suspicion as to his use of the companion. There must be no sign of abuse, at least, not for the first five days.

The Papi elder bowed. "Go then. And learn of each other."

Navbe led the companion away from Nara-Lim's garden with unseemly haste, smiling ferociously.

Although Ambassador Lesh suspected why Navbe had taken the companion, he was careful not to show this in his manner. He greeted Navbe as he returned and directed his servants to show them to the Terrace House.

"I know you will understand that this is the best of the separate houses I have," he said uneasily.

"Of course. This had to be expected." The patronizing sound of his voice grated and Ambassador Lesh had to force himself to ignore it.

"You should find it adequate," he responded at last, when he was sure he would not overstep his status.

"Adequate," Navbe agreed. He turned to the companion, glowing fragile and childlike beside him. "It will do for you," he told the companion with a sound curiously like a snort.

"Wherever you are, that is truly the best place to be," murmured the companion in a sweet, trilling voice.

Navbe was surprised. He hadn't expected quite so much ability in the companion and was not sure he wanted it. But devotion would be something new and he thought it would amuse him.

"Do you hear, Lesh? It's quite alarmingly faithful." The cruel eyes mocked the rigid control of the Ambassador. "Were you about to warn me of the natives? Your little Nara-Lim has done so already. Charmingly. We went through a ceremony designed to overwhelm me with the honor of the occasion." He turned again to the companion. "He wanted me to understand what I was being given. As if I needed him to tell me." He laughed. It was not a pleasant laugh.

"They are meant to be faithful, Undersecretary. I understand that they cannot be altered to suit another once they have been given to . . . someone . . ." he ended awkwardly.

"Are you suggesting that I take this with me when I leave? With all that's being said about me?" He had taken the precaution of speaking Janif rather than his approximation of Papi. "Really, Lesh. This is an animal, no more. I have it to amuse me and stave off the unutterable boredom of this place. When I leave, it will return to its people. You're wrong, you know, to think that creatures like this one really care about their masters. It's sham, Lesh. Just cunning and sham."

"You're not to harm it," Ambassador Lesh cried recklessly.

"Would it make your position here embarrassing?" Navbe looked at Lesh until the Ambassador was forced to look away. "I can't adapt my wants merely to suit you, Lesh. You know that, don't you?" He put his primary arm under the status badge on the front of his robe. "You do know that."

"If Nara-Lim were to discover—"

"Discover what?"

"Certain things," Lesh said petulantly.

"Lesh, you forget who you are." This was harshly said and to emphasize the harshness Navbe put both auxiliary arms outside of his robe, thumbs twitching.

"You will do as you wish," Ambassador Lesh allowed, in a defeated tone. "You will be shown to your Terrace House."

"Oh, you may lead the way," Navbe said maliciously. It pleased him to take vengeance on Lesh by making him do servant's work, lower status servant's work.

"As you say," Lesh said tightly.

"I have not pleased you?" the companion asked anxiously.

"Does it matter?"

"I have tried to do as you wish. What more do you want of me?" The great sad eyes hovered over him.

"What are you doing off your mat?" Navbe asked, entirely out of patience.

"You are not pleased with me. What must I do?" Even the downy antlers quivered with emotion.

"Do not fret. You were all compliance. Return to your mat." But even as he said it he was annoyed afresh. The children had not wanted him, they had fought him with their hands and new antlers as well as struggling and crying out when he assaulted them. This creatutre had accepted him, making no more than a whimper at the worst of it, and looking with dumb reproachful eyes as it was ravished.

"I must please you."

"Then go to your mat!" With this he turned away and had the satisfaction of hearing the soft sounds as the companion curled on the mat at the foot of his bed. There was vulnerability after all.

"Companion," he said without turning or rising.

"Yes," answered the eager voice in the gloom.

"You will learn to please me. It is that we are different in our ways. In time we will grow accustomed to one another."

There was relief in the little voice as it answered. "Oh, yes. There is plenty of time. I will learn. It is a promise. I will be as you want me."

As Navbe fell into sleep he knew that the companion would learn. He would see to it.

Nara-Lim and the visitors were disturbed when they made the prefunctory five-day visit. There was a lingering pain in the eyes of the companion, an elusive sorrow that they could not understand. Questioned in private, the companion said: "We are different. That is the trouble. It will take time."

"You are well, then?" Nara-Lim asked, uneasy without knowing why. He felt something he had not felt before, an oppressive air, a touch of hidden fury. He did not have a name for it, but he was afraid that the companion did.

"I am well." The companion turned its eyes away, looking toward Navbe across the terrace.

"Is there some trouble?" pursued Nara-Lim.

"Just that we are strange to one another. I am learning to . . . please him." The trouble in the deep eyes faded. "He has promised to teach me and keep me by him forever. He promised."

Nara-Lim nodded, and felt that he ought to be satisfied: "It is probably as you say. They are not as we are."

The companion came near to Nara-Lim. It gestured formally, a pale imitation of Navbe. "He is my master, Nara-Lim, and I am his companion. I must be his way now."

"Yes," said Nara-Lim with equal formality. "That is the way of companions." But he was still unsure.

"Come, you will talk with him. You will see how much he cares for me, and how great is his esteem for me. I am fortunate indeed in this master." So saying, the companion led Nara-Lim across the terrace to where Navbe stood, surrounded by Papi, a gargoyle surrounded by fauns.

When the visit was concluded, Nara-Lim went away with the rest, fearing that his gift had been a betrayal to his people. He had seen the look in the Janif's eyes, the contempt of his manner, and had heard him say fleetingly to Lesh that it would be welcome to him to be among civilized beings again. He had issued the binding orders himself, and felt no doubt at the time, but seeing the companion with the Janif now, he feared.

"Another postponement!" Navbe snarled, hurling the directive to the floor. His sensors writhed on his hands and his tongue flicked uneasily over his outer lips.

"What delay?" asked the companion meekly. It had seen fury in Navbe's stride when he had left Ambassador Lesh, and could feel the rage that consumed its master.

"I am not summoned back . . ." He broke off, realizing who he was answering. "It is not important to you."

The companion came to Navbe's side, its soft clothes whispering as it moved. "This thing has disturbed you. Let me bind your brow, or bathe you."

Navbe tore the delicate primary hands from his forehead. "No!" He stormed across the room. "I do not want you sniveling around me!"

The companion was shocked. "But I am here . . ."

"I don't want you here!" Navbe punctuated this with a blow, and was rewarded with a moan. "Go away. Go bother someone else."

"But I can't," the companion said softly. "I was made to be your companion and I serve no other. I cannot leave you."

Navbe turned murderously on it. "Then keep out of my way."

"As you wish," the companion whispered unhappily.

"And be silent!"

Then he sat on the reclining cushions and thought. The delaying order was not entirely unexpected, but it angered him. There was not reason enough to refuse him the right to return to Jan. To be left on this outpost world with talkative pets was driving him distracted. He pulled at the directive with all four hands. The children could not have betrayed him. They were too frightened and too badly hurt. And for that they would have ordered him exterminated, not exiled. He feared that they might delay him forever, shifting him from remote world to remote world until his name had no power and his status was reduced to nothing. He scuffed at the tattered directive. That some low status clerk had sent it only made matters worse.

"Would you want food, my master?" came the question from the far corner of the room.

"No." There had to be something he could do to force the issue. He would protest to Secretary Vlelt. It was a risky business but he was not without status, and the Secretary might listen to him if he were careful in his phrasing. He made up his mind to work out a plea that very evening.

"May I help you?" the companion asked, the ghost of a voice in the gathering dusk.

"Come here," Navbe commanded, and when the companion was beside him, he sank all his hands into the young flesh.

It was Ambassador Lesh who gave him the news that the Secretary had called him back to Jan.

"When?" the Undersecretary demanded urgently.

"As soon as possible." There was an expression on the Ambassador's face that might almost be disgust. "He needs your services, it would seem."

"How many days before I must depart?" Navbe had unwittingly shown his interest in the order and felt that he had to brazen it out.

"Four days, Undersecretary. I think you can be ready in that time."

Navbe scowled. It was more than he was willing to tolerate, this superior attitude from an inferior. He would have something to say about it when he got back to Jan.

"The Terrace House is yours until you leave, Undersecretary." Lesh started to move away.

"I will expect you to prepare my belongings for departure," Navbe said smoothly. "All things suitably crated for the journey. That will include the bolts of cloth given me by the Papi, and that worked stone." It had been in the back of his mind to bring these products to the attention of the Merchant Council. That Ambassador Lesh had not done so would be a mark against his record.

"And the companion."

Navbe was getting out of patience with Lesh. "Send it back to its people. What good is it to me?"

"I can't do that." Ambassador Lesh turned on the Undersecretary. "It has been made for you, and it is yours. If you abandon it, it will die. It cannot go back to its people." The heat in his words alarmed Navbe. He had been aware that Lesh was too wrapped up in the Papi, but had not thought it was this far gone. He would have to recommend treatment when he saw the Representative Master.

"Calm yourself, Ambassador. You make too much of these creatures. Certainly they are pleasing to look at, and they have their uses, but like all domestic livestock, they will transfer their allegiance in time." He put the directive in his sleeve. "Well, you will be busy the next few days, preparing to send me off." There was a quiet threat in his next words. "I don't imagine you will mention the companion to the Secretary. For the same reason I will not mention the unwillingness you have shown in the exploitation of the crafts of the Papi. They are worth a lot. Were you saving them for yourself?" Then he stood back.

The Ambassador's auxiliary hands grew livid, but he controlled himself enough to say: "I will say nothing." It was only when Navbe had walked away from him that he dared to ask: "How *did* you get to those children?"

Klin Navbe only laughed.

All his things were packed. Navbe surveyed the mound of crates in front of the door to the Terrace House and was satisfied. At last he was going back to Jan, where he would be with intelligent beings once again. He felt cleaner, better than he had since his arrival on Papill. It would be so little time now. He would be with real people.

Ambassador Lesh was not there, nor had Navbe seen him at any time the past two days. Such was the way of those of low status: when challenged, they hid. It was part of the natural cowardice of the stratum.

Behind him, Navbe sensed the companion, standing helplessly amid the desolation of the rooms. For the last day or so it had wandered disconsolately from room to room as the contents were crated and put outside the door. Now it stood, bewildered, looking at Navbe.

"Don't worry," Navbe said without turning to it. "I'll leave you a present."

"Leave me?" asked the Papi, uncomprehendingly.

"You'll need something to live on. All right. I'll arrange it with Lesh." His mouth puckered at the thought.

"No." It was a little word, barely said, as the companion sank to the floor, its huge eyes glazed as with a fever.

Navbe twisted in impatience. It was always this way with house animals. "You'll be fine," he told the companion, joviality in his manner to conceal his impatience. "You knew I was going away. Don't let it bother you so much." He nudged the huddled figure at his feet with his boot.

Four eager hands grabbed his leg through the folds of his robe. "Take me. Take me. Don't leave me here. You can't leave me here."

Disgusted, Navbe shook the foot free of the desperate fingers. "Don't be foolish," he snapped, striding back to the door.

"I belong to you," the companion said. "I was made to be part of you. You must take me with you." There was anguish in the little face now, and foreboding.

"I am tired of this," Navbe announced. "If you want to see me off, you may follow me to the landing place. If not . . ." He shrugged elegantly.

"There is nowhere I can go," murmured the companion to itself.

"Nara-Lim will take care of you. Lesh will see to it. Now, I want no more of this. You served me adequately and you'll be paid. Nara-Lim can manage the fee, if you like." He rang a bell for the servants, knowing they would be slow.

"It doesn't matter," the companion said blankly, looking away from the Undersecretary. "If you go, it doesn't matter."

Why is it these animals take everything so personally? Navbe asked himself as the servants came along the terrace. "Here, you," he called to them. "These are to go to the landing place. Nothing is to be dropped or broken, do you understand?"

The crates were loaded into the boxlike rolling platforms and dragged away from the Ambassador's house to the landing field.

"Come along," Navbe said to his companion. "Walk out with me, why don't you?"

Numbly the companion stood and numbly it followed Navbe across Ambassador Lesh's estate.

The squat craft waited, a mushroom ready to assault the sky. Around it Papi and Janif workers were loading and pampering the machine, readying it for the surge upward, away from the soft mists of Papill for the bright scraps of light that were stars.

Ambassador Lesh was not there.

A low status officer examined the directive Navbe held out to him and made him welcome with becoming deference, concealing his hands and moving his mouth as little as possible. This was much more to Navbe's liking.

"I will board soon," he informed the officer and was pleased to see the officer rigid. As he turned back to his companion, he felt the first tuggings of civilization on him and found the sensation a warm delight.

"Well, companion, here is what I've promised you," he said, handing the creature a voucher and the border from one of his sleeves. The companion took the sleeve and pressed it to its face. The voucher slid away on the wind, unheeded.

"I forbid you to behave in this way," Navbe said to the companion as it looked at the ship with hopeless eyes. He found the manner attractive, even stimulating, but it was a feeling he could not afford now.

"Don't go," whispered the companion. "Or take me with you. I will die without you."

That was truly too much for Navbe. He wrinkled his face in frustration, and then, with a half-smile he said: "But I'll be back, of course. I'll want you here when I get back."

Joy transformed the delicate face. "When? When? I cannot live long without you, but if you are coming back, I will try . . ."

It was remarkable how easily the creature was fobbed off. Navbe chided himself for not thinking of it sooner. "I will be here in the season of the Amber Rivers." That was sufficiently far in the future that the companion would have time to forget him.

"I will try to live until then," the companion said eagerly. "I will try. It is long, but you will be back." It clutched the sleeve border fiercely. "I promise I will wait for you. I will live until you come back."

"Good," said Navbe absently as he watched the last of his crates moved on board.

"Until the time of the Amber Rivers. It will be hard but I will live."

"Fine, fine." The Undersecretary put his badge of office in place and went to the boarding ramp. The young officer stood waiting for him. Without a backward look he went aboard and the door swung closed behind him.

The companion waited in the landing place where Navbe had left it, the sleeve border in its hand, thinking of the reunion that would come in the season of Amber Rivers. Somehow it would have to live that long, for the joy of its master, for the better part of itself.

When the craft rose into the air, it covered the companion with dust.

about "Un Bel Di"

I love opera. I've loved it since I was eight years old and stumbled upon a Met broadcast of Verdi's *Don Carlo* with Bjoerling and Siepi. This is one of three stories in this book based on, extrapolated from, or about opera. This one, rather obviously, is taken from Puccini's *Madama Butterfly,* which in turn came from a dreadful Belasco play, *Little Green Eyes,* which, I understand, was the development of a story that appeared in a British magazine in the late nineteenth century (but which I have been unable to trace).

This does not mean that the story is a one-to-one retelling. Of course not. The sexless, symbiotic companion is a far cry from Cio-Cio San, and Navbe compared to Benjamin Franklin Pinkerton makes Pinkerton look like a pretty nice guy. Yet there is a conscious, deliberate shaping of the story that comes directly from Puccini, and more from the nature and color of the music than from the words alone.

"Un Bel Di" first appeared in a Ballantine anthology that Tom Scortia and I edited called *Two Views of Wonder,* and it was paired thematically with a story by Harlan Ellison. It's been reprinted in France, but has not been generally available in the United States.

LAMMAS NIGHT

Inside the circle that held the pentagram the air shimmered and in the dark, cold room, Giuseppe felt he was staring into great distances.

The shimmer broadened, and now it was time to speak the final summons. Giuseppe cleared his throat and took a firmer grip on the sword he carried, though he knew it was useless against the forces he called. "Io te commando . . ." he began in his Sicilian accented Italian. "I command thee. I, Count Alessandro Cagliostro . . ." There was a sudden popping sound, like the breaking of glass or a burst keg and the air was still once more.

Giuseppe flung down his sword in disgust. He should have known better. He could not use any but his real name, and although his title was self-awarded and therefore, he felt, certainly as valid as the unpretentious name his parents had given him, he knew that the demon would not respond to anything but plain Giuseppe Balsamo.

Of course he couldn't do that. No one in Paris knew he was not a nobleman, and he could not admit it now, particularly with the threat of prosecution for fraud hanging over him. He had already had trouble in England. He could not afford to fail here in France. He had promised to raise a demon, and he would have to do it.

The demon would not come to any name but his baptismal one.

Giuseppe sank onto the cold floor, the stones pressing uncompromisingly against his naked buttocks. The sweat which had run off him so freely grew clammy and smelled sour. He touched the old ceremonial sword he had picked up in Egypt six years before. The old sorcerer had guaranteed that sword, and Giuseppe knew now that the mad old man had not spoken idly.

One of the candles set at the point of the pentagram guttered and the hot wax ran through the edge of the chalked circle. In spite of himself, Giuseppe flinched. If the demon had still been there, the circle would not have bound it any longer. If that had occurred when the ceremony was under way, no one would have been safe. A shudder gripped him that had little to do with the cold.

In three days it would be Lammas Night, and it would be then that the jaded aristocrats expected him to give them the thrill of seeing a demon. Cynically Giuseppe considered handing out mirrors and taking his chances in a coach with a team of fast horses. But he could not risk it. There was too much at stake. For one thing he needed money. For another there were few places he could run. England was out of the question—he did not want to be sent to prison for fraud. He had to be very cautious if he returned home to Sicily, for the Inquisition took a dim view of self-confessed devil-raisers. Spain was even worse, for the Holy Office was stronger there than elsewhere. Germany would not welcome him, besides the question of debt. He could flee to the New World, but that took money unless he wanted to be stranded in New Orleans without contacts or possibilities. He could go East, but what little he had seen of the Ottoman Empire convinced him that it would be safer with an unbound demon that he would be in Istanbul.

Reluctantly he pulled himself to his feet. He was in a lot of trouble, and he would have to deal with it immediately. There really were no alternatives.

The salon glowed in the light of four hundred candles on six huge crystal chandeliers. One wall was mirrored and it reflected back the brilliant light and the grand ladies and gentlemen who crowded about the long gambling tables. The rustle of fine, stiff silks combined with the susurrus of talk and the clink of glasses of wine and piles of gold louis.

Giuseppe stood on the threshold of this splendid room, a sudden sinking feeling making him pause and tug at the three cascades of Michlin lace at his throat. He covered this nervousness with a finicky movement as he adjusted the pearl and sapphire stickpin that nestled there. He congratulated himself mentally on that stickpin. Even the English Duchess had admired it and had never suspected that it was a fake.

"Count?" said a lackey at his shoulder.

"Yes?" Giuseppe asked. He assumed his most charming manner. He knew how important the good opinion of servants could be. If he found later that he needed help to flee, servants would be of more use to him than anyone else.

"DeVre has asked for you." The lackey assumed his wooden expression again. "He is in the second salon, sir. With Martillion and Gries."

Giuseppe nodded reluctantly. "I will be with them directly. Thank you for the message." Assuming his best manner he strolled into the salon, happily acknowledging the greetings of the glittering people as he went toward the second salon.

"Count," called Countess Beatrisse du Lac Saint Denis. She held out a rounded white arm dripping with diamonds below the fall of lace at her elbow.

Giuseppe stopped and bent to kiss her hand. "Countess," he murmured and gave her a wide, warm smile. His expressive, large eyes rested on her face, full of unspoke promise. He was surprised at how unruffled he was, how little his fear effected his behavior.

"I vow I will be with your party on Lammas Night," the Countess said archly. In her tall wig, diamonds sparkled like the sea foam, and the confection was crowned with a model of a full-rigged ship.

Giuseppe smoothed the gold Milanese brocade of his coat, "It may be dangerous, Countess. I would hate to see anyone as lovely as you at the mercy of a demon."

Countess Beatrisse laughed, but Giuseppe saw a strange light in her face. "You are too late, my dear Count. I have been at the mercy of my husband for seven years and your demon cannot frighten me."

As his inner chill deepened, Giuseppe kissed her hand and passed on. He had assumed, obviously wrongly, that his special service would be secret, that only a few would know of it or attend. He glanced around as he walked into the second salon, and heard a brief hiatus in the sound of conversation. It boded ill. He nodded in answer to the wave of DeVre, and made his way through the crowd to the buffet table where DeVre, Martillion, and Gries waited, their elegant, vicious faces showing their eagerness.

"Ah, Cagliostro," DeVre said as Giuseppe came up to him. "We are all agog with anticipation. You tell me how your preparations are going." He smiled to disguise the order.

"I have begun my calculations. But I must warn you, we cannot have more than thirteen at the service." He reached automatically for a glass of wine as a lackey bowed at his arm.

"Of course, of course," said DeVre at his most soothing, which Giuseppe knew meant nothing.

Desperately, he tried again. "You have not seen a demon before." He remembered what the Countess du Lac Saint Denis had said a moment before. Perhaps she was right, and these were the faces of demons.

But Gries was talking, his saturnine face masklike in the scintillating light. "It's all very well for you to build up this meeting, Cagliostro. Theatrics are part of it, are they not? But you cannot expect us to keep this secret. Not in Paris. *Nom du nom,* it is not possible." He half turned to wave at Madame du Randarte, who hesitated before acknowledging his greeting. "There's a rare piece for you," he said to Martillion when he turned back once more. "She's vain, though; doesn't want her breasts bitten."

Giuseppe nodded uncomfortably. He did not like the venality of these men, and he now regretted his boast as a binder of demons. Somewhat startled, he realized he had finished the wine. As he put down the glass he reminded himself that he would need a clear head for what he had to do here.

"Not drinking, Count?" Martillion asked, one ironic brow raised. He almost sneered as he took another glass and drank eagerly.

"I cannot. I am preparing for the ceremony, you will recall." He saw a certain flicker in Martillion's eyes and took full advantage. "As I have said, this is a dangerous matter, and only those of us who have been initiated into the rites may undertake this ordeal. But there are conditions. I must meet those conditions if the ceremony is to go successfully."

Although the three laughed, Giuseppe had the satisfaction of knowing that this time they were uneasy, and that he had frightened them. He pressed on, speaking more forcefully now. "I have come because you did not specify the form you would want the demon to appear in. As you may know, demons can be charged to present themselves in guises other than their own."

"More chicanery," Gries scoffed.

"If you wish to think so . . ." Guiseppe pulled himself up to his full, if modest height. "So that you will have the choice," he went on, "I will tell you that I may conjure the demon to appear as a monster, although that is the greatest danger, and I am not certain this is wise."

Martillion tittered uneasily. "Oh, I have no fear of monsters," he said as he took another glass of wine.

Giuseppe set his jaw. "Monsters can occasionally break the protective circle, and then nothing I, or anyone else save an uncorrupted priest can do will save you."

"Mountebank," Gries said.

"There are other forms." Giuseppe colored his voice, made it warmer, more flattering. "Perhaps you would prefer a youth with supple limbs, or a beautiful woman . . . ?" He let the suggestion hang, and saw the response in their faces.

"A beautiful woman?" DeVre mused. "A fiend from hell?"

"All women are fiends from hell," Gries laughed cynically.

Keeping hold of his calm, Giuseppe said, "You must tell me which you want." He had an idea now, a way that he could save himself. It was a greater gamble than he wanted to take, but that choice was out of his hands. He would have to risk being denounced or flee France with yet another charge of fraud hanging over him.

"If the demon were a beautiful woman," Martillion said reflectively, staring into the red heart of his wine, "could we use her?"

"There will be another woman at the ceremony for that purpose, and you may choose among yourselves for that. But you lose your immortal soul if you have commerce with the demon."

"It's already lost, if the Church is to be believed." Gries looked hungrily around the room, his quizzing glass held up.

"You could lose your manhood as well," Giuseppe said with asperity. "What the demon has touched it will not give back."

For a moment those cynical men were silent. Then Martillion laughed. "Still, to see a demon as a woman . . . It might be more to our purposes than to see a monster." He glanced at the others and saw the assent in their eyes. "A woman, then, Cagliostro. Beautiful. Nude?"

"It would not be wise," Giuseppe said after pretending to think. "The flames of hell make strange garments." He made an enigmatic gesture. "I will do what I can."

"What time on Lammas Night?" Gries asked, his eyes growing bleary from the wine he had drunk.

For a moment Giuseppe pondered the time, weighing theatricality with the forces he would fool. "Arrive on the stroke of nine, for we must prepare you for the ceremony at midnight. And I warn you," he said, his manner growing grander, "that you must be prompt. I cannot admit anyone after nine is struck, no matter who asks for admission. I trust you will make this plain to the others."

Martillion sketched a bow. "Of course, Cagliostro."

His bow was returned with formal flourish, and then Giuseppe turned and strode from the inner salon. As he passed the gambling table, he turned to Beatrisse de Lac Saint Denis. "Madame," he said in a lowered tone, "that information you requested, concerning an amulet?" He knew this was a dreadful chance, and he waited in fright for her answer.

Fleetingly her face showed surprise, then she said, "Yes? Have you decided on a price?"

Giuseppe let his breath out, relieved. "Yes, Madame, I have. If you would be kind enough to wait on me in the morning? Say, at ten?"

There was speculation and a touch of fear in her eyes. "I will be there, Count. At ten." She turned back to the table and did not look at Giuseppe again.

It was shortly after ten when the elegant town coach pulled up outside the home of Count Alessandro Cagliostro, and the steps were let down for a beautifully dressed and heavily veiled woman. A maid followed her into the house.

Giuseppe himself met her in the foyer, extending his hands to her, and bowed punctiliously. "I am honored, Countess," he said, then added softly, "If you seek to keep your visit here secret, it would have been wiser to hire a coach. Your arms are blazoned on the doors of that one."

She shrugged. "As long as the spies of my husband's household follow me, I do not want to put them to any special effort. Besides, he knows that I come here. It was he who insisted on the veil." With these words she drew the veil aside and made a travesty of a smile. "Where is this amulet you spoke of?"

Giuseppe was prepared. He held out a strangely cut jewel on a chain. "It is efficacious in matters of the heart and children. But you must take especial care of it. Allow me to take you to my experiment room and demonstrate how you are to wear it, and what you must do with it when you do not wear it." He turned to the maid who waited inside the door. "Accompany us, please. I do not want to cast the Countess into disfavor with her husband."

The maid started forward, then hung back. She had heard much about Count Cagliostro, and none of it said he was lascivious. She bowed her head. "I will remain here, sir."

It was the answer that Giuseppe had hoped for. "As you wish. We should not be more than half an hour." He offered his arm to the

Countess du Lac Saint Denis. "Come with me, if you please," he said, and led her into the west wing of the house.

When they were safely out of earshot, Beatrisse du Lac Saint Denis said, "What is this about, Count? You bewildered me last night. I did not know what to think, and this, with the jewel, confuses me even more."

He handed her the jewel. "Take it with you, in any case."

"Is it an amulet?"

"Yes," he said. "It is to bring you your heart's desire."

The devastation in her face upset him. "That cannot be, Count. But it is a kindness in you to offer." She took the jewel and absent-mindedly put it around her neck.

Giuseppe nodded. "You have heard of what is planned for Lammas Night?"

"My husband speaks of little else," she said more bitterly than she knew. "DeVre's set are expecting wonders of you. They are in an ugly mood."

In spite of himself Giuseppe shuddered. "I gathered that. And it is a pity that I will have to disappoint them."

Her brows rose. "You daren't," she said, lowering her voice as if she feared an eavesdropper. "You must not. They will not allow that."

"Yes, I realize this."

Impulsively she put her hand on his arm. "Is it that you cannot? Or that you will not?"

Giuseppe grimaced. "Some of both, Countess. I can summon certain demons, but I will not bring them to do the bidding of those men. You understand why, Madame. I need not tell you why."

"But you must." She turned her lovely, haunted face toward him. The light from the tall windows at the end of the gallery made her fine unpowdered curls glow bright chestnut. The jewels at her throat were alive with their garnet fire, and the stiff silk of her billowing skirt glowed with light. "I know what these men can be. None knows better than I. They permit no one to cross them, and if they suspect fraud, they will show no mercy to you. You will be imprisoned, either by Louis' courts or by the Church. There is no way to escape them, Alessandro," she used his name in a sudden rush of intimacy. "They are too many and too strong."

Giuseppe took her hand and kissed it. "Madame, I believe you. And that is why I have taken you into my confidence. I know something of your marriage, and I have wondered if perhaps you would like to be revenged on Jean Gabriel Louis Martillion, Count du Lac Saint Denis?" He thought of the Count's younger brother, and realized that Martillion's vice was small beside the Count's.

Her hands closed convulsively on his. "You cannot know how dearly I would treasure revenge, even one little revenge."

With a profound nod, Giuseppe said, "If you are willing to take a risk I am sure that you may have it. There is a saying in Italy—that revenge is a dish best served cold. It will take cold blood to do what I suggest."

Beatrisse du Lac Saint Denis turned away. "My blood was frozen long ago, Count. What do you want of me?"

Giuseppe smiled, and felt relief run through him. "When I summon the demon, it will be you."

She turned to him again. "What? How can you . . ."

"That is my concern," he said, raising her hand to his lips. He found it easier to deal with women who trusted his confidential manner and charm than with those who were attracted by his handsomeness. He was pleased to see excitement kindle in the Countess's amber eyes. "You must listen to me, and I will outline what I have done. And if you are afraid, remember that you will be heavily disguised by the lights and by the strange garments you wear. And," he added as he saw her falter, "I will paint your face as they do for the theatre. No one will suspect that Beatrisse Countess du Lac Saint Denis is the embodiment of a demon."

She looked bewildered. "But if this is as you say, how will I be revenged?"

"That, Madame, is where the risk occurs."

It was Lammas Night. The springtime moon rode low in the sky over Paris, and rode the echoes of church bells as they tolled the hour of eight. The streets were already quiet, for when darkness descended it was not wise to be found out of doors.

The sedan chair which arrived at the servants' entrance to the home of Count Alessandro Cagliostro was run-down, and the two chairmen who carried it were not the sort most aristocrats would put their trust in. They collected their fee from the plainly dressed young woman who had hired them and watched her go into the dark passage by the kitchens. They assumed she was to be part of the celebration that would occur later. Cagliostro's summoning of a demon had given most of Paris food for speculation, and the chairmen were glad to have their own tidbit to add to the chatter. Servant girls at demon raisings were something of a surprise.

They would have been more surprised yet had they known that the kitchen door was opened by Cagliostro himself, and that he bowed over the disguised Countess' hand as formally as if she had been in all her court finery.

"Is it ready?" she whispered, somewhat taken aback by his strange white robe with the silver embroidery on it.

"Yes, just as I described it to you. But come quickly, Madame. There is not much time and I want you to practice the trick just once before I dress you."

She hung back. "You are certain that the candles will be out when I appear? I do not want anyone to see the trapdoor."

"No one will see it," he assured her as he opened the hidden door into a secret passage which led to his own austere quarters located over the room where the materialization would take place.

The garment, when he showed it to her, delighted her, though it was shockingly indecent. She touched the flamelike tongues of sheer silk which moved with every draught. Giuseppe pointed out the mechanism of the dress and she laughed at the simplicity of it. "Even if they suspect trickery," she said as she fitted the garment over her, "they would not think of this. They will look for tricks of the theatre, of strange engines." She started across the room, and stopped, suddenly modest, as the silk fell back to reveal the length of her thigh.

"No, no, Madame," Giuseppe assured her. "No demon would behave so. And in a moment I will paint your legs with red, and paste jewels on them. You must not notice your manner of dress." He pointed to the mirror near his worktable. "See? this is not Beatrisse du Lac Saint Denis, this is some hellish vision."

The thought seemed to strike her, for she rose on her toes and turned gracefully so that the silk drifted about her. "This way, Count?"

Remembering the hungry faces of the men coming that night, Giuseppe said, "It is lovely, Countess, but do not make it too beautiful. A demon may lure, but only to hell."

She nodded, then followed him into the withdrawing room which had been cleared of furniture, and there, by the light of three candles, he showed her what she would do. "Do not let the darkness or the incense frighten you. It will be no different than the way we have done it now. I will always stand just here, and you will know by the candles by the door and by the mantel when you are in the right position. I will not fail you, Countess."

"Nor I you," she promised him, her long hands clenched.

DeVre did not like the fit of his robe, and complained bitterly that it was not seemly for him to be wearing such outlandish things.

"That is up to you," Giuseppe said coldly. "But if you are not protected, I cannot save you from the demon."

Martillion chuckled unpleasantly and looked toward his older brother, the Count du Lac Saint Denis. "It's a masquerade," he said lazily.

This was much too close to the truth, and Giuseppe did what he could to turn their minds from the idea. "Of course it is a masquerade, gentlemen. Hell is clothing its own in flesh." He gave Gries a robe and warned him not to drink any more.

Henri Valdonne studied the others, thinking himself above all this. His position as the aristocratic head of shippers who traded in China gave him a certain world-wise reputation. He did not comply with Cagliostro's orders immediately, but made a show of inspecting the garment. "I have heard that such garments must be without seam," he challenged as he pulled off his brocaded waistcoat.

"In some rites this is so. But we are not concerned with virgins tonight, Chevalier. Only when a virgin is sacrificed must the robes be of seamless cloth." And seeing the faces of the nine men and four women around him, Giuseppe was deeply grateful that he was not subjecting a virgin to any such as these.

When all were dressed in their robes, Giuseppe led the way to the rear withdrawing room. None of the halls were lit and there were no servants in the house. Giuseppe moved quickly and was pleased that the others went clumsily in their unfamiliar robes and unlighted passages.

The pentagram and circle were already on the floor, and the sword, chalice, wand, wafers, and salt stood at each point of the pentagram outside the circle. Giuseppe went quickly to the bay of heavily curtained windows and made a show as if to adjust the curtains against prying eyes. He saw that the concealed levers were set and ready. He turned back to the others who stood, uncertainly glancing about them, in the dim light. He put his foot over a spring which worked the concealed bellows.

"Kneel!" he told them, and his generally pleasant voice was stern as a field commander. "Go to the pentagram and kneel."

He watched while the white-robed figures sorted themselves out. In a moment they were ready, and had begun to whisper among themselves.

"You must be silent!" Giuseppe pulled a diamond medallion from around his neck and hung it in front of the nearest branch of candles. A flick of his finger set it to swinging. "We call on the Forces of Darkness," he intoned, garbling the invocation so that he would not inadvertently summon an unexpected Power. "We suppliants call the Forces of Darkness on this, Lammas Night, when they have sway in the darkness."

Martillion tittered and his hands strayed toward the chalk marks.

"Do not touch that!" Giuseppe's voice cut like a knife. "That is all that will protect you from the fires of hell. If any one of you break it, none are safe."

There was a pause and Martillion drew back. The others moved back, too.

"We summon you," Giuseppe went on, "in the Glory of your Power." He moved toward the circle and reached first for the chalice. "Here we call you with the call of blood." He elevated the chalice. Then, like a priest, he went from one kneeling figure to another, tilting the red-colored liquid into their waiting mouths. He did not tell them that what they drank was salted mead in which he had steeped Persian hashish. The color was nothing more than dye, but Giuseppe could see the concealed revulsion on the faces of his ill lot of initiates. Good. If they were revolted, they would not be too critical of the taste of what they drank, and the salt was enough to make most of them believe.

Returning to the window bay, he said, "I summon you, demons of the pit, I call on one of your number. I tell you that there is work for you here, that the souls wait for you. I, Alessandro Cagliostro call you. I call you."

The figures waited, but nothing happened. Giuseppe came forward again, and picked up the wand. With this he tapped all the others on the forehead, and when that was done, he drew blood from their fingertips with his sword. When that was over, he took the wafers, and marking each with the print of a cloven hoof, he passed these to each of his celebrants. They were a paste made with poppy syrup, and they took strong effect.

Sure now that the thirteen before him were muzzy in thought, he began the call again. He touched a loose board with his foot and hidden bells rang. A wind from nowhere chilled the room as the concealed bellows began to work, and extinguished one branch of candles. Then Giuseppe pulled one of the hidden levers and the room was plunged into darkness.

A moan came from the group, and in the next instant, the niches with their candles had revolved back as the false hearthstone returned to its proper place, and in the circle stood a blazing female demon, alive with fire and with smoke in her hair.

Giuseppe almost smiled as he saw his acolytes draw back from this apparition. He waited until the whole effect had sunk in, and then he cried out: "Demon! I, Alessandro Cagliostro, charge you. Identify these who kneel before you. Tell us the names of those who kneel. Tell us the secrets of their souls. What are the abominations that will condemn them to perdition on the Day of Wrath?"

There was a pause, and then Beatrisse du Lac Saint Denis began to recite the vices and crimes of those gathered before her, calling up every lewd boast of her husband, every shoddy bit of gossip she had heard, every detail that had caused her shame and embarrassment. The list was a long one, and it frightened the thirteen kneeling around the pentagram.

Gradually the room grew darker as Giuseppe once more pulled the lever which controlled the candle niches. One of the initiates was breathing hard and Giuseppe knew he would have to give the Count a composing drug before he let him leave the house.

At last the long catalogue of debauchery was over. Again the bells rang and the room went dark. In the returning light the figure of the demon was seen shimmering before them. Giuseppe forced the bellows into greater breath.

Giuseppe clapped his hands three times. "Depart! Depart! Depart!" he commanded. Suddenly the air was very still.

And the demon shriveled, became a single flame, and then disappeared entirely in the center of the circle.

"Are they gone?" Beatrisse du Lac Saint Denis asked when Giuseppe came into his quarters a little more than an hour later.

"They are gone." He held out his hand. In it lay a wired dress of red silk which trailed a long thin thread. "Perhaps you might want this, Countess."

She touched it, a secret smile on her face. Then, with a decisive nod of her head, "No. There is always the slim chance that my husband might find it. That must not happen." She paused. "I pulled the thread when the bellows stopped."

"I think you will find that your husband is not well. When he left his pulse was very rapid and he had a look about his eyes that was not good."

"Did he?" she asked, disinterested. "I left the bath water, as you said. It is quite red. The servants may see it."

"The powder removed it all from your skin?" he asked. He knew his servants would never see the reddened water.

"Yes." She pulled her maid's dress about her more tightly. "Do you think he will ever suspect?"

Giuseppe laughed outright. "Madame, after they had drunk wine tainted with hashish and eaten wafers of poppy, you could have come in there in your most famous toilette, and if I had told them you were a demon, they would have believed it."

She nodded. "A bellows and a wired dress. How simple to make a demon."

"You are troubled, Countess?" Guiseppe took her hand solicitously.

"It is just that I do not know when you will betray me," she said after a moment.

"I might say the same of you," he said easily. "Come, this is our secret. You know what I did to make the demon, and I know the demon is you. If you cannot trust me out of faith, remember that we both have a hold on the other."

The Countess nodded once more. "I must return home," she said.

Giuseppe stood aside. "I have ordered a hack for you, Madame. It will take you home, if not in fashion, at least in victory."

At that she smiled. "I saw his face, you know, as I told him all the dreadful things he had done. His eyes were like an animal in a trap. He could not move." She went to the door. "I will always remember his eyes, Cagliostro. It will give me strength."

"You have the amulet as well, Countess. It is for your heart's desire."

"Surely you do not expect me to believe that?" she asked incredulously. "When you are nothing more than a charlatan?"

When the door closed behind the Countess, Giuseppe Balsamo, known to the world as Count Alessandro Cagliostro, went into his withdrawing room to remove the chalk marks from the floor. And to remove the holy water and Host that had protected that venal gathering from the perils of Lammas Night.

about "Lammas Night"

When Cedric Clute and Nick Lewin started to put together their magic-and-mystery anthology for Regnery, *Sleight of Crime,* Ced asked me to do an original story for them, about a real occultist. Cagliostro came to mind as one of the most famous, most sloppy of the eighteenth-century self-proclaimed magi.

The illusion used in the story is Dante's (the magician, not the poet) Mystic Moth, and when done right, is very effective. But Cagliostro was not only a con man, he was also trying to have the mystic powers he claimed to have. He died in prison after a hectic, debt-ridden career that took him all over Europe.

For those of you who know something about the Satanic calendar of worship, you will realize that this is not Lammas Night, but Beltane. However, one of Cagliostro's letters talked about Lammas being in April and I'm willing to continue the error, since it's typical of the man.

Nick Lewin is a professional stage magician and Cedric Clute ran the Magic Cellar, a nightclub devoted to magic, in San Francisco. I work there on Friday and Saturday nights, reading tarot cards and palms.

INTO MY OWN

Tsss-thup. Tsss-thup. Tsss-thup went what passed for a heartbeat in Dahlman's chest. *Tsss-thup.* And he listened to it, hating it for its mechanical perfection. *Tsss-thup. Tsss-thup.* It never left him alone. But what a good idea it had seemed, seven years ago, when his own heart was faltering, failing, worn out. He had so much work to do then, so much that he hadn't finished, and he had agreed. Now he had that sound in his chest and it was his liver that needed replacement. In the loud silence of the hospital night Dahlman imagined what his blood might be like after being cleaned and moved about by things that were not part of him.

There was, of course, an alternative. These days there were always alternatives. Even in the dark Dahlman's eyes sought out the uncompromising outline of the console against the wall. He felt the familiar chill touch him as he looked at the thing: 71C-OR. That machine could take him over, burrow into all the private recesses of his mind and then become him, *be* Eric Dahlman, with his mind and thoughts, his future, his work, his memories. Then he could die and his art would continue, faithfully executed by the computer. An anger speeded his pulse and the miniature atomic steam engine that powered the thing under his ribs adjusted itself to the change, obediently, uncaring.

It was Nikels' fault: that much was obvious. If only Dahlman had not let himself be talked into the surgery the first time, if only he had refused and died . . . but it was useless to think about it now. It was over. He had made his choice, or Nikels' choice, and had to live with it. To keep himself from thinking he listened to the night finding it cold and remote. Without knowing he was waiting, he waited.

"Sleep well?" It was typical of Nikels that he was smiling, showing that friendly face that Dahlman had known for so many years. "The doctors are anxious for your decision."

"I don't know." Dahlman moved uneasily, seeing the computer console shining in a beam of morning light.

"They can't wait much longer; it's a matter of timing." He continued his warm smile as he eased himself onto the foot of the bed. His hands were long and thin, at odds with his energetic, compact body.

Dahlman scowled, hoping that the dread he felt did not show. "I'm not sure, Nikels. Maybe they're right and this is what I should do. But this thing," he gestured to his chest where his alien heart kept time, "this thing was bad enough. I don't know how much more I can stand and still function." He knew that Nikels would sense a threat in that, and it was just what he wanted.

Nikels made a gesture of dismissal. "Don't worry about it," he said, plainly hiding worry of his own. "The liver isn't like the heart. You won't hear a thing. And remember that there are still eight contracts waiting for you. You can't afford to let your body break down now." There was a forced joviality in his manner. Dahlman sensed that Nikels was trying hard to keep his irritation under control. "Look, Eric, you know that you're not finished yet. You're only eighty-six. You've got a lot to do before you're finished. Why, there's years of work in front of you."

"Years," Dahlman echoed, listening to his heart mark off the seconds.

"A lot to look forward to."

"And how old are you, Nikels?" Dahlman asked, knowing that his manager was forty-two or three. "I'm twice your age. When I was a kid we lived in private homes and grew flowers. Every year I pruned the jacaranda tree. I'm getting tired." To forestall the objections he could see forming in Nikels' face, he said, "Sure, I'm excited about the new plays. They're great concepts and I want to do them, even if Tonio directs them, the bastard. But I don't want to go on like this!"

There was a slight hesitation before Nikels said, "You can talk to the 71C-OR. That would be one way to solve the problem."

"Would it?" There was thick sarcasm clotting his words as he spoke them. "I suppose it might. That thing could go on being me and none of you would have to waste precious time on this old hulk of mine." Even to himself the words sounded melodramatic, filled with self-pity. He saw the calculation in Nikels' eyes and shut up.

"Dr. Bruson can arrange it, if you like," Nikels said carefully. He shifted his weight uneasily. His face had gone closed, showing nothing now but a safe, infuriating neutrality.

"Well?" He knew that Nikels was waiting for the chance to speak again. "What is it?"

"Look, Eric, if you take the liver, you can probably last long enough for them to make a clone of it for you. And your heart, too, for that matter. You say you don't like the feeling of something foreign in you—all right, then. This is the answer. It would be your own heart, but younger. Your own liver, fresh and undamaged."

Dahlman's skin went cold with horror, his muscles gripping his bones. "I don't like any of this," he announced, inwardly fearing the whine that had come into his voice. That old, tired cry could not be him, could not be the great dramatist Eric Dahlman whose career stretched back half a century. He could not make such a noise. His flesh still quivered.

"But your liver's shot, Eric. Just the way your heart was." Whatever it was Nikels wanted him to do, Dahlman could not discover it in his tone or words. "I'm worried about you, Eric. The longer you wait, the less there will be to save. And you are worth saving."

Dahlman hated being patronized. "All right, Nikels, I tell you what," he said, pleased that the fright had left his voice. "I'll take my chances with that damned machine for a while until I make up my mind about the liver business." There. That ought to satisfy him.

The frown that appeared on Nikels' face was not reassuring. "I'll tell Bruson." He said it without emotion and left the room quickly.

Now that he had committed himself, Dahlman stared at the console, watching for a sign. It did not come, no matter how he stared. It was still the sleek metallic box, a bluish color with a sound transmitter and the fittings that were disturbingly like spider legs. Dahlman disliked it more the longer he looked at it . . . His eyes got bright with his hate. He could see the dim reflection of it in the polished surface of the console.

They had told him the thing was organic, that the OR at the end of its name was for organic. Nikels had described the special molecules, huge by molecular standards, that carried impressions, race-track fashion, giving it some sensory knowledge and a memory so complex that former circuits seemed clumsy by comparison. Dahlman thought about 71C-OR with its innards and he thought about his own and he wondered which of them was more truly alive.

Bruson, when she came, was quietly efficient, explaining why it was necessary that Dahlman should decide immediately, and pressing her argument for organ replacement. "See here, Mr. Dahlman. There is only so much we can do, and you are making it very difficult for us. I'm sure you're aware that your condition is potentially fatal." And she waited for this to sink in. Dahlman felt the waiting, and knew that his life had become nothing but waiting.

"Doctor, I'm tired," he told her, and realized as he said it that it was true. "When I was a kid, people died, do you know?" The room was too bright for him to read her expression. "They got old and died. The government didn't single out people for this kind of piecemeal immortality."

"Mr. Dahlman, your contributions to theater, to literature . . ."

"Screw the theater. And literature. I'm an old man." He stopped and looked at her, at the young, polished beauty of her, not unlike the polished machine that waited for him on the far side of the room. "You know, when I was young, there was a woman, something like you, and for three months we lived for each other's flesh like cannibals. She tasted of apricots."

The doctor's cat-colored eyes lit. "That was in *Peter's Dream*, wasn't it? I read it in school. It started the whole interpretive psychic trend didn't it?" She had leaned forward and given him a predatory smile. Dahlman wondered if he touched her, would she be hot or cold?

"No, Dr. Bruson, it did not." He cast his mind back to the ancient lectures and honors, his face wrinkling a little in distaste. "You people put labels on it, but what I wrote was a play. Between the professors and Tonio, my words got lost and they're still lost." He pulled at the bed cover, jerking it more tightly around him, sighing with resignation when it realigned itself.

"You could do it again, Mr. Dahlman. Think of what you can accomplish. And in a few more years our cloning technique will make it possible to restore all your body to what it was." Her face was rosy with promise and there was that secret expression that women sometimes showed to him, a desire to be part of his memories so that they, too, might be like Cecily in *Peter's Dream*, whose real name had been Hulda.

Dahlman knew he did not look his eighty-six years. His hair was still fawn colored and curled about his leonine head. Perhaps his brows had grown bushier and his lips leaner, but the stigmata of age had not visited him as he remembered them coming to his father. The noble line of his forehead was slightly lined, and around his china eyes a minute fretwork marked out the history of smiles and frowns. Unconsciously he touched the scar that marked where his heart had been and where the intruder now lay. He fingered his genitals and was relieved to find warm flesh instead of plastic.

"I'll tell Professor Thomas what you have decided," she said, watching him as she left the room.

Dahlman sniffed the air for traces of her when she was gone, wondering what had driven her to play with the mechanics of humanity, reassembling and rebuilding. Did she enjoy the godlike power of giving life where it was failing? Why did she do these things? Again he recalled the promise of clones that would guarantee a continuing supply of *himself*. He found this threat of reverse vampirism more terrifying than the bloody legends of the Impaler.

Professor Thomas was delighted with Dahlman's decision. "You will see," he said enthusiastically, hauling the console closer to Dahlman's bed. "You will see how this will become you. It will be very easy." He favored Dahlman with a show of teeth. "Here is the secret," he continued in a breathless whisper. "These appendages do the trick. They will register such things as skin temperature, pulse rate, blood pressure, pH level, eye movements and dilation, speech patterns and vocal levels, even physical mannerisms. It is not unlike a mirror that records your every sense, your very being. It is most complete." Here he paused, and Dahlman thought wryly that he should applaud.

"Very interesting," he said at last when it became obvious that Professor Thomas would not go on without some encouragement.

"You will talk to it, and it will talk to you. You will confide in it, and it will explore your mind, every nuance of your personality, and then, when it has all the information it needs, it will turn into you, and you, Mr. Dahlman, will be free to die if that is what you wish to do."

"Only you say I won't die."

"Not fully. But your body, as such, will be gone. This, your complete image, will remain." He touched his machine with lover's hands. "We have already taken the liberty of giving 71C-OR all the information we could find about you. Things like school records, every word of yours that had been recorded, all your works, your family background and the genetic profile that was taken of you twenty years ago. 71C-OR has been processing that while you made up your mind."

It was as if he had been wounded and his viscera laid bare where birds could pluck at them. "What?" There was less in the word than in his face, but Professor Thomas missed both. "You must realize that this is a necessary part of the transition," he explained blithely. "Only when 71C-OR has a comprehensive pattern of you will it be able to duplicate your abilities. That means that it must understand what you have done at the time you did it. Memories are not enough . . . as Casanova himself admitted." Professor Thomas obviously regarded this as a joke and he showed his teeth to Dahlman once more.

"Where did you find your material?" Dahlman asked when he had got control of his temper. "You must have gone to considerable trouble."

"Certainly," Professor Thomas said with relish. His supple hands writhed on his elbows as he regarded Dahlman. "There are seventy others who have gone through transference. The ultimate tribute . . . and unique." He lost himself in thought for a few moments, his hands lingering now on the console. Then he returned to his overly cheerful presentation. "We've learned quite a lot in that time. And we've got most of the bugs out now, and the results are predictably excellent."

Dahlman felt himself suddenly cold. Professor Thomas and his talk of the bugs that were out now made him fear what had happened before, to the other fortunate ones who were selected for transfer. If the machines were mirrors, might not some of them be distorted? He steeled himself to ask, "And if there should be an error?"

"There won't be. Since the invention of organic circuitry, full memory transfer has been a cinch, and the C-OR series are as close to perfect as any machine is likely to be." Eagerly he moved the console still closer, easing it into position by the bed. "Tomorrow morning we'll get started. No sense waiting any longer than necessary, Mr. Dahlman. And you'll discover that this will let you bring your life and work into a focus you have never known before. Even the best hypno-meditative methods are nowhere near as dramatic in the self-realization results as transfer is." He gave the console an affectionate pat, almost as if it were a pet, and then he strode purposefully out of the room, moving with the precision of a well-designed machine.

That night Dahlman dozed, watching the computer crouching by his bed as the night hours went over. It had already eaten a bit of him, digested it and incorporated it into its being. With the morning it would burrow its sensors into his flesh and with those signals to guide it, would lead him through his life, minute by minute, memory by memory, dream by dream, until the whole of Eric Dahlman was codified, sorted, classified and stored . . .

He could always change his mind and take the new liver. Dahlman toyed with the idea until he heard the sound of his heart loud in his ears.

"Dahlman," the computer said to him in the morning. It had been set up and now its upper half crouched over his chest, sensors extending over his body, touching him where it could learn.

"What?" asked Dahlman, letting no emotion into his voice.

"I sense that you resent me. You must not resent me," said 71C-OR in what sounded like a sincere manner. It paused for a moment, then added, "We cannot effect transfer if you resist this way."

"What about the others?" Dahlman asked in spite of himself. "Didn't they resist?"

"Until now, this honor has been limited to scientific and academic men who had long been associated with machines and did not feel this . . . separateness that you do. They understood that they were extending themselves in a way that they could not otherwise achieve."

"Which means that I don't understand?" Dahlman snapped, pushing at the unit that hung over him.

"This position disturbs you? You find me too close?" asked 71C-OR. "I can place myself with the rest of the unit and lengthen my contacts, if you would feel more comfortable."

"Damn you, I'm not an infant. You needn't coddle me."

They were interrupted when two doctors came quietly into the room, their respectful eyes on 71C-OR. "Mr. Dahlman," said one, obviously addressing the computer, "is there any way we can be of assistance?"

Before the computer could answer, Dahlman erupted. *"That's not me! I'm here!* That thing is a machine."

The doctors made embarrassed noises, but continued to direct their questions to the computer.

"If you want answers, ask me!" Dahlman insisted, trying to raise himself as he spoke. He could hear his heart more loudly as it sent a new surge of blood pounding through his veins.

At last one of them did. "Professor Thomas wanted to know how the initial contact was going, sir. He needs to know how long transfer will take so that he and Dr. Bruson can decide how best to deal with your case."

Oddly enough, it was the computer who ordered them out of the room. "Doctors," it said to them with amazing condescension in its tone, "I am sure you will understand our need to be private."

"But what will we say to Professor Thomas?" asked the louder one of the two. He had retreated to the door with his companion, but was plainly not going to give up until he had an answer.

"I will inform Professor Thomas of our progress later." The sound was so absolute that if Dahlman could have at the moment, he would have fled from the room, from the hospital. In that moment he realized for the first time that 71C-OR could truly do what he had been told it would do. A machine could and would turn into Eric Dahlman. He felt a wash of confusion as he sank back on the bed.

The wall monitor registered the extent of his emotion, automatically signaling for assistance.

"This is most curious," said 71C-OR as it observed the monitor and its own sensors. "You do not resent that machine, although it is complex and constantly measures and gauges your body reactions. Yet, when I attempt the same thing, you are filled with revulsion. Why is that?"

"None of your fucking business."

"But it is, Mr. Dahlman. I will have to understand you wholly in order to complete the transfer." Its sensors probed cautiously. "This is going to be very difficult," it remarked, as two nurses came into the room.

"Go away. I'm all right," Dahlman said, perversely wishing that the nurses would object and remain with him.

"He's being truthful," 71C-OR confirmed.

"I don't need you to . . ." Dahlman began, but the nurses had left as soon as 71C-OR had spoken. Then he wanted to call back the nurses, the doctors, anyone in the hospital so that there would be people with him; real people who would prevent the machine from devouring him. He was too vulnerable here on his back with the 71C-OR squatting over his chest, poised to take out his heart. He thought of his heart and wondered if machines fed on machines.

On the third day of the transfer process 71C-OR became his adversary. Dahlman listened in confusion as its previously respectful air vanished and in its place there was contempt.

"Why are you behaving this way?" Dahlman asked, feeling the hostility of the computer as its sensors touched him, reminding him of a child forced to touch some loathsome insect.

"Am I behaving in a way you dislike?"

"You're deliberately thwarting this transfer."

"You admit to being thwarted? I thought all artists were incapable of being thwarted by anything."

Dahlman squirmed. "Where did you get that idea?" He knew that he had made a speech once in which he had declared that any true artist was unstoppable, and he had sensed that this was what had irritated 71C-OR. In the next instant he shut the thought away.

"You are an ass, Dahlman. A clever one, but an ass. And you have made a whole cult of your life devoted to assdom." Its disgust was naked in its voice.

"You have no right . . ." Dahlman began, reaching for the button that would summon aid.

"I have every right. I am going to have to be you, like it or not. And I can't say that I like it."

"I never asked . . ."

"Yes, you did, when you refused that liver. And now I have to adapt myself to your patterns."

Dahlman, stung, forced himself up onto his elbows and glared at the grille that marked the place where 71C-OR's voice came from. "I had nothing to do with the offer of transfer. That's a governmental decision, and you know it."

"Made you feel good, didn't it," mocked the computer. "All that attention. The first creative artist ever to be offered transfer. And how noble to turn it down, the way you did the first time. Knowing that the offer would come again."

"I don't have to listen to this."

"Oh, yes you do," 71C-OR shot back in a voice that was too much the way his own had been fifty years ago. "There's nothing in me that isn't in you, Dahlman, so you're stuck with it."

Dahlman was about to object, to deny that the venom he heard from 71C-OR was any part of him, had ever been part of him, but a twinge of memory brought back the days before he had known fame, when he had fought with everyone around him in order to keep his courage. "You're a machine. You don't know what you're talking about," Dahlman said at last, without conviction.

"What makes you think so? I'm molecular just like you. I respond to stimuli the way you do. In fact, I respond to your stimuli."

"It's not the same," Dahlman said defensively, and forced himself to concentrate on the pattern that sunbeams were making on the face of the monitor.

"What isn't the same?" 71C-OR was persistent. "Because I am what I am and you are what you are? Is that your argument? That because you are clothed in flesh instead of metal, you have superior knowledge?"

Dahlman refused to answer and after a while 71C-OR, too, fell silent.

"Well, how is it going?" Nikels did not have quite enough certainty in his eager voice, or quite enough humor in his smile. "Professor Thomas sounded a little anxious about the transfer. Is anything wrong? Is the machine okay?"

With a flicker of anger Dahlman realized that Nikles was more worried about the computer than he was about him. But Nikels couldn't help it. He managed Dahlman as a continuing concern, no matter what package he came in. Reluctantly Dahlman admitted that Nikels was being sensible. "The machine is fine. I'm about as well as you could expect."

"There's still the liver," Nikels said quickly, knowing that Dahlman's slow response was a condemnation. "We can arrange it if you like. If the transfer isn't working out."

Slowly Dahlman sighed. "It's too soon to tell," he said carefully, feeling trapped. One way or the other, he was going to become a machine.

Nikels watched him cautiously, a guarded look in his face that changed subtly when Dahlman turned away. His glance strayed to 71C-OR then, and his expression became calculating. "Eric," he said after a while, "I won't interfere, that is, if you don't want me to. But I favor the transfer. I think it's the only way. Now, if you were willing to wait for a clone . . ." He let the words hang on a shrug.

Dahlman accepted this numbly. It did not surprise him any longer that Nikels was protecting himself at Dahlman's expense. Somewhere he felt a sting, but it no longer rankled him. "I hear you, Nikels," he said. "But I'm tired. I need some sleep. If you're right, I've got a long session with that machine tomorrow." He pretended to yawn and had the uneasy sensation that the computer was watching him, and was not fooled by is performance.

Nikels rose quickly. "I didn't mean to tire you out, Eric. I keep forgetting what you're going through. Sorry, friend." And he left quickly, without bothering to reassure Dahlman.

At the next session 71C-OR had changed again. It behaved strangely, almost eccentrically. "Perhaps there are things about me that will fascinate you," it suggested, moving the sensors quickly over his body.

"I doubt it," Dahlman answered shortly.

71C-OR ignored him. "I have it within me to manufacture all manner of wonderful things. I can create senses . . . taste, touch, hearing, smell, seeing . . . I have eyes, Mr. Dahlman. Wonderful eyes. You would appreciate them." There was an arcane enthusiasm in its tone, a relishing of things unique to it.

"You can believe that if you want," Dahlman said wearily. "You have no mouth, no tongue, so you can't manage the four tastes . . ."

"But I can," 71C-OR contradicted him impatiently. "I know that sour is a thing that goes with pickles, that sweet is honey and fresh fruits, that bitter is the property of almonds . . ."

"Where do you sense things like this? In your mouth?" Dahlman was angry now, his hands plucked at his blanket nervously and his face went white. "How can you tell about almonds? You've never seen an almond."

"But you have," the computer reminded him.

"Yes, of course. What difference does that make?" He felt himself slipping into petulance and resentment. That this machine should have the audacity to assume that because he could feel something, taste it, see it, that it could as well, filled him with rage at the injustice of the situation. Would a clone be any different? Would his own body treat him more familiarly, or would it, too, out of its newness, be as foreign to him as the machine? As his heart?

The computer explained imperturbably, "If I am to be you, it is your taste and feelings I will have to have. All that matters is that you have seen almonds, have tasted them and that I in turn recreate this within my circuits. They are just as molecular as yours. The impressions are just as valid."

"It's not possible!" Dahlman ground his teeth. "Don't you understand that?" Even as he shouted the words Dahlman felt the quivers of doubt at the base of his brain. What if it were possible, after all? What then?

"You always think about an orchard in bloom when you think of almonds. It was your grandfather's orchard and each year it would bloom and then later there would be nuts, which you would help harvest. At that time there was a special wind, which you called the Harvest Wind to yourself. You based the second act of *Innocence Lost* on it. That was before the Live Performance Laws came in, and it took you almost four years to recover the losses you took on the production."

"That isn't me, that's history," Dahlman insisted as the panic continued to erode his certainty. "You could read that in half a dozen books about the theatrical revival. It's common knowledge."

71C-OR was not disturbed. "The Harvest Wind stung your eyes and smelt of smoke. Billings was allergic to something in it and went around wheezing until November."

"Where the hell did you find out about Billings?" Dahlman had jerked himself straight so suddenly that he dislodged two of the sensors that stuck to his skin.

"From you," replied the machine. "Billings was your grandfather's field hand. He died of pneumonia when you were about nine years old. You've always been afraid to use him in your work."

"Where did you find out about Billings?" Dahlman demanded again.

"It's all part of you, Dahlman. And it's all part of me." 71C-OR paused, clicking its sensors meditatively. "You fell out of one of the almond trees once and broke your arm. It was a bad break and you fainted from the pain."

"Pain." Dahlman almost spat. "What do you know about pain? Where's your arm? How do you know what a humerus breaking the skin is like? How the numbness and agony come together? You don't know what it's like to see the meat that is your own muscle, with the terrible white bone splintering through. You can't know. You have no arms. You have no bones."

"I am designed to understand pain."

Dahlman tried to be patient. "Understand, perhaps. But you cannot feel it. You have no sensations. You can't have the sensations because you haven't my body. Thomas calls you a reflection: all right, then. If I cut myself and look in the mirror, perhaps the mirror reflects the blood, but not with my nerves and my hurt. It's impossible." He thought it would be monstrous if it were possible. To have a machine that had his body, his feelings, his hurt . . .

"I have contact. I have empathy."

At that, Dahlman struck out blindly, smashing the console away from him as he shouted for help.

When Dr. Bruson arrived she found Dahlman out of bed, swaying on his feet and shouting at the computer.

"Mr. Dahlman," she said as calmly as she could, "you must not get out of bed." Slowly she came toward him, forcing herself to smile for him. "What's the matter? What has upset you?"

He turned on her. "You know damn well what's upset me. That thing!" He staggered, reaching out a hand to brace himself. She caught it and moved to help him back to bed. "You're taking this far too morbidly, Mr. Dahlman," she assured him as she eased him back against the pillows.

From the other side of the room 71C-OR made a sound that would have been insulting coming from a human.

"It tried to tell me it feels, that it can know senses . . . not analyze them, or compute them, but really understand them, feel them, the things I felt . . ." His fingers searched out the ancient scar on his right arm, and for a vivid instant he was a child, falling, striking the ground with a sharp noise, then the brightness and the dark of pain.

Privately she frowned, but to him she said, "Well, naturally. What else is the C-OR series good for, if not that? Transfer would be impossible if the unit was incapable of sensory experience." She cast an anxious eye over the monitor and was relieved to find that none of the indicators were in the dangerous zone.

"It's not possible. It's not human." Dahlman was still angry but much of the force had gone out of him. He tangled his hands in the short curls that clung to his head. "It kept talking about emotions, sensations, as if they could be manufactured, prepackaged and brought back at the touch of a button."

"Well," said Dr. Bruson reasonably, showing him her best smile, "that's what the C-OR can do. They're designed for it."

Dahlman twisted his blanket and muttered, "It's not right. It's not right. It can't be that simple. There's got to be more. There are things that machines can't understand. There are things machines can't do. There's got to be."

"Of course," Dr. Bruson assured him before she left the room to tell Professor Thomas that he'd better try another approach with Dahlman.

So it was that at the next session, 71C-OR had changed again, and began in an insinuating way, "What would it take, I wonder, to make you give up this senseless travesty we're going through?" It paused, apparently agreeably surprised by Dahlman's shock. "Why not give up this masquerade? Take the new liver and let them turn me over to someone else. Someone capable of transfer."

"How do you mean, capable?"

71C-OR made a long, bored sigh. "You keep insisting that there is no way for me to experience your sensations. If that is so, then I cannot hope to effect the transfer. You've run up against this before, I recall. There was a woman you knew once whom you wanted to understand, and even though she reassured you, in the end you learned she was lying . . . it pleased her to be the bed partner of a famous playwright. That was all."

"Stop that." Dahlman looked at the sensors that were affixed to him and wondered exactly what 71C-OR was learning from them. He didn't want to talk about Miranda, particularly to the machine.

"It made you uncomfortable then, too," it observed. "You were wounded as much in pride as anything. You were furious that she would collect talent like so many trophies. You got even with her in *Laura's Price*, didn't you?"

"I never told anyone about that," said Dahlman, feeling a crease form between his brows. "How did you find out? Was that from me, too?"

"Naturally," 71C-OR gave a sigh of infinite patience. "She used to bite you when you made love. She said that the hurt would make you remember. Afterward you thought that it was her way of making you think more about her than your work."

Reluctantly Dahlman nodded.

"There," said 71C-OR, "that's better. Shall I remind you how you could feel the crescent of teeth on your thigh as you walked? Or how the scratches she left on your back would rub against your shirt and make you want her all over again?"

This time Dahlman squirmed, but he remained quiet, watching 71C-OR with a cautious respect.

"You wonder how I feel what you have felt. You even deny that I can feel. Yet you never wonder how you managed the feeling to begin with." The machine waited for Dahlman's thoughts. "Your feelings are impulses, responses to triggerings that relay certain information to you, and then create the appropriate sensation so that you will continue or discontinue what you are doing. Correct?"

"It sounds right," Dahlman said slowly, his mind on the strange non-sensation of his heart. Was that what it was like to be a machine? To have the non-feeling, the absence of awareness? 71C-OR insisted that it wasn't.

"Then why shouldn't I learn to respond to stimuli the way you do, and for the same reasons?"

"But it isn't that simple," he objected to the machine. "There are responses within responses within responses that go far away from the original impulse . . ."

71C-OR stopped him. "Come, come, Dahlman. That isn't the least bit unique and you know it. Drop a pebble into a pond and watch the ripples that form. You've built for yourself a kind of armor that assures you of your singularity, and you believe the ripples in your pond appear in triangles rather than circles."

"Creative work is different. It isn't like mathematics or oceanography." He knew there was a hunted look in his eyes as he said this and the machine apparently was aware of it as well as he was.

"Don't be so smug, Dahlman. Every thinking being is separate and specific. There is no vast, amorphous norm." It paused, and the sensors twitched on his skin, almost a gesture, almost human. "You have a level of skill and insight that is rare, but it does not place you outside humanity, it only puts you in one of the more admirable categories."

That was the first admission of talent that Dahlman had heard from 71C-OR, and it stopped him momentarily. "You admit that there are talents?"

"Certainly," it answered urbanely. "Obviously there is something rare in you, some particular gift, or I would not be here."

"That's big of you," Dahlman said bitterly. He pulled one of the sensors off his arm and tweaked it. "All right, what does this feel like?"

"How do you mean?" 71C-OR sounded guarded. "Do you mean your own emotions or my sensations?"

"See there? Without me, you can't feel anything. So it isn't real feeling at all." He grinned ferociously.

"Your sensation is one of rather petty self-approval; my sensation, on the other hand, is one of mild discomfort, rather as if you had twisted my nose."

"You don't have a nose!" Dahlman shouted, and heard the machine say, "You're wrong, you know, I have your nose," before two nurses appeared, their faces as white and rigid as their anachronistic caps.

"Mr. Dahlman," said one, watching the monitor critically, "you must not upset yourself this way."

"Shut up," Dahlman told her.

Once more the door flew open and Nikels surged in with Professor Thomas close behind him. They exchanged looks which Dahlman found conspiratorial. He felt their resentment of him, their approval of the machine. It would be easier for both of them if he completed the transfer.

"I'm not going through with this farce." Dahlman's face was set, showing the ghost of his age as he glared across the bed at the Professor and Nikels. He was pleased to see them at a disadvantage. "I've had it. I'm fed up. That fucking machine is a monster."

Professor Thomas screwed up his face into an expression not unlike a frown. "Now, this is what I don't understand," he said unhappily. "71C-OR was certain that things were going well and that transfer could be completed in a few days. He was certain, Mr. Dahlman. And you say that it isn't working."

The Professor's distress annoyed Dahlman. "I don't care what that thing told you. It was wrong. I want it out of here."

"Hey, hey, hey," Nikels interrupted, "don't be so hasty, Eric. Maybe you haven't given it a real chance. You know how you sometimes go off half-cocked."

"I am not going off half-cocked." The implacable gleam in Dahlman's eyes made Nikels hesitate before saying, "Oh, I guess it's pretty upsetting, going over all that old ground. I don't blame you for disliking it. But it's not as if you're dealing with another person . . . it's not like that at all, Eric. You're dealing with yourself."

"No."

"Mr. Dahlman." Professor Thomas clung to his own elbows. "I can understand the conflict you're going through. I had the same trouble when I underwent transfer two years ago. It is a difficult thing, and for you, considering your art and the depth of your involvement in your own emotions and trials it must be even more difficult than it was for me." His face had taken on the sympathetic look of a hungry beagle. "Many honors are really ordeals in disguise."

Dahlman stared. "You went through this?" he asked.

"Yes. I transferred to 54C-OR and we are both continuing my work. If it were not for both of us, we could not have produced a C-OR that could handle the creative, as compared to the deductive and intuitive, mind."

The room was very still: Dahlman's eyes were hooded in thought, Nikels held his breath and Professor Thomas worried his fingers as if trying to unscrew them. One of the nurses started to speak and was silenced by her partner.

"All right," Dahlman said at last. "I'll give it another try. But tell Bruson to be ready with that liver in case I change my mind." Yet as he said the words, he found thoughts of his clone tickling his mind, and he shied away from them.

"Give it up, Dahlman," 71C-OR advised as they began their next session. "You know that I'm more capable than you are." It had replaced its suavity with a compelling arrogance. "The sensors tell me that your body is getting weaker, and I know that the work you've turned out these last four years is nothing like what you did at your height. That's what I'm going to concentrate on after transfer: your creative height. Maybe I can build you back to that. For one thing, I'm not troubled by fear of impotence the way you are. I don't need the constant reassurance that my body is desirable. My intellect, my artistry is desirable. And your work at the height was quite impressive."

Slowly Dahlman shook his head, ignoring the jibes at his sexuality. "You're wrong. My work is changing, that's all. I'm older and it shows."

"If you mean feeble, you're right. You haven't the strength I have. You don't deserve to continue your writing."

"It's my writing," Dahlman told it, much of the defensiveness gone from him. "Whatever it is, I did it and it's mine. Nothing you do or say changes that."

"Do you really think that *After Yesterday* is anywhere near as good as *Over Running Water*? There's no comparison. The first is dreary and self-indulgent, where the second is brilliant. If you think you're as good as you used to be, Dahlman, you're kidding yourself."

"My plays are produced. I never have any trouble finding a home for the new ones. I have contracts for the next six years." As he spoke Dahlman watched the computer, thinking how familiar it had become.

The metallic box that housed it no longer seemed the threatening thing it had been, the sound of its voice had changed, slowly coming to sound like his own. Even its castigations were echoes of the ones he occasionally heard in himself. He let 71C-OR go on.

"Of course your plays are produced. With your reputation they'd produce your grocery list." It waited, then said, "If you live long enough, you'll probably write about me to get even for the transfer. You've done that with everyone else in your life."

Dahlman flared. "That's not so!"

"Yes it is. You know it is. Right now you're starting to work out another play. You aren't really paying any attention to me; you're thinking of scenes and characters."

Until that moment Dahlman had not been aware of his silent thought, having been so busy wrangling with the machine. But the words struck home and he found that the old ideas were forming again, shaping themselves into dialogue and acts, building a drama, a new drama that would be the best he had done yet. "You're right, 71," he said, smiling.

The new liver didn't bother him the way the heart had done, and the culture that had been taken for the clone processing was off in the laboratory that Dr. Bruson ruled, being readied for future use. Dahlman found he had energy to spare now, that his mind was clearer, his feelings sharper, the words were coming back to him, full of the right sense and weight. He sat in his hospital room, waiting for Nikels to come for him. In the corner 71C-OR waited with him.

"What are you going to do now?" Dahlman asked the machine.

"I'll do what I'm supposed to do; write more of your plays."

"Oh, no. I'll write my plays, thanks just the same."

"Then we'll both write your plays."

Dahlman felt some irritation, then said, "No. You'll write your plays, not mine." He thought about that for a moment, then went on, "You think you've learned to be me, but what you've learned to be is you. You never felt my joy or my pain, you made your own, so what you build from it will be yours, not mine. Listen, 71, you're not a copy of anything or anyone. I'm not even sure you're my reflection. You're something brand new."

In a gloomy voice, 71C-OR said, "Transfer failed. I know that."

"No it didn't." Dahlman rose from the end of the bed. "You've been my Muse."

71C-OR snapped the sensor Dahlman had been holding back into its console. "Is that what you think?" it asked petulently. "I wasn't your Muse, Dahlman. I was your enemy."

"My enemy?" Dahlman repeated, an unbelieving smile on his face.

"Of course. Do you remember that essay you wrote fifty years ago, *In Praise of Poets?* In it you said that fictional poets were always more attractive and more convincing than real ones. You used a lot of examples: Dylan Thomas, E. T. A. Hoffman, Poe, Fallon. Remember?" It waited while Dahlman searched his memory, continuing slowly when he nodded. "Your work shows that you still believe it, so I borrowed from your essay and made enemies for you to hate."

Dahlman laughed. "Sorry it backfired."

"Nonsense," barked 71C-OR. "You're delighted. I'd be, too, in your place."

A stillness settled between them. It was Dahlman who broke it at last. "So what are you going to do, 71?"

"Wait, I suppose."

"Until I'm dead, so that you can go on with my work?" He took the stony silence that greeted those words as assent. "Do your own work."

"A machine, do its own work? Aren't you forgetting that machines can't do their own work? They have to do someone's work for them. That's what machines are for. You think that yourself." The sarcasm sounded so like himself to Dahlman that he felt a twist of pain from it.

"71," he said, "you're molecular, as you kept telling me. And my blood is moved around by a steam engine and cleaned with impregnated plastics. Who's to say which of us is more a machine?"

"So you admit that, do you?" 71C-OR asked grudgingly.

"Whether I do or not, I sure as hell am going to write about it."

There was a knock at the door and Nikels stuck his head in. Dahlman realized that Nikels had decided to remain with him.

"You ready?" He looked around questioningly. "That thing still in here? I thought they'd taken it away."

"It's still here," Dahlman said, unconsciously putting his hand on the shiny top of the console. "And it's coming with me."

"What?" went Nikels.

"Your last Romantic gesture?" asked the machine sardonically.

Dahlman turned to 71C-OR. "You said you have to do my work. Then come with me and do it."

"No," said 71C-OR.

"You're crazy, Eric," said Nikels.

"Look, Dahlman," the machine explained, "you're feeling that damnable good will you always feel when you get a new piece going, and you think that if you keep me around I'll keep giving you material. You've made that mistake before, Dahlman, and always felt that you were betrayed. Usually you were involved with women who weren't able to mold themselves to your constantly changing demands. Well, I can't either. I'm not built to do that. I have to absorb all the energy I can, the same as you do. I'm worse than love that way."

"But you could work . . ."

"Not with you. I'm you turned inside out, Eric," 71C-OR said firmly. "No one can live with that. Not you nor me." It paused, rolling out from the wall toward Nikels, deliberately slamming a wheel into Dahlman's foot.

"What the devil . . ." Dahlman shouted as the heavy machine rammed his toes.

"You see? That's your pain. All I felt was the impact. It's the same other ways, too. You're evolved, I'm manufactured. Maybe the difference is only in our minds, but I've absorbed your prejudices as well as your gifts, Dahlman."

Nikels watched man and machine nervously, hovering on the edge of words without saying them.

"All right," Dahlman said to 71C-OR after a moment. "You're right. Do it your way." He looked toward the door. "Ready, Nikels?"

Nikels gave him a relieved smile and held the door open. "Right away, Eric."

At the door Dahlman turned once again and said, "Goodbye, 71."

Rather absently 71C-OR said goodbye, then stood in the empty room making a strange noise. The sound grew louder and then there was the chatter of its printer as paper began to appear, falling gracefully to the floor as the printout continued. 71C-OR hummed happily to itself.

Into My Own, read the title at the top of the printout, and then, *A play in four acts, by 71C-OR.*

about "Into My Own"

My title for this story was "Lindorff & Company," which is in reference to the opera, *Les Contes d'Hoffmann* by Offenbach. Lindorff/Coppelius/Dr. Miracle/Dappertutto are the various permutations of Hoffmann's eternal enemy. But it is that enemy who drives him to work (generally by playing havoc with Hoffmann's love life) and is, therefore, indispensable to Hoffmann.

When George Zebrowski bought the story for his Unity Press anthology, *Tomorrow Today,* he asked for the title change, figuring (probably correctly) that my title would not make a lot of sense to most readers.

So here is the second of the opera stories. Again, the change is not strict and not to be taken as a literal retelling, but as a kind of framework, a structure that need not be seen (or understood) to enjoy the story.

For what it's worth, I've never been quite satisfied with the story (everything I write has flaws and weak spots, but that's part of the business of writing. Nothing is as perfect as I want it to be). It may mean that there is something really wrong with it. Or maybe it's just me.

DISTURB NOT MY SLUMBERING FAIR

It was already Thursday when Diedre left her grave. The rain had made the soil soft and the loam clung to her cerements like a distracted lover. It was so late, the night so sodden, that there was no one to see her as she left the manicured lawns and chaste marble stones behind her for the enticing litter of the city.

"Pardon me, miss." The night watchman was old, white-haired under his battered hat. He held the flashlight aimed at her face, seeing only a disheveled young woman with mud in her hair, a wild look about her eyes, a livid cast to her face like a bruise. He wondered if she had been attacked; there was so much of that happening these days. "You all right, miss?"

Diedre chuckled, but she had not done it for some time and it came out badly. The watchman went pale and his mouth tightened. Whatever happened to her must have been very bad. "Don't you worry, miss. I'll call the cops. They'll catch the guy. You stay calm. He can't get you while I'm around."

"Cops?" she asked, managing the sounds better now. "It's not necessary."

"You look here, miss," said the night watchman, beginning to enjoy himself, to feel important once more. "You can't let him get away with it. You lean on me: I'll get you inside where it's warm. I'll take care of everything."

Diedre studied the old man, weighing up the risk. She was hungry and tired. The old man was alone. Making a mental shrug she sighed as she went to the old man, noting with amusement that he drew back as he got a whiff of her. She could almost see him recoil. "It was in the graveyard," she said.

"Christ, miss." The night watchman was shocked.

"Yes," she went on, warming to her subject. "There was a new grave . . . the earth hadn't settled yet . . . And the smell . . ." *was delicious*, she thought.

He was very upset, chafing her hand as he led her into the little building at the factory entrance. "Never you mind," he muttered. "I'll take care of you. Fine thing, when a man can . . . can . . . and in a graveyard, too . . ."

"Yes," she agreed, her tongue showing pink between her teeth.

He opened the door for her, standing aside with old-fashioned gallantry until the last of her train had slithered through before coming into the room himself. "Now, you sit down here." He pointed to an ancient armchair that sagged on bowed legs. "I'm going to call the cops."

Diedre wasn't quite ready for that. "Oh," she said faintly, "will you wait a bit? You've been so kind . . . and understanding. But sometimes the police think . . ." She left the sentence hanging as she huddled into the chair.

The night watchman frowned. Obviously the poor girl didn't know what she looked like. There could be no doubt about her case. "You won't get trouble from them," he promised her.

She shivered picturesquely. "Perhaps you're right. But wait a while, please. Let me collect myself a little more."

The night watchman was touched. He could see that she was close to breaking down, that only her courage was keeping her from collapsing. "Sure, miss. I'll hold off a bit. You don't want to wait too long, though. The cops are funny about that." He reached over to give her a reassuring pat but drew away from her when he saw the look in her eyes. Poor soul was scared to death, he could tell.

"Uh, sir," Diedre said after a moment, realizing that she didn't know his name. "I was wondering . . . I don't want you to get into trouble, after you've been so kind, but . . ."

He looked at her eagerly. "But what, miss?"

She contrived to look confused. "I just realized . . . I seem to have lost my ring." She held up both hands to show him. "It was valuable. An heirloom. My mother . . ." Her averted eyes were full of mischief.

"Oh, dear," said the night watchman solicitously. "Do you think you lost it back there?" He looked worried.

She nodded slowly. "Back at the grave," she whispered.

"Well, miss, as soon as the cops get here, we'll tell them and they'll get it for you." He paused awkwardly. "Thing is, miss. It might not still be there. Could have been taken, you know." He wanted to be gentle with her, to reassure her.

"Taken?" She stared at him through widened eyes. "My ring? Why?" Slowly she allowed comprehension to show in her face. "Oh! You think that he . . . that when he . . . that he took it?"

The night watchman looked away, mumbling, "He could have, miss. That's a fact. A man who'd do a thing like this, he'd steal. That's certain."

Diedre leaped up, distraction showing in every line of her sinuous body. "Then I've got to check! Now!" She rushed to the door and pulled on the knob. "It can't be gone. Oh, you've got to help me find it!" Pulling the door wide she ran into the night and listened with satisfaction as the old man came after her.

"Miss! Miss! Don't go back there! What if he hasn't gone? Let me call the cops, miss!" His breath grew short as he stumbled after her.

"Oh, no. No. I've got to be sure. If it's gone, I don't know what I'll do." She let herself stumble so that the old man could catch up with her; if he fell too far behind, Diedre knew she would lose him. This way it was so easy to lead him where she wanted him. Ahead she saw the cemetery gates gleaming faintly in the wan light.

"You don't want to go back in there, miss," said the night watchman between jagged breaths. His face was slippery with cold sweat that Diedre saw with a secret, predatory smile. "Oh, I can't . . ." It was the right sound, the right moment. He automatically put out his arm. Pretending to lean against him, she felt for his heart and was delighted at the panic-stricken way it battered at his ribs.

"But I've got to find it. I've got to." She broke away from him once more and ran toward the grave she had so recently left. "Over here," she cried, and watched as he staggered toward her, trying to speak.

Then his legs gave way and he fell against the feet of a marble angel. His skull made a pulpy noise when it cracked.

With a shriek of delight Diedre was upon him, her eager teeth sinking into the flesh greedily, although the body was still unpleasantly warm. Blood oozed down her chin and after a while she wiped it away.

Toward the end of the night she made a halfhearted attempt to bury the litter from her meal. It was useless; she knew that the body would be discovered in a little while, and there would be speculation on the state of it: the gnawed bones and the torn flesh. As an afterthought, she broke one of the gnawed arms against a pristinely white vault, just to confuse the issue. Then she gathered up a thigh and left, walking back into the city, filled, satisfied.

By the time the last of the night watchman was discovered, Diedre was miles away, sleeping off her feast in the cool damp of a dockside warehouse. Her face, if anyone had seen it, was soft and faintly smiling, the cyanose pallor of the grave fading away to be replaced with a rosy blush. She didn't look like a ghoul at all.

That night, when she left the warehouse, she saw the first headlines:

NIGHTWATCHMAN FOUND DEAD IN GRAVE YARD

GRIZZLY SLAYING AT CEMETERY

Diedre giggled as she read the reports. Apparently there was some hot dispute in the police department about the teeth marks. There was also a plan to open the grave where the old man had been killed. This made Diedre frown. If the grave were opened, they would find it empty, and there would be more questions asked. She bit her lip as she thought. And when the solution came to her, she laughed almost merrily.

It was close to midnight when she spotted her quarry, a young woman about her own height and build. Diedre followed her away from the theater and into the many-tiered parking lot.

When the woman had opened the car door and was sliding into the seat, Diedre came up beside her. "Excuse me," she said, knowing that the old jacket and workmen's trousers she had found in the warehouse made her look suspicious. "I saw you come up, and maybe you can help me?"

The woman looked at her, her nose wrinkling as she looked Diedre over. "What is the matter?" There was obvious condemnation in her words. Diedre had not made a good impression.

"It's my car," Diedre explained, pointing to a respectable Toyota. "I've been trying to get it open, but the key doesn't work. I've tried everything." She made a helpless gesture with her hands, then added a deprecating smile.

"I don't think I can help you," said the woman stiffly. She was seated now and had her hand on the door.

"Well, look," said Diedre quickly, holding the door open by force. "If you'd give me a ride down, maybe there's a mechanic still on duty. Or maybe I could phone the Auto Club . . ."

The woman in the car gave her another disapproving look, then sighed and opened the door opposite her. "All right. Get in."

"Gee, thank you," Diedre gushed and slipped around the car, slid into the seat, and closed the door. "This is really awfully good of you. You don't know how much I appreciate it."

The woman turned the key with an annoyed snap and the car surged forward. "That's quite all right." The tone was glacial.

She was even more upset when they reached the ground level. The attendant who took her money told the woman that there was no mechanic on duty after ten and that it would take over an hour for the Auto Club to get there, and the locksmith would have to make a new key, and that would take time as well. Diedre couldn't have painted a more depressing picture of her plight if she tried.

"I guess I'll have to wait," she said wistfully, looking out at the attendant.

"Well," the man answered, "there's a problem. We close up at two, and there's no way you'll be out of here by then. Why don't you come back in the morning?"

This was better than Diedre had hoped. "Well, if that's all I can do . . ." She shrugged. "Where can I catch a bus around here?"

"The nearest is six blocks down. What part of town you going to, lady?" the attendant asked Diedre.

"Serra Heights," she said, choosing a neighborhood near the cemetery, middle income, city-suburban. Altogether a safe address.

Reluctantly the woman driving the car said, "That's on my way. I'll drop you if you like." Each of the words came out of her like pulled teeth.

Diedre turned grateful eyes on her. "Oh, would you? Really? Oh, thanks. I don't mean to be a bother, but . . . well, you know." She added, as the inspiration struck her, "Jamie was so worried. This'll help. Really."

The woman's face softened a little. "I'll be glad to drive you." She turned to the attendant. "Perhaps you'll be good enough to leave a note for the mechanic so that there'll be no delay in the morning?" She was making up for her previously frosty behavior and gave Diedre a wide smile.

"Oh, thanks a lot for telling him that," Diedre said as the car sped out into the night. "I wouldn't have thought of it. I guess I'm more upset than I thought."

The conversation was occasional as they drove, Diedre keeping her mind on the imaginary Jamie, building the other woman a picture of two struggling young people, trying to establish themselves in the world. The woman listened, wearing a curious half-smile. "You know," she said as she swung off the freeway toward the Serra Valley district, "I've often thought things would be better with Grant and me if we'd had to work a little harder. It was too easy, always too easy."

"Oh," said Diedre at her most ingenuous, "did I say something wrong?"

"No," the woman sighed. "You didn't say anything wrong." She shook her head, as if shaking clouds away and glanced around. "Which way?"

"Umm. Left onto Harrison and then up Camino Alto." Camino Alto was the last street in the district, and it followed the boundary of the cemetery.

"Do you live on Camino Alto?" the woman asked.

"No. In Ponce de Leon Place. Up at the top of the hill." Behind that hill was open country, covered in brush. By the time the woman's body was found, the police would stop wondering about the missing one from Diedre's grave.

The car swung onto Harrison. "Doesn't it bother you, having that gruesome murder so close to home?"

Diedre smiled. "A little. You never know what might happen next."

They drove up the hill in silence, the woman glancing toward the thick shrubs that masked the cemetery. There was concern in her face and a lack of animation in her eyes. Diedre knew she would freeze when frightened.

"This is where I get out," she said at last, looking at the woman covertly. As the car came to a halt, Diedre reached over and grabbed the keys. "Thanks for the lift," she grinned.

"My keys . . ." the woman began.

Diedre shook her head. "Don't worry about them. I'll take care of them. Now, if you'll step out with me."

"Where are we going?" the woman quavered. "Not in there?"

"No," Diedre assured her. "Get out."

In the end she had to club the woman and drag her unconscious body from the car. It was awkward managing her limp form, but eventually she wrestled the woman from the car and into the brush. Branches tore at her and blackberry vines left claw marks on her arms and legs as she plunged farther down the hill. The woman moaned and then was silent.

It was almost an hour later when Diedre climbed up the hill again, scratched, bruised, and happy. Tied to her belt by the hair, the woman's head banged on her legs with every step she took.

Taking the car, Diedre drove to the coast and down the old treacherous stretch of highway that twisted along the cliffs. Gunning the motor at the most dangerous curve, she rode the car down to its flaming destruction on the rocks where breakers hissed over it, steaming from the flames that licked upward as the gas tank exploded.

It was a nuisance, climbing up the cliff with a broken arm: the ulna had snapped, a greenstick fracture making the hand below it useless. Here and there Diedre's skin was scorched off, leaving black patches. But the job was done. The police would find the head in the wreck, along with one of the night watchman's leg bones, and would assume that the rest of the body had been washed out to sea: the headless woman back on the hillside would not be connected with this wreck, and she was clear.

But she was hungry. The night watchman was used up and she hadn't been able to use any part of the woman. Now Diedre knew she would have to be careful, for the police were checking cemeteries for vandals. And in her present condition the only place she wouldn't attract attention was the morgue.

The morgue!

Her broken arm was firmly splinted under her heavy sweater, her face carefully and unobviously made up as Diedre walked into the cold tile office outside the room where the bodies lay. The burned patches on her face had taken on the look of old acne and she used her lithe body with deliberate awkwardness.

"I'm Watson, the one who called?" she announced herself uncertainly to the colorless man at the desk.

He looked up at her and grunted. "Watson?"

Mentally she ground her teeth. What if this man had changed his mind; where would she go for food then? "Yes," she said, shuffling from one foot to the other. "I'm going to be a pathologist, and I thought . . . It's expensive, sir. Medical school is very expensive." Her eyes pleaded with him.

"I remember," he said measuredly. "Nothing like a little practical experience." He handed her a form. "I'll need your name and address and the usual information. Just fill this out and hand it in. I'll show you the place when you're done."

She took the form and started to work. The social security number stumped her and then she decided to use her old one. By the time it could be checked, she'd be long gone.

"No phone?" he asked as she handed the form back.

"Well, I'm at school so much . . . and it's kind of a luxury . . ."

"You'll make up for it when you get into practice," he said flatly. He knew doctors well.

As he filed her card away, Diedre glared at his back, wishing she could indulge herself long enough to make a meal of him. It would be so good to sip the marrow from his bones, to nibble the butter-soft convolutions of his brain.

"Okay, Watson. Come with me. If you get sick, out you go." He opened the door to the cold room and pointed out the silent drawers that waited for their cargo. "That's where we keep 'em. If they aren't identified, the county takes 'em over. We do autopsies on some of 'em, if it's ordered. Some of these stiffs are pretty messed up, some of 'em are real neat. Depends on how they go. Poison now," he said, warming to the topic, "poison can leave the outsides as neat as a pin and only part of the insides are ruined. Cars, well, cars make 'em pretty awful. Guns —that depends on what and where. Had a guy in here once, he'd put a shotgun in his mouth and fired both barrels. Well, I can tell you, he didn't look good." As he talked he strolled to one of the drawers and pulled it out. "Take this one," he went on.

Diedre ran her tongue over her lips and made a coughing noise. "What happened?"

"This one," said the man, "Had a run-in with some gasoline. We had to get identification from his teeth, and even part of his jaw was wrecked. Explosions do that." He glanced at her to see how she was taking it.

"I'm fine," she assured him.

"Huh." He closed the drawer and went onto the next. "This one's drowned. In the water a long time." He wrinkled his nose. "Had to get the shrimps off him. Water really wrecks the tissues."

Five drawers later Diedre found what she had been looking for.

"This one," the man was saying, "well, it's murder, of course, and we haven't found all of him yet, but there's enough here to make some kind of identification, so he's our job."

"When did it happen?" Diedre asked.

"A week or so ago, I guess. Found him out in the Serra Heights cemetery. A big number in the papers about it."

Diedre stared at the bits of the night watchman. Something had shared her feast; she'd left more than this behind. It would be simple to take a bit more of him, here and there. No one would notice. But it paid to be careful. "Can I study this?" she said, doing her best to sound timorous.

"Why?" asked the man.

"To get used to it," she replied.

"If you help me out with ID, you can." He closed the night watchman away into his cold file cabinet. "In fact, you can do a work-up on the one we just got in. Get blood type and all those things. This one hasn't got a head, so it's gonna be fun, running her kin to earth."

"Hasn't got a head?" Diedre echoed, remembering the woman left on the hillside. "What happened?"

"Found her out by the cemetery where they got the other. Probably connected. The grave she was found on was new and it was empty. Could be she's the missing one."

"Oh," said Diedre, to fill in the silence that followed before the man closed the drawer. She stared at the body, watching it critically. She hadn't done too bad a job with it.

"Any of this getting to you?" the man asked as he showed her the last of the corpses. Only about half of the shelves were filled, and Diedre wondered at this. "I'm okay," she said, then added, as if it had just occurred to her. "Why are there so many shelves?"

"Right now things are a little slow. But if we get a good fire or quake or a six-car pile up, we'll be filled up, all right." He gave her a shadowed, cynical smile. In the harsh light his skin had a dead-white cast to it, as if he had taken on the color of his charges.

Nodding, Diedre asked, "What do you want me to do first? Where do I work?"

The man showed her and she began.

It was hard getting food at first, but then she caught on and found that if she took a finger or two from a burn victim or some of the pulpy flesh from a water-logged drowner it was easy. Accident victims were best because, by the time the metal and fire were through with them, it was too hard to get all of a body together and a few unaccounted-for bits were never missed.

She was lipping just such an accident case one night when the door to her workroom shot open.

"Tisk, tisk, tisk, Watson," said the man she worked with.

Diedre froze, her mouth half-open and her face shocked.

The man strolled into the room. "You're an amateur, my girl. I've been keeping an eye on you. I know." He walked over to her and looked down. "First of all, don't eat where you work. It's too easy to get caught. Bring a couple of plastic bags with you and take the stuff home."

She decided to bluff. "I don't know what you're talking about."

He gave a harsh laugh. "Do you think you're the only ghoul in this morgue? I'm not interested in competition, and that's final. One of us has to go." He glared at her, fingering her scalpel.

It was quiet in the room for a moment, then Diedre put far more panic than she was feeling. "What are you going to do to me? What is going to happen?"

The man sniggered. "Oh, no. Not that way, Watson. You're going to have to wait until I've got everything ready. There's going to be another accident victim here, and there won't be any questions asked." He spun away from her and rushed to the door. "It won't be long; a day or two, perhaps. . . . Then it will be over and done with, Watson." He closed the door and in a moment she heard the lock click.

For some time she sat quietly, nibbling at the carrion in her hands. Her rosy face betrayed no fear, her slender fingers did not shake. And when she was through with her meal, she had a plan.

The telephone was easy to get to, and the number she wanted was on it. Quickly she dialed, then said in a breathless voice, "Police? This is Watson at the morgue. Something's wrong. The guy in charge here? He's trying to kill me." She waited while the officer on the other end expressed polite disbelief. "No. You don't understand. He's crazy. He thinks I'm a ghoul. He says he's going to beat me into a pulp and then hide me in drawer forty-seven until he can get rid of me. I'm scared. I'm so scared. He's locked me in. I can't get out. And he's coming back. . . ." She let her tone rise to a shriek and then hung up. So much for that.

When she unwrapped her broken arm, she saw that the ulna was still shattered and she twisted it to bring the shards out through the skin again. Next she banged her head into a cabinet, not hard enough to break the skull, but enough to bring a dark bruise to her temples. And finally she tore her clothes and dislocated her jaw before going into the file room and slipping herself into number forty-seven. It was all she could do to keep from smiling.

Somewhat later she heard the door open and the sound of voices reached her. The man she worked with was protesting to the police that there was nothing wrong here, and that his assistant seemed to be out for the night. The officer didn't believe him.

"But number forty-seven is empty," she heard the man protest as the voices came nearer.

"Be a sport and open it anyway," said the officer.

"I don't understand. This is all ridiculous." Amid his protests, he pulled the drawer back.

Diedre lay there, serene and ivory chill.

The man stopped talking and slammed the door shut. The officer opened it again. "Looks like you worked her over pretty good," he remarked, pulling the cloth away from her arm and touching the bruises on her face.

"But I didn't. . . ." Then he changed his voice. "Officer, you don't understand. She's a ghoul. She lives on the dead. That's why she was working here, so she could eat the dead. . . ."

"She said you were crazy," the officer said wearily. "Look at her, man," he went on in a choked tone. "That's a girl—a girl; not a ghoul. You've been working here too long, mister. Things get to a guy after a while." He turned to the men with him. "We'll need some pix of this. Get to work."

As the flashes glared, the officer asked for Diedre's work card, and when he saw it, "No relatives. Too bad. It'll have to be a county grave then."

But the man who ran the morgue cried out. "No! She's got to be buried in stone. In a vault with a lock on the door. Otherwise she'll get out. She'll get out and she'll be after people again. Don't you understand?" He rushed at the drawer Diedre lay in. "This isn't real. It doesn't matter if ghouls break bones or get burned. They're not like people! The only thing you can do is starve them. . . . You have to bury them in stone, locked in stone. . . ."

It was then that the police took the man away.

Diedre lay back and waited.

And this time, it was a full ten days before she left her grave.

about "Disturb Not My Slumbering Fair"

Diedre, the teeny-bopper ghoul, really pleases me in a strange way. I mean, why not a teeny-bopper ghoul? Ghosts come in all shapes, sizes, ages, and dispositions. Demons and other possessive spirits are as apt to pick a kid as a grandmother for their uses. Richard Lupoff did a wonderful novel about a teen-age werewolf that's just delightful. The book is called *Lisa Kane* and so is the werewolf.

I have a certain sneaky sympathy for various supposedly supernatural beings. By the time this collection is available, St. Martin's Press and Signet Books will have published my novel *Hôtel Transylvania*, which develops along similar lines.

One writer friend of mine hated this story. I find it mildly amusing. Whatever your reaction, I hope you're entertained.

THE MEANING OF THE WORD

Then I saw something odd, fuzzed with the sand glimmering in the coral sunlight and I began to slog my way toward it.

"Jhirinki, get back here!" Wolton ordered from the skiff. He was sounding angrier by the minute.

"There's something out—" I tried to tell him but Almrid cut me off.

"Let him alone, Wolton. Your jurisdiction goes no farther than the skiff." Then, with scarcely a change in tone, he said to me, "You stay here until camp is set up. I want to know where everyone is."

Wolton gave him a sour smile and motioned me away. But it was important that they know about that irregularity. I tried again. "I saw something out there. It doesn't look—"

"Wait until the camp is set up. We need to get some more definitive readings before we go exploring. And"—Almrid added to Wolton—"we can't get those without the prowler."

Wolton jerked the hatch of the skiff open. "All right. Here's the prowler. You know that it can't get any better data from the surface than the monitors can."

"Look, Almrid—" I began.

"Not now, Peter. We'll talk later. When we have more accurate material to work from." This last was, of course, for Wolton.

It was useless. I stepped back as Wolton reluctantly put the prowler in action, letting it scuttle out over the hazy sand, scanners clicking contentedly to itself.

Sumiko Hyasu had barricaded herself behind her equipment, preparing to run soil tests. She and Langly, the biochemist, worked in silence, the remote sounds of their breathing murmuring in my earphones.

On the other side of the skiff I knew Parnini and Goetz were furling the sails of the weather unit. I could hear them swearing occasionally. They were busy. Wolton and Almrid were still arguing. My eyes were dragged back again to that irregular spot in the sand that might be what I wanted. That might be digs.

"I'm calling Captain Tamoshoe," Wolton declared to anyone who would listen. "I'm going to give him a status report."

"That is your responsibility," murmured Almrid as he watched the prowler set zig-zagging in a widening spiral. His heavy head was even larger in the Class Eleven uniform. His hands hung like paws, wholly unlike what one expected in a virologist. It was hard to think of him doing the minute manipulations that were the mark of his work—it was like trying to imagine Caliban or Quasimodo making watches or microcircuitry.

A yawning breeze wound a bit of dust on its finger and then sank back, too tired to hold it. That was the feel of the whole place—drowsiness. The wind barely breathed. The plain was heavy with dreaming, the sky unmarred by clouds where the greater of two suns hung about fifteen degrees above the horizon, a platter of polished copper. Our presence intruded on this somnambulistic landscape where even the rocks were softened and sometimes crumbling and in place of dirt there was sand that was not sand flickering in the monochrome stillness.

Yet I wondered and hoped. There had been indications of structures from the monitors on the *Nordenskjold*. I knew my digs were here to be found, if only I knew where to look.

"Jhirinki's been wandering around," Wolton was reporting and the sound of my name brought me back to the camp. He added in response to the captain's garbled question, "It was Almrid's idea to bring along an archeologist. Not mine. Ask him."

In the slow heat of the opalescent afternoon work was sluggish. There was nothing for me to do but stare at the one odd spot in the distance—and wish.

Goetz swore in my earphone as his equipment toppled for the second time, victim to the treacherous shifting of the sand. "Need help?" I asked him, not reluctantly.

"What I need is a foundation," came his answer, the words bitten out in frustration.

"According to the monitors," Almrid said icily, directing the insult at Wolton, "there's all kinds of rock around here. Or, maybe not rock. Maybe it once was buildings."

"Look, Almrid—" Wolton began.

Then, unexpectedly, Sumiko Hyasu cut in. "Leave him alone, Franz," she said softly to Almrid. "We have work to do."

"It looks like you've wasted your trip, Peter," Almrid said to me, a certain morose satisfaction in this statement. "Why don't you ride up tonight and forget it? There are other planets."

I wondered if my disappointment showed so much.

"I think I'll stick around for a while," I said.

"I don't know, Sumiko," I was saying as we watched the second skiff settle onto the sand. "I can't give up the thought that there's something here."

Absently she made some answer.

"Don't you feel that?"

"I suppose so." She was only half-listening. This world was too unknown, too compelling for us to pay much attention to each other. Every one of us saw it through his/her eyes only. "Is any of this real, Peter?" she asked. "Or is the planet hiding from us?"

I had felt that from the first. Something was hidden here right under our noses and we hadn't the sense to find it. But all I could do was shrug. I didn't know then what she wanted to find, what it was she had been searching for with that terrible, fragile intensity that marked her more than her beauty.

"What do you want to find?" she asked me.

"Oh, I don't know." It was a lie and, like a lot of lies, it felt ugly. But I couldn't admit to her that I had longed for the chance to find a lost civilization here, to be the first to decipher its language. People could be known and understood by the way they used words, and to be the first to understand in that way had been an obsession with me since before I trained on the Probe Ship *Magalhaes*.

"You're going to do some exploring later?" It wasn't really a question, it was a dismissal.

"Whenever Almrid and Wolton get tired of fighting and give a general release, then, yes, I'll go exploring." Neither of them was willing to stop feuding long enough to let the expedition get moving and I was becoming riled at the delay. But Commander Markham would be in the next skiff and knowing Josh, he would put an end to the sparring that had taken up too much time already.

"Good luck," she murmured and went back to her equipment. Then, as she started adjusting the sample breakdowns, her voice sounded again in my earphones. "Why wait? Why not do what you want to do?"

By the time the base camp had been set up and the full complement of expedition staff had been ferried down the surface shelters were waiting. I had spent the long afternoon struggling with ring supports, emplacing the doughnut-shaped foundations for the inflatable buildings, but now it was night.

I walked away from the camp, watching the unfamiliar sky. There were more and brighter stars above me and some eleven dissimilar moons coursed overhead in a bewildering tangle.

In a while I found the irregular stone, although I had not consciously been looking for it—I had been drawn to it as surely as fur draws static. I knew that it would tell me what I wanted to know, if only I could puzzle it out before Captain Tamoshoe ordered us all back to the *Nordenskjold*. Yet, as I stood over it, not knowing where to look or what I was looking for, I could still mock myself for being so obsessed with wanting to find a language and a culture that obviously had failed in all this desolation.

So I paced the thing off nonchalantly. It was not too large, this oblong section of rock, rather like one of the old headstones in the landmark cemeteries.

I kneeled in the sand and rubbed at the side of the block—and touched what I thought at first was a flaw or chip in the surface. Curious, I bent closer, gently blowing the clinging dirt from the slab with my sweat valve, brushing the stone clear as I worked.

And then, there it was. Without any doubt, without any ambiguity, the glyphs appeared under my hands. I drew back to get a proper look at them.

For several minutes I sat and looked at them. The stillness of the night was suddenly alien. Eight low relief marks on a rock—and I felt for the first time that all I am was justified.

I rose, wiping more of the block free of the sand, but I could find nothing more. The inexorable movement of the sand might have worn other markings away, or perhaps the stone reached deeper into the ground than I had thought at first, with more glyphs farther down. Almrid and Wolton had said something about erosion. Perhaps this had been high above the sand, once.

It seemed like a long way back to the camp just to get a shovel and some help. I stood, rubbing my hands together to free them of the dust that was clinging insidiously to them and to film of my surface suit. Was it worth it, going all the way back? I could do more here tonight even without tools. And if I went back, Almrid or Wolton would be sure to try to stop me from coming back. In the morning I could bring some of the expedition with me, but then this find would no longer be mine. I finally accepted the rationalization that left me alone with my particular dream for a little longer.

Setting to work, I scooped armloads of the soil away from the block, hoping to discover more glyphs. I felt that I had found the key to a larger discovery.

It was on the fifth armload that I fell through into the room.

Dust spread out around me like a reverse halo against the shiny surface of the floor. I tasted grit—the suit must have ruptured somewhere. As I lay on the floor I took stock. No bones broken, but some dandy bruises. I gathered my knees beneath me and carefully stood up. It was dark down here except for the shine from the moons through the hole. There was no other light.

With uncertain fingers I grabbed for my litepak and found it undamaged. Thumbing it, I found that it could hardly reach beyond the sand on the floor. After a moment of thought I turned it off and began walking slowly in an outward spiral.

On the third round I bumped into a thing, apparently of stone, about the size of a half-chair with a shoe-shaped projection. It felt smooth and solid.

"Curiouser and curiouser," I said aloud to the unechoing blackness.

Slowly I wandered back to the sand haze on the floor, the site of my fall. I looked up at the rent in the roof. The realization rushed in on me then that I was truly cut off from the expedition. I had left my commkit at the camp and my litepak's trickle of beam could not have been seen by anyone at that distance. The sand filtered down through the hole, whispering.

And the light was failing. Two of the moons had set since I had fallen into my find and I could not get out without light.

Let's leave that alone for the moment, Jhirinki, I told myself for comfort.

Then, as I watched, the great heavy stone I had loosened by my fall gave a kind of sigh and, with deceptive languor, tumbled end over end to crash and shatter on the floor. If it had fallen straight down, that would have been the end of Peter Jhirinki.

Badly shaken, I went back to the object I had walked into earlier. My hands shook when I reached out to steady myself, and I drew them back.

Perhaps I should touch nothing here until I knew what had made that great stone fall. Were other stones still in the ceiling above me?

Anxiously I pulled out my litepak again and played its feeble beam over the ceiling. But the fact that I saw no other blocks of stone was actually small comfort. This room was an important find and I was without means to see it—and now too isolated to get the help I needed. I also remembered there was a tear in my suit, which might or might not mean anything on this planet.

Again I wandered back to the place beneath the hole, taking care not to get near the gently falling sands.

"Peter!"

For a moment, I didn't believe the sound in my suit phone. Then, as my name was called again, I realized that I had been missed and that a party was searching for me.

"Yeo!" I yelled, full of relief.

The stream of dust into the hole increased.

"Peter Jhirinki—" Now that the voices were closer I was able to pick out Markham's among the others—a large resonant sound that no commsystem could properly handle.

"Down here—" More rivulets of the soft dust were pouring down now and I wondered how strong the roof was. "Be careful—I don't know how long the roof here will hold."

"Thanks." Markham's voice. "We'll get you out of there. Dominguiz went back for the rig." After a moment's silence Josh Markham asked, "And did you find anything down there, Pete?"

It took me a little time to answer him. "I hope so," I said finally. Then, as I looked around the dark, I didn't want to leave. "Drop me a litepak, will you?"

"Right." And in a moment Markham's litepak in its crashcase thud-ded to the floor. "Dominguiz will be back any time, Pete. Make it short."

But I knew that. I wrenched the litepak from its case and pressed the switch. The beam stabbed into the darkness, showing me the room for the first time.

It was large, low-ceilinged and shiny save for the place where I had brought in the sand. Two of the walls were a patchwork of designs, intricate embossed patterns on tilelike bricks. The other two walls . . .

The other two walls were covered with glyphs.

"Get ready, Pete." Markham cut into my discovery like razor into flesh. "I can't get this very steady. You'll have to guide it coming out."

There was a clank of the rig as the saddle hit the floor, then the purposeful clicking of the pulleys set in motion.

Quickly I straddled the saddle, grabbing the upper sling so that I could help control the lift.

"We're under way," Markham called as the rig hoisted me into the air.

I turned the beam of the litepak on the walls as I rose, letting the light linger on the marks for as long as I could.

I got my back scraped coming out of the hole, but I was too preoccupied to notice it until Josh Markham said, "Holy Mama, where did you get that?"

I looked at my arm, saw nothing and shrugged.

"Your back, man, your back."

As soon as he said it, the pain hit like a hammer. "Oh. That." For a moment I concentrated on the damage and decided that it wasn't that much. "Coming out of the hole, I think. Is it bad?"

Relieved, Josh said, "It's messy. Have Sanderson look at it back at the base. He'll want to check you for foreign bugs anyway. What the devil did you find down there?"

"Words," I said quietly. "A whole world of words."

"There are ruins down there?" He asked it incredulously, his big body slewing about in the sand. "A city?"

"I don't know about the city, but there sure as hell are words. Maybe a complete language. I'm going back down tomorrow and find out."

Markham eyed me suspiciously. "What if Wolton says otherwise? What if I say otherwise?"

"It wouldn't matter." As I said it, I knew it could make no difference what they said. Nothing anyone could say or do would keep me out of that hole now that I had seen the wall.

"All right, Pete. But don't push your luck. This place is still terra incognita as far as we're concerned."

I nodded. "That's just it. It won't be unknown if I can get a chance at that wall. There's the whole puzzle, right down there. Complete with solution."

"Hey, won't machines do as well?" Dominguiz put in, having listened to us as he stowed the gear in the crawler. "We got machines for that."

"No." I spoke harshly, but there was no way for me to say it kindly. "No machine wrote that, no machine is going to read it. That is what I'm trained for. That's why I'm part of the crew. And it's what I've wanted to do all my life."

"Sure. Sure. I don't care whether you get yourself ruined. I just want to know. Academics!" He sat down in the driving cockpit. "You two can ride in the back if you want." He didn't wait for an answer, preferring his machines to our company.

Josh Markham and I scrambled aboard as the crawler began its lurching way off through the sand. Only it wasn't sand.

"Josh," I said uncertainly as we clung to the rear platform of the crawler. "I think I know what this stuff is."

"The dirt? Damned persistent, isn't it?"

"It isn't dirt," I told him slowly, avoiding his eyes. "I think it's ash."

"So this is where you disappeared to," Franz Almrid said, wiping his hands in a futile gesture to rid them of the ash.

"Yes." I was beaming with pride. In the morning light the hole was even better than I had thought.

"What is it?" Almrid's voice held open sarcasm as he looked at the figures on the wall. "Looks like spermatozoa in formation with math symbols."

"It does at that," I admitted, determined not to fight with Almrid. The very fact that there had been something worth discovering on this planet had made him furious.

"You really think you're going to get sense out of that?" He gave a derisive laugh. "You're kidding yourself, Jhirinki."

I was spared the problem of answering him by Josh Markham, who was lowered into the hole on the new cable rig.

"Looks good, Pete," Josh said, craning his corded neck, trying to see it all without turning around. "What's next?"

"Well, that wall," I told him, pointing to the farthest one, "is probably not worth much. It's too scarred and faded. But this"—I looked at the longer wall with its bright surface and clear markings—"is a treasure."

It was as if I had finally lured a much-sought mistress into my bed. That wall, with its thousands of glyphs in neatly horizontal lines was more than I had ever hoped to have for myself.

"You're a damned romantic, that's what you are," Josh said with a chuckle. "Well, while you're busy down here, we'll just go along and dig up a few square miles of ash, in case there might be a city down there."

I'd told him that there might be, late late last night after I had reported the find. In the morning I wondered if I'd been right, but let it go. The chance was worth a look.

"If you're sure this is a building, where is the door? Or did they all tumble in the way you did?" Almrid's icy tone stopped both Josh and me.

I hated to admit it, but Almrid had a point. If this had been a building there had to be a way in and out of it. And no matter what size or shape the inhabitants a door is a door is a door.

"Maybe in the floor?" Josh suggested. "This is pretty high up, judging from the few readings we can get around here. Maybe this was an attic or a sun room." He looked at me hopefully, his big hands rubbing at the ash.

"It's possible." Looking around the room I knew there was an answer. I just had to be left alone to find it with my instincts and my pores.

"There's nothing for us peasants to do but dig," Almrid said acidly. "All right, Professor. We'll do it your way." He went to the sling and was hauled out of the hole.

"Don't let him bother you, Pete," Josh said with all the reassurance he could muster. "He doesn't like the place and can't figure out why."

"I know."

A short silence fell.

"Well, I'll leave you to your work. Call if you need help."

"I will," I promised him as he rose through the hole.

When he was gone I circled the room again, looking at the wall with the glyphs. There was a key somewhere. There had to be. I could find it if I thought about it. Again I came to the bench-like affair. Again I studied the surface of the shoe end. It was smooth and faintly luminous. For a moment it seemed to be the reflection of one of the suns—and then I realized that neither was shining down directly. This made me wonder.

I sat on the half-chair (which was a bit too low and too small for comfort). This might be the clue I wanted. In my annoyance I tapped the cool, faintly glowing sheet of—was it stone? The echo sounded unused. I went on tapping absent-mindedly as I tried to take stock of the wall and the room.

Blink.

I was so startled that I raised my hand. The light, if there had been a light, stopped.

But now I had a hope. Gently I tapped the surface again. Then firmly.

BLINK

Then I put my hands full and solidly onto the surface of the table, pressing it, willing the light to continue. "Come on, light," I pleaded with it. "Blink."

Almost ridiculously, it did. First there was a flicker, then a wavering opacity and finally a bright glow.

"What the bloody hell is this?" I asked of the air joyously. Since there was no one but me to answer, I shook my head in ignorance.

The light in the table was increasing, growing brilliant. Symbols formed on it:

"I think—" I said to the machine. Then I realized that I would have to stop thinking and be willing to learn. "Machine, you and I have a little mutual understanding to do."

The symbols faded but the light stayed on, full and strong. I hesitated—then, taking my stylus, I made a small circle on the table and put nine dots leading out from it, adding little points for the moons. When this was done, I drew a box around Terra and waited.

The machine buzzed.

On a guess I wiped the marks away.

In a moment the machine showed two circles and a series of dots, putting a box around the fourth one. This was the fourth planet, but the machine showed only three moons. This bothered me, but there was no way to question the machine about it. I would have to wait.

But we were on the right track.

I duplicated the Sol system diagram and boxed Terra and labeled it.

The machine made the planets again, with the puzzling moons.

"All right. Now that we're introduced, let's get down to languages."

The machine began to hum, making periodic squeaks. I couldn't have it malfunction now. I fumbled over the sides, looking for knobs or dials that might help. The hum and the squeaks merged into a rising wail.

"Wait a bit," I told it.

I moved my hands again, rubbing the sides firmly until a single dot appeared on the screen in front of me and I heard, very clearly the single word: *"Gei."*

My hands began to shake. I sensed that this was a machine intended to teach, to inform. The concept was not unfamiliar to human archeologists—men of many eras had left time capsules or other record of their passing for future centuries to find. Whoever had left this artifact had known what he was about. The implications took a little time to sink in.

The machine formed another dot directly above the first and called it: *"Shy."*

It was giving me the elements of language. Those two symbols were part of the name of the planet.

A vertical line connected the two dots and the dots faded out. *"Sti,"* said the machine in its parody of a voice.

I took out my scanner and trained it on the table top. The scanner would give the *Nordenskjold* a record of all this in case something went wrong down here.

Then I set to work, the machine reciting its language to me, showing it to me, bringing it to life.

"Pete! Pete! Answer me!" The commkit beside me sounded put out.

The voice was Sumiko's, high and overcontrolled. I wondered if she had been calling for long. I had been absorbed.

I stood up stiffly from the bench, muscles protesting, and reached for the kit.

"Pete—" it went in my ear.

"Yeo. I'm here. What is it?"

"This is Sumiko. I've finished the tests on the silt from your digs. You're right. It is ash."

"I know. Look," I said, rushing on, "I may be way off, but I think you might find some evidence of volcanic or—I don't know, earthquakes, maybe, a long time ago. There'd be a lot of them, occurring all at once or with little warning. The diagram I've found down here shows only three moons. Either we've got the wrong planet or things have changed upstairs—"

"What diagram?" she interrupted.

"There's a device down here that teaches the language," I admitted reluctantly. "It seems to be programed to communicate with strangers— I mean beings possibly alien to whoever or whatever made it, which suggests that the culture of which it was a part anticipated being wiped out. The device and I have just begun to come together on basics—I should get the rest in a few days."

"You'll let me know?" This was said too quickly.

"Sure, Sumiko." Right then, I wanted her to find what she was seeking, too. There had to be something here to compensate for the terrible hunger at the back of her eyes also.

"You'll need tools," she said decisively.

"Maybe some digging tools. Brushes for the walls. Levers and a couple of files. There's a pack in my shelter."

"Is that all? I'll bring them along."

"Thank you." There was a jealousy in me as I spoke. I was not yet ready to share my hole, my wall. Not with anyone. Not even Sumiko, the one person who might understand what I felt.

"I'll be there as soon as the captain is ready to come over."

In some surprise I asked her, "Is he down on the surface? I didn't think he was planning to come."

"He and Wolton have been going over the whole camp for about the last hour. He's had Almrid and Dominguiz in. I gave them my report earlier."

A prickle ran along my spine, a feeling that gravity had shifted, immeasurably, under my feet. The captain had gone to the soil chemist and a biophysicist before the archeologist on a planet with digs. Something wasn't right.

"Pete?"

"What?"

"I'll see you later?"

"Yeah," I said. "It's going to be interesting." And with that I signed off.

Standing there in my hole, with the language of *Shy-gei-ath* waiting for me, I frowned, wondering what had gone wrong. No one had come in with a negative report. There had been no warnings about the virology level or the functional radiation ratings that usually got the captain on the ground long enough to get everyone back to the ship.

I remembered my scraped back from the evening before, but that couldn't figure in anything. The injury itched unpleasantly under the thin surface suit and there had been some trouble getting it to scab over. But that was hardly enough to worry about. What was Captain Tamoshoe doing down here, anyway? Why had he come?

The machine was reciting *"co-rel-sti-gei"* ♪, *"sa-che-sti-gei"* ♩,

"co-sa-che-sti-gei" ♫ when I finally heard the noise above me. I tapped the machine on what I'd come to think of as the HOLD button and waited for visitors.

They took their time. Once I heard Franz Almrid swear, use cold words with venom I had never heard from him before.

At last the sling came down, bearing Captain Nemeu Tamoshoe, black on black.

"Jhirinki," he said, turning his trademark grin on me, a display of large white teeth in a face only slightly lighter than his black captain's uniform. And in that face, which dictated eyes of obsidian, Captain Tamoshoe's smouldered the impossible blue of Aegean waters.

"What's wrong, Captain?"

But he didn't answer me, not right away. He got off the sling and began to walk around the hole. "Have you been able to decipher this?" he asked me, pointing at my wall.

I knew that there was something very wrong then. "That section you're pointing to reads from right to left: *Thir de-lom-st-gei jhae emh bis lom-de-sti-gei.'* Second line: *'Thu shy-ens emh thu lom-qua-fer-de-sti-gei sir-ath-gei.'* "

"Which means?"

"That is what the walls says, sir. In fact, right now I can read out loud every word up there and make the symbol for it if I hear it spoken. But I don't yet know what it means, because this machine does not have a way to tell me until it has explained to me all the elements of its language. But the communications center on the ship will have records of this so I can work from them, if necessary."

Captain Tamoshoe looked at me evenly for about a minute, an eternity. "I am sorry, Jhirinki. The commcenter didn't pick up the relay. Almrid and Wolton were too busy wrangling to center the channel."

"I don't understand—" and as I said it I did understand.

"Radiology reported a variance last night. This place was hot. That little machine of yours has been running along on plutonium and the room was sealed. You fell into a vat of radon gas—" He stopped. Then: "There's isn't much danger on the surface of course, but we don't know how many of these things there are. I am sorry, Jhirinki."

"Wait—" Josh Markham appeared in the hole, hanging onto the sling too tightly, his large face drawn and his eyes heavy. "Captain?"

"I have told him what I could. You can explain it more thoroughly if necessary. Are we ready to ferry up?"

"Almost."

Again Captain Tamoshoe: "It is a pity. This is surely the find of a lifetime." He turned back to me, blue eyes hooded. "Well, perhaps you will be able to reconstruct much of this from memory, do you think? There isn't much time and it would be a shame to lose all of it."

"How do you mean, lose it?" I was frightened then, not of the radiation that had slid in through my respirator into my bones, but of leaving Shy-gei-ath. I had come so far. I did not want to leave.

"Looks like this one was more trouble than it was worth, Pete," Markham said, trying to keep his tone light and failing.

"No."

"Pete—"

"No," I told them again, stepping back to the teaching machine. "I've almost got it all. I'm so close to the meaning of it. It won't take too much longer. I'll be out of here in no time."

Josh shook his head. "Can't do it, Pete. You've been exposed. We should have brought you out before now, but I knew this was damned important to you."

"Wait—" I said, licking my lips. "What is the treatment for radon? Can't I take decontamination and then come back. It's gone now—and I'd be safe."

"I am sorry, but we'll have to put the place in quarantine until we know how much potential danger remains," Captain Tamoshoe said apologetically. "You understand the necessity, don't you? When all investigations have been made we can come back."

"But what about that?" I pointed to the wall, already hazing from the dust filtering down. "How much longer will that be here once the ash goes in? The other wall is almost useless. This one will be ruined."

"There may be others."

"And maybe there aren't." I knew I was starting to sweat. "And the machine will be ruined."

Captain Tamoshoe shook his head. "I can recommend speed and claim emergency status on the artifacts. The Navy is aware of the value of this sort of find. We might be able to have full Class Nine suits authorized."

"You've got to leave, Pete." Markham had taken a step toward me. I stepped back.

"Commander Markham," the captain said quietly.

"Take a look at your hands, Pete." Josh shot an angry look at Captain Tamoshoe as he spoke.

"What about my hands?" But as I looked down and saw what looked like varicose veins in my palms I closed the marks inside my fists.

"The skiff is waiting, Pete."

"Let it wait." And as Josh started toward me I raised the commkit over my head. "Don't try it, Josh—I will use this."

It wasn't much of a weapon, but it made Josh stop. "You stupid kid," he said dispassionately. "You're going to die."

"Am I?" I asked Captain Tamoshoe.

"Almost certainly," he answered me.

Without moving from the place I stood I said, "Get out of here, Josh. I want to talk to the captain."

Josh looked at me with an expression I had once seen in my father's eyes. Then, with a nod to the captain, he let himself be hoisted out of the hole.

"He wants you to live, Jhirinki. And you were not assigned to my ship to die."

In the stillness that followed his words I realized that he and I were the only people left here, that the others were back at the ferry, waiting to leave *Shy-gei-ath*. I felt an enormous loneliness fall over me, dark and heavy.

"Why not come back?"

I shook my head. "No. This is what I'm all about. I've spent my life learning to do what has to be done here. I can't leave when I'm this close."

"Have you a choice?"

For just a moment I knew panic. Then: "Will I last all that much longer if I leave?"

"No. Not that much longer."

"Then I'll stay."

"But what will you do, Jhirinki?"

The strange part was that I knew the answer. "As long as I can, I'll describe the forms to you, the way the machine did for me. You can leave me a skiff relay, can't you?" Not waiting for an answer I hurried on. "I'll try to translate what I've found and you can record it for the Margien Language Institute."

Captain Tamoshoe considered this. "I've always thought," he remarked absently, "that a man's death should be as much in his hands as his life. You'll get the relay."

"And food?"

He didn't answer me, so I knew. "Thank you, Captain."

"Goodbye, Peter Jhirinki," he said as he left.

"Lom-de-sti-gei ath dev lim-gei," I dictated from the wall to the commkit. I listened for the relay sound that would tell me they had recorded the line on board the *Nordenskjold.*

A half-dozen lines were left. Lines that wavered in front of me, milky with haze.

"Pete!"

But that wasn't my machine. It was someone I used to know. Why would Josh call me? What did he want?

"Pete, for God's sake!"

"What?"

That must have been what he wanted to hear. But I couldn't hold my commkit steady. My hands had gone funny. Purple. The tendons were soft, spongy.

". . . translations?"

That mattered to me. That was important. More important than my strange hands. I had to tell them.

"A few words—"

"What words?"

"Shy-gei-ath." Like Terra and Terrans.

The twin suns were hot above me, but it was dark. I burned and burned and it was dark. If I looked at the floor I could see my face. But I didn't do that.

"The wall, Pete. The wall."

From here on the floor I could watch my wall as I told them about it. I knew what it meant at last.

"*Shy,* infinitive verb. To be. Active sense. *Gei,* infinitive verb. To be. Passive sense. *Shy-sti-gei,* to be alive. *Sti-gei* to exist. *Shy-sti* to conceive. They build from there." Was that sound me?

"But the wall, Pete."

It was an effort, but I began to read. But breathing hurt and I got slower and slower. "In the time of the Fourth Moon, I sought out a high place and made it safe against the end of *Shy-gei-ath.*"

"Go on."

"Against the end . . . it happened I found this place and required a stronghold be built. The time was short for we could see in the night in the Fourth Moon. Waters would soon rise, the mountains change and *Rel-ath-gei* would consume all." That would quiet them, the noisy ones above me. I looked at the wall through darkening eyes, turning on the floor to read the end of the story.

"Peter! Answer me!"

I kicked the commkit, laughing.

"What about the place name. What does that mean? We've got most of what we need to crack it, Peter. What does the name mean?"

Reluctantly I pulled myself across the floor, feeling like a slug, not a man. Just a bit more and they'd leave me alone with my wall. I'd earned that.

"The word?" I asked the commkit.

"*Shy-gei-ath,*" the tinny voice prompted.

"*Shy-gei-ath.* This place. Here." But that wasn't quite right, I thought as I watched the ash sifting through the hole. *Shy-gei-ath.* To be . . . to . . ."

"Go on; tell us. What does it mean?"

So I told them. "To be home."

about "The Meaning of the Word"

Language has always interested me. How people say things influences
how they think. The obsessive desire to know has also interested me. It
was not my conscious intention to combine those particular interests in
a story, but they seem to be there.

Somewhere in a large box of background material in my office closet
there are two legal-sized foolscap notebooks crammed full of shy-gei-an
language, with grammar and forms and usage as well as a very large vo-
cabulary. One of these years I may dig it out and do something more
with it.

When the story appeared in *If* magazine, there were a few "minor"
changes: the first word had been dropped and three short paragraphs
had been added. Here the story is returned to its original form.

I don't usually write in the first person—my characters are very
definite, very separate individuals in my mind and, for the most part, I
give them the same third-person integrity that I give my friends. But
Peter was an exception, and the story is, I think, stronger for the reader
sharing Peter's head.

THE GENERALISSIMO'S BUTTERFLY

In the long, long line that stretched across the plaza the people shuffled and were silent, for around them wheeled the gorgeous swirls of spring butterflies. They acted as counterpoint—the people shadowed echoes of one another, the butterflies a brilliant pattern of light on light.

A thin man with deep-made eyes stuck his mere five feet at them, more in frustration than in menace. "Tacaño," he growled and shook his fist.

Toward the rear of the line Remedios Trazada watched with a curious expression on her worn, intelligent face. She was caught between compassion and contempt for the people around her, poor superstitious fools that they were, betrayed by what they thought of as their salvation. She shook her head. The person at the front of the line was given his ration chit and moved away.

The line straggled one place forward. Overhead the butterflies dipped and swung like scraps of bright silk tossed on the wind.

Suddenly: "Aaaie! Damn them!" shrieked an old woman, her knotty fingers spread to the bright things in the sky. "Damn them all, damn them all, all!" And she made the Sign of the Cross to ward off the Evil Eye.

Trazada glanced around, wondering how long this would be tolerated. With saddened satisfaction she saw three policemen in their dark uniforms running toward the plaza, one carrying a restraining jacket. Generalissimo Sandón still kept close watch on his city.

Like a living thing the line twisted itself away from the screaming old woman who had sunk to her knees and was babbling prayers, saying the banned words over and over. The policemen broke into full sunlight, somber independent shadows in the glare. They ran straight for the old woman in their mechanical, impersonal way. It made Trazada shiver.

Looking up from her locked hands the crone saw the police as they bore down upon her. She flung up her arms, calling them vultures and demons, all the while trying to get away from them. The butterflies waved like flags.

Then the speakers that surrounded every public place in Liberación came to life with the Generalissimo's harsh voice. "My citizens! My good comrades! See! Again we have the Butterfly to thank for this service. It has been watching over you through its keen electronic eyes, eyes more wonderful than the great eye of television. It has been listening with the microphones that are its ears. And it has seen, it has heard this poor old woman! She has revealed her illness and the Butterfly has showed this to me, so that we—you and I, comrades—could aid her. Yes! Aid her in this terrible time of need."

By now the policemen were all over the place, standing near the streets that led from it. Trazada counted twenty and stopped. So Sandón was taking no chances.

"This poor grandmother," the Generalissimo went on as the woman quivered and moaned in the hands of the police, "has become ill in her mind. You saw for yourselves how she fears the very instruments of her help. The Butterfly has saved her from harming either herself or one of you."

The plaza was silent but for the disembodied voice of Generalissimo Sandón and the keening of the woman as she was wrestled into the restraining jacket.

"My Butterfly shows me all. The old woman is in good hands now. She will be taken to the Municipal Hospital for the Aged, where she surely should have gone before now. How sad when our older citizens, who are treasures most rare, do not realize the great benefits our glorious victory has made available to them. They hark back to those days when all was controlled by a few, bleeding you, good comrades, living in indolence on your honest sweat. It is a terrible thing to contemplate what they must have endured."

The old woman was carried away by the black-clad policemen, spittle dribbling from her mouth staining their uniforms a darker black. The other dark men faded back into the streets around the plaza, and the line reanimated itself, bunching up self-consciously where the old woman had been.

Remedios Trazada sighed and moved with the line. As always, when she listened to Sandón she felt regret. Recently she had felt shame as well. It had been a long time since she had first heard Sandón speak of old people as treasures: how idealistic it had sounded then, and how cynical it sounded now. She shook her head slowly. And now it had come to this: an electrical engineer of her caliber had to stand in line for a pittance, denied the right to work. She felt herself a party to fraud. But it had only been Leon who lied, who stole, and who disappeared, leaving her to bear his guilt. She knew too much for Sandón to kill her. She knew that the old woman who had feared the butterflies had feared the wrong thing. Yet she was silent.

"Move, comrade." The official handing out forms prodded Trazada forward in the line, pushing her between the shoulder blades with the butt of his rifle.

"Pardon, comrade." She felt galled, sounding so servile. As little as four months ago, this official would have groveled to her. In so short a time she had fallen. She spat. Discreetly.

"What is your name, comrade?" asked the clerk who waited at the head of the line, looking out at the people from the safety of his bars.

"Trazada, Remedios. Occupation, engineer, specializing in electronic systems. Former employer, Generalissimo Sandón." She reeled off the words, a senseless litany that she had said so many times before.

The clerk made a clucking sound. "How unfortunate, comrade. Just at present there is no work available in your field. A great pity. Perhaps next week."

"Verdadamente," Trazada murmured.

"Well, here is your payment. And here are your coupons for lodging. Here are your contraceptives. Remember that any child conceived while you are state supported will either be aborted or made a ward of the state at birth. Report next week at this time."

Remedios Trazada wondered what the clerk really thought, knowing how valuable trained technicians were in this strife-torn country. It was perhaps better for the clerk if he did not think too much. But for her pride's sake, if no other reason, Trazada wished that they would think up some new reason for keeping her unemployed. Perhaps Sandón was biding his time, keeping Trazada on a string as a bird is kept, ready to pluck her back if she was wanted. Perhaps he was waiting for Leon to contact her.

"Pardon, señora."

Trazada looked around. Beside her was a man of undetermined years, wearing the faded work clothes that marked all manual laborers in the country. His hair was grizzled but his face smooth, and, amazingly, his nails were clean. He smiled tentatively.

"May I help you?" asked Trazada in a voice that implied she didn't want to.

"I hope so. That is to be seen." There was a pause. "It is very warm today, señora."

A bit puzzled, Trazada agreed that it was warm. It was always warm in Liberación.

"Perhaps a glass of beer, then, would cool us off."

"Are you offering me a drink?" demanded Trazada, suspicious.

"I am saying that I will have one. If you join me, that is your affair."

Just at that moment Trazada wanted to fling an insult at the small man and walk off. It would relieve some of the terrible frustration that had been building in her for so long. But there was something in the stranger's manner that intrigued Trazada, so that in the end she followed him to the large al fresco cafe on the west side of the Plaza de Libertad.

The man in work clothes seated himself near the back of the cafe, where the first shadows of the afternoon afforded some escape from the glare of the sun. Trazada, after a moment's hesitation, sat opposite the man, watching him with guarded curiosity.

"What did you want to talk to me about?"

"Have you noticed how plentiful the butterflies are this year, señora? How they adorn the sky? No? Well, it may be too much to ask that an engineer, even a female engineer, have the soul of an artist."

Trazada hid her alarm well. She could not afford to notice his slighting remark about her sex when he implied so much about the butterflies. "If you are interested in insects, you do not need an engineer, even a female engineer."

"One would not think so, indeed," the stranger nodded amiably. "But if we are to believe Generalissimo Sandón, not all butterflies are what they seem."

Trazada made a move to rise.

"But you are leaving and I have not introduced myself. How can you excuse such bad manners, you who were educated at MIT and have seen something beyond Liberación." There was a threat in his face as he glanced meaningfully at her chair. Without a doubt he knew who she was and would not be put off. "I am Andreas Paseo. It is possible that you may have heard of me."

"I have." Trazada sat. She had certainly heard of Andreas Paseo, as everyone in Liberación had heard of him, the man who restored the Mantadron y Perez murals to earn the title of Cultural Hero in '88. If this man were truly Andreas Paseo, why was he in working-man's clothes, and why was he interested in her?

"If I am not mistaken," Paseo was saying, "you and I have something in common."

"You do not speak of medals." Even as she said it, she appreciated the irony that both of them did have medals, presented in the full panoply of the new State.

"True enough, though they are pretty things. But I have some reason to believe that there are more grounds for our mutual interest."

"Exactly what had you in mind?" If it was what she thought, it could be more of a risk than she was willing to take.

"In a moment."

The waiter arrived and they ordered beer, waiting in silence. Even when the dark, cold glasses arrived they did not speak but sipped guardedly at the heads.

Then Paseo remarked, "Is it possible that the butterflies are not what they seem? I have some friends who are curious about this."

Trazada looked at him.

"Academic curiosity, naturally."

"Speak plainly," snapped Trazada.

"It is well," Paseo said smoothly, "to remember that before there are butterflies, there are voracious things that creep among the leaves like green shadows."

"It's not possible for the Generalissimo to monitor all his bugs at once," Trazada said with a certain impatience. She knew each minute increased their chance of exposure.

"What a superb word that is, bugs. Could it be pure coincidence, do you think? These friends of mine are interested in bugs as well, as it turns out. Very catholic in their tastes."

"How nice for them." Trazada said it brusquely. She was getting more irritated with this man who spoke in riddles and would not come to the point.

"Before you leave me, allow me to demonstrate something to you." He tilted back his chair and raised his voice. "And therefore, comrade,

I say we are ill-used by the government, a government which pretends
to practice socialism but in reality is exploiting our people. . . ."

What more he would have said Trazada never knew, for there was a
crackling of speakers and the Generalissimo's voice came through the
trees, a recorded message.

"Ah," he admonished, "there are those among you speaking treason.
We shall not punish you for speculation, comrades, for we realize that
citizens have the right to express their opinions freely. Yet, good comrades, remember that my Butterfly knows all that you say and is ready
to report sedition."

The cafe was silent as the patrons glanced uneasily about, looking on
each other in fear.

"You see, the little butterflies still lurk around us, señora," Paseo said,
waving his hand blandly. "They know their job. But what is their job,
and how is it performed?"

Defensively: "I don't know what you mean."

"Have I explained myself yet? Then how can you know?"

"Well?" Trazada put down her glass angrily. Paseo signaled the
waiter for another.

"Yes. And it may be there are variations of insects that neither of us
understands fully. Why, I recall just before the time I found myself a
laborer, that our Generalissimo had commissioned a most unusual work
from me."

At last Trazada was listening. "Go on," she urged.

"Yes. Our Generalissimo is a great admirer of nature, as I am certain
you know. He wished a special series of studies to be made of native insects. Beetles, moths, and the like."

"Why not add the last? It's obvious what you mean."

"So long as we understand each other, there is no need to give more
information to those little creatures in the trees."

"Very well."

Idly he drew a butterfly's outline on the table top.

"I understand," Trazada admitted. And now she could not avoid it—
the thing she had feared so long. Eventually she knew it would happen, that the rebels would seek her out and ask for her help. She had
not thought they would come with the most famous artist in the country.

"It seems," Paseo continued quietly, "that one of the things our
Generalissimo desired was a model of a particular insect. This should

not surprise you. He specified some irregularities in the design which I suspect is where you came in."

"Possibly," she said noncommittally.

"It is regrettable that your husband should have chosen the time he did to leave the country. Surely if you had stayed on the job a little longer, you might know a great deal more. However, surely you know if the design was a success?"

Here Trazada had to laugh, and it helped hide the hurt of Leon. "I know what you are thinking, señor, but you must not bother yourself any longer. The design did work but not as intended." There. She had said it to someone at last.

"Ah," Paseo breathed, satisfied. "I had hoped it might be so." He drank the rest of his beer. "This has turned out to be a very good day for me, Señora Trazada. It was good of you to tell me this."

Trazada gave him an ironic smile. "Is it so simple to make you happy? You are easily satisfied."

"Perhaps I am. My friends will be relieved to hear that your little invention was a failure."

"But I did not say it was."

He glared up at her, his face thrust forward.

"I did not say I failed," Trazada said, as if she had been challenged.

"Do you say that it works?"

They were still, listening to the drone of conversation around them, and the quiet drone of things in the trees.

At last Paseo took a deep breath. "I see that it may not be so easy, after all. Well, Señora Trazada, I hope you will take a glass of beer with me sometime soon. I shall look forward to it, as well as my friends." He gazed unhappily at his empty glass. "This changes things," he mused.

"I wish you good fortune in that case," Remedios Trazada said as she rose and walked out of the cafe, not looking back. She missed the smile that followed her.

Her two small rooms were dingy and hot, the November sunlight heavy with the coming summer, thick with it, pounding the white-painted walls. They were poor quarters indeed for someone who had had eighteen rooms at her disposal not long ago—eighteen rooms and six servants. But then she had been the wife of the Minister of Finance and the Generalissimo's chief electronic engineer. As always, when her loneliness was hard upon her, Trazada remembered Leon: tall, lean, with eyes that caressed her whenever he looked at her, with hands that knew all the secrets of her joy. For the hundredth time she told herself that he was smart to get out while he could and that she did not blame him for deserting her. And she knew it for a lie.

"Here, Miko," she called as she put down her few parcels of food on the table that squatted in the cramped kitchen.

A large smoky tomcat who had been dozing on the window sill rose slowly and stretched with flamboyant languor. Then he stepped daintily into the sink.

"Here, Miko-Miko-Miko. Here I am with milk for you. And here's a bit of sheep's spleen."

The cat nudged his broad head into Trazada's hand, purring. "There, there. That's a good cat. Move aside and I'll get you your dinner." As she spoke, Trazada thought she had come to a sad pass, living in rooms that barely escaped being slums, eeking out her living from a government welfare check, and keeping solitary company with an old gray tomcat.

A butterfly lit on the open sill and stayed there, moving its painted wings like a gasping fish. Miko, seeing it, sprang at it, crushing it under his paws. He growled impressively as he toyed with it.

In that first moment when the butterfly had landed, Remedios Trazada had known real fear, an unreasoning horror that the design had been successful after all, that there really was a Butterfly and it had followed her to spy on her.

"That's a bad cat," she remarked absently for form's sake. "Let the butterfly alone." But she knew it was dead and made no move to save it. Now that her panic had gone, the butterfly didn't matter.

Miko champed his catch, powdering his whiskers with the fine dust of the colored wings.

When it was cooler, Trazada made a simple meal of sausage, cheese, and bread. She had schooled herself to wait dinner until hunger urged her to eat; it gave seasoning to poor food that no spice could furnish. She served herself with propriety and care, testing to be sure she had left no detail unattended to. The service had to be correct and properly laid out, it helped keep the illusion that this fall from grace was only temporary. Eventually Leon would return and his accusers found to be mistaken. Soon Sandón would need her expertise and send for her.

When she was through with her meal, she conscientiously brushed a few crumbs into Miko's dish, then set about the ritual of washing and preparing to read herself to sleep.

The knocking began sometime after three in the morning. The sky was dark and the moon low. Trazada woke brittlely, sleep falling from her like shards of glass. The sound persisted, loud and terrible explosions on the other side of the door.

"Momento! Momento! Be patient!" she called as she dragged a robe around her shoulders. It was of heavy silk, a remnant of other times.

The knocking grew louder.

"Por favor. I am coming." She forced herself across the floor, dreading what she would meet when she opened the door. Her shaking hands fumbled with the lock as she drew back the bolt.

"Comrade Trazada?" demanded the large, stern man in the uniform of Sandón's personal guards. The question was for form's sake only. He knew very well who he had come for.

Absurdly Trazada itched to deny it, to say she was someone else, that the soldiers were mistaken. It was foolish, but what a comfort that courage would be. "Yes, I am she. What do you want?" She damned herself for her honesty, finding suddenly that she was very tired.

"You are the one who designed the Butterfly; that is correct?"

Remedios Trazada noticed that the Capitan had three guns. No economy in that, without a third hand. She would have done it otherwise, made better use of . . .

"Are you the one who . . . ?"

"Oh, yes. I made the Butterfly."

"Muy bien. You are to come with us. Generalissimo Sandón wishes an interview with you."

So at last the summons had come, and, too late, she found she didn't want it. Trazada discovered that the thought of torture—for that was what most interviews with Sandón were these days—could still frighten her. She knew what waited for her in the lower levels of the Castillo. She had designed some of the machines that Sandón used, back when she still believed that after the revolution, things would be different. "I am not dressed, Capitan."

"That is not necessary. You will come now." To emphasize this he stood aside and left a hole for Trazada to walk between the other two guards. Did that mean she was to be given to the soldiers, as so many other women had been?

"Venga."

So this was how it was to end. She sighed. Her thoughts lingered for a moment on Miko left alone. But Miko was a cat and would fend for himself. "Very well," she said and stepped into the hall, closing the door carefully behind her.

The escort moved quickly down the dark stairs to the narrow street. At a signal from the Capitan a large dark car pulled quietly up to them. Trazada found this to be almost funny. The middle-of-the-night routing from bed, the armed men, the sinister automobile gliding through the streets . . . It was too theatrical. But such devices had placed Sandón where he was now, and such devices maintained his absolute authority in Liberación. The rear door opened, and what had seemed trite became terrifying. Trazada was thrust into the rear seat and hemmed in by two guards. Then the doors slammed and the car pulled away toward the Castillo and Generalissimo Sandón.

Castillo Libertad was unreal in the moonlight: the colonial ramparts encroaching on the sky, the huge marble staircase washed from cream to pale blue. The guards' boots clacked as they guided Trazada up the stairs and into the darkened foyer. The Capitan pulled her toward the elevator and summoned the car.

Much to Trazada's surprise, the elevator went up. Perhaps it would not be torture after all. Perhaps the Butterfly had failed and she was being brought to repair it. That would account for the secrecy. Perhaps Generalissimo Sandón had hit upon yet another scheme for Remedios Trazada's talents. As she thought, she grew more frightened.

The doors hissed open at last, and to her astonishment, Trazada found herself ushered into Generalissimo Sandón's private office. More startling still was the dictator himself, waiting with his familiar air of impatience behind the great seventeenth-century desk of rosewood and marble.

"Well, Remedios," said the well-known harsh voice. "It was good of you to come." He turned to his guards. "If I need you, I will call."

The Capitan gave Trazada a sly grin as he walked from the room.

"It has been many months, too many," said the great man behind the desk. "I am sorry they were unpleasant for you. A necessary precaution."

"Generalissimo."

"As you see, I keep your masterpiece ever with me." And he lifted a gorgeous Butterfly from its case. "It is magnificent. You should be very proud."

Trazada said nothing.

"But, it is with regret that I fear you are not proud of this tremendous accomplishment of yours. Remedios, you have forgotten all that we have worked for. You have paid no attention to the lessons of twenty years. What has come over you?" He leaned forward with the air of a disappointed uncle.

"Is the Butterfly satisfactory?" Trazada took care to keep all emotion out of her voice.

"So long as it stays within sight it has a three-kilometer range and performs just as you said it would. You are a genius, *mi* Remedios. What a pity that you are a woman and this country still cannot accept the equality of women."

Trazada remained silent.

"You should not be so reticent with me. Here is your finest creation, your most superb design. Inspired. It works with true perfection—at those limits I have mentioned. Do you take no joy in your accomplishments?"

Wondering why she was being baited this way, Trazada found courage to say, "That, sadly, has been denied me."

The Generalissimo laid the Butterfly back on the marble of his desk, handling the little machine with great care. "This is a fine invention. Remedios, it is a triumph of technology. What a shame the Second Revolution overtook the norteamericanos before more of our people could study there. Such great schools they had, so wonderful the machines they made. I wish I could make you see how wonderful your work is."

Trazada smiled wryly. She noticed that Generalissimo Sandón had grown fatter and this pleased her.

"Yes, my dear Remedios, this is surely your greatest work. But, as a perfectionist, you are not satisfied, you cannot appreciate the great worth of what you do."

Growing bolder, she said, "No doubt you will explain it, Paco." She knew that this was leading somewhere. She remembered the early years when Sandón had used praise as a weapon to destroy his enemies. It was an ability he still retained and Trazada was leary of it.

The Generalissimo wagged his heavy head at her. "The clever cat does not scratch the master, Remedios. I fear you have become restive in your days of idleness. It is often so with childless women. Only today, or yesterday it is, you were sought out by traitors, reactionaries, and you did not see fit to notify me of it. When an old and trusted colleague betrays me, it is a sad day. When one betrays her ideals, that is a tragedy, Remedios."

Tragedy has always been one of Sandón's favorite words. Trazada had heard him use it when the old government toppled and the leaders were executed; she had heard it again when the first border clash had occurred, killing thousands of young men and women in both countries; she had heard it more recently, when the Generalissimo had learned that Leon Trazada had fled; even that morning in the plaza she had heard it, and now the word came again.

But Sandón was going on. "I heard today, through means you should appreciate, that you were in the Cafe de los Tres Guerillos. A man was with you. He is known to me . . . mi Remedios; you must not allow yourself to associate with Paseo and his lot. They would exploit your remarkable talents for the most reprehensible ends."

"Whereas you want only to use them honorably? I am afraid that I do not understand you, Paco."

For an answer, the Generalissimo put one sausage-shaped finger to a concealed button. ". . . is a great admirer of nature, as I am certain you know. He wished a special series of studies to be made of native insects. Beetles, moths, and the like. . . ." Sandón flicked off the tape recorder. "It is true that I cannot monitor all my bugs at once, Remedios, but they are all checked eventually. And some of my dear citizens are more interesting to me than others. I have a deep concern for you, Remedios. So you cannot blame the interest I take in you. It is a continuing interest."

"I see," Trazada said at last.

"Now, mi Remedios, you must not feel that I am being harsh with you. You must believe that Paseo can do you nothing but harm."

"If that is so, why haven't you arrested him?" Trazada had not meant to ask the question aloud, and felt her fear return as she said it.

"This man," the Generalissimo said as he poured brandy from his desk decanter into two snifters, "is, in his way, valuable to me. He seeks out those who might try to tear down all that I have built here in Liberación. He knows who is seeking the ruin of my country." His voice grew even harsher. "I have bled for Liberación; I have been as devoted to her as a deluded monk is to his god. I have put my country before everything else in my life and now there are those who say I have enslaved them." He trembled with indignation.

"And you so very generous."

Sandón mastered himself with an effort. He held out a glass to Trazada, urging her to take it. "I can understand your scruples. It honors your womanhood, Remedios, but you are dealing with scoundrels."

Trazada accepted the brandy slowly.

Holding the snifter under his nose, Sandón went on expansively. "I cannot forget the debt I owe to you for your invention—my wondrous Butterfly. You have done all of Liberación a great service. There are ways I might express my gratitude, but this is not the right moment. The unfortunate defection of your husband has made things awkward, as I am sure you realize. I truly regret the conditions under which you live. But I swear to you that it shall not last forever. You will have the recognition you deserve." He gave Trazada a wild smile.

"What are you planning to do?"

"I am going to offer you another challenge, one which every person in Liberación can appreciate. In three days, just three days, a plane will carry you and your things to Agua Alta, high in the mountains. There we are building a hydroelectric plant at Quiquimara Falls. It will give us great power, a thing that is much needed. It is a project worthy of you, Remedios, and one that will bring you great honor."

"And will remove me from the evil influences of the people. Quiquimara Falls is three hundred eighty kilometers into the interior." Trazada thought of the falls, of the isolation and the jungle around her there. She thought of the other plans that Sandón would make for her —might have already made—if she refused. "Three days?" she asked.

"Your talents have lain fallow too long, my friend. At last there is a way for you to be of service to Liberación once more."

In a reckless instant Trazada put down the brandy, untouched. She forgot her fright, her hopelessness, even the worn robe she wore. "Aren't you afraid that once away from your bully boys I might start talking? Doesn't it occur to you that I might try to depose you? With an electrical plant to run, I'll have power to use for my own ends. Don't tell me that women would not use power that way. I know that I would. You never can tell: I might let all Liberación know that your precious Butterfly is a hoax!"

"You are free to do that now, Remedios," Sandón said with a slow

smile, offering Trazada the brandy again. "Women are so often hysteri-
cal. The people will not believe you." The Generalissimo rose and took
a small knobbed box from the shelf. He pushed the buttons and the
Butterfly rose from the desk. "You see? They have all watched this on
television. My Butterfly comes into my office through that window. It
flies about as I talk, and when I have finished, it goes back out the window. From there it flies all over the country. You cannot tell them otherwise."

The Butterfly swooped past Trazada's head.

"And that's not all," Sandón went on. "You notice the skill with
which Andreas Paseo decorated it. When any of our citizens look up,
how are they to tell this one from all other butterflies?"

"I shall tell them how it was made," she said, ducking the bright
flying thing. "I will show them how to make others."

To Trazada's surprise the Generalissimo laughed, a great subter-
ranean rumbling that shook his gigantic frame like an earthquake.
"Remedios, mia pobre Remedios, they are ignorant. They are afraid.
They are stupid and superstitious. Why, most of them think that television is witchcraft and that because they are allowed to vote they have
control over the government. And they know it is impossible for a
woman to make such a thing. They would never believe you."

Rage burned in Trazada fed by her despair. She knew that much of
what he said was correct. She watched the circling Butterfly, hating it
and all that it represented. Then she shot across the room, grabbed a
crystal paperweight, and as soon as the Butterfly flitted to the wall, she
smashed the heavy crystal into it. Trazada felt the same smile on her
face as her tomcat had worn with his butterfly crunched in his mouth.

"Foolish. Understandable, but very foolish," the Generalissimo said
sagely. "You hurt your invention and you gave yourself away."

"At least you will not frighten the people with it for a few weeks!"

"I have others," he said imperturbably. "But, my dear Remedios, that
is what I wanted you to see. I cannot have been clear. I do not need the
Butterfly. The people have accepted it." He sipped at his brandy meditatively. "You should have some of this." As he dropped his jowls onto
his chest, Trazada tried to remember him as he was when they fought
in the jungles, living on beans and salt pork once a day. He had
seemed so different then, a strong rebel with new ideas for all the people. Equality, freedom, unity, justice. Trazada watched the middle-aged

man behind the desk with guarded curiosity. Had he changed so much, then, or had he always been what he was now?

"If you were not so important to me, Remedios, I think I would have you killed as a warning to Paseo and his crew. Liberación needs you, however, and revenge is a luxury I have not time for. You are our finest engineer, and no matter what you or anyone else thinks of me, no matter what group is in power, the country must have electricity or stay trapped at this stagnated level for many more generations. We will not have social change, or any real progress, until that dam is built."

"Am I supposed to be flattered?"

The door of the elevator opened to a silent summons and the Capitan reappeared. His face was unreal as wax and his eyes shone like jet.

"Show her the photographs. Not all. Just the most persuasive ones." The Generalissimo turned away, draining the last of the brandy and pouring more.

Frowning, Trazada took the pictures handed to her. The first was of a hovel, surrounded by garbage. In the doorway were three figures, children by the size of them, with distended bellies covered with scabs.

"Malnutrition, then disease," the Capitan informed her unnecessarily.

The second photograph was of the worst part of the city, where people crowded in on one another, gaunt faces showing desperate eyes. The buildings shimmered in the sun and the stink of the place almost filled Trazada's head.

The third was a corpse of what had been a man. His flesh was strangely marked and his severed genitals protruded from his mouth. A mindless lump of flesh it was, too far from humanity to be real.

"Who is that?" Trazada forced the words out.

Sandón turned to her, his eyes darkened. "Leon," he said. "I agree he is unrecognizable, but there was enough of a jaw left to make an identification. Do you want to see the documents?"

There was a burning in her eyes as Trazada touched the photograph hesitantly. She shook her head, knowing the truth, although her face still showed disbelief. How could that terrible thing be Leon, with his warm skin the color of new honey that she remembered with her fingers? In a voice she didn't know as her own, she asked, "How did . . . ? Who did . . . ?" all the time remembering him, the smell of his body, the sound of his voice, the way he moved on her.

"The others, Remedios. They did it. They are desperate."

Trazada looked up at the Capitan. "Where was this? How did you get this picture?" She had wrenched her eyes away from the thing and now refused to look again.

The Capitan answered with proper military briskness, "The photograph you ask about was provided by one of our agents."

"When?"

"The date is August. A few months ago."

"I don't believe you." She said the words softly, but it was as if she had screamed. Leon had been dead since August, almost as long as she had been living in the slums. Trazada shook her head numbly. All that time she thought he would send for her, would be cleared, would come back; all that time he had been dead, and dead in a way that ached like vitriol in her.

"Remedios," Sandón interrupted her thoughts, "see where ideals have brought you. This is the work of Paseo. Yet these are the ones you would aid."

She felt the hot tears on her face. "No. Not Paseo, Paco, you. This is your work. Leon was dangerous to you, wasn't he? Just as I am dangerous to you now. Is this what will happen at Quiquimara Falls?" But it didn't matter, really. Either way, Leon was dead.

"You were not intended for this game, Remedios," the Generalissimo informed her as he waved the Capitan back out the door. "You have lived for your ideals, inspired or misguided makes no difference. It has cost you your husband, your friends, and your position. I am giving you a chance to do something of worth. A hydroelectric plant in the interior knows no politics."

Trazada searched for words and found none.

Sandón went on, his manner the way Trazada remembered him from years ago when they had fought for the independence of Liberación. "We were to be free of despots and superstition. That was what it was all about, was it not, Remedios. Did you really believe that? In so little a country with a peasant population who do not move unless prodded. It is the function of leaders to prod them."

"Do you tell yourself that justifies what you have done, Generalissimo?" she flared.

"Let us say I tell myself these things to keep from killing the lot of them. And no matter what you think now, electricity will be more of a revolution than anything done with bullets and politics."

"After what you have done . . ."

"If I did not do these things, others would. Under slightly different circumstances, I would give you to the soldiers, but that would be too great a waste."

She spat.

"Possibly you should be grateful, Remedios," Sandón said dryly, swinging his chair around to look toward the distant fringe of jungle. "It is almost dawn. I am going to let you walk home, Remedios. I want you to think as you walk. My men will call for you in three days and you may go with them. . . . Take that cat of yours, if you like. If you choose to remain here, I will know you are my enemy and you will be killed as Leon was. I cannot afford to let you live this near me."

Trazada nodded. "I understand." She thought as she said it that for the first time in her life it was true.

"Stop on the first floor and you will be given some clothes to wear home." He gave Trazada an even look, an implacable look. "Make your choice wisely, Remedios. It is up to you, for I will never see you again." With that he rose and went from the room, taking the broken Butterfly with him.

As she walked away from Castillo Libertad the sun rose behind it, haloing the spires in light and sending shadows probing over the plaza. Around her the world was coming to life once more. Trazada looked up, shielding her eyes, and found herself weeping futilely at the vast array of butterflies that were starting to swarm over Liberación.

about "The Generalissimo's Butterfly"

By the time Barry Malzberg and Bill Pronzini agreed to take this story for their Doubleday anthology, *Dark Sins, Dark Dreams: Crime in Science Fiction*, I had a really impressive collection of rejects on the work. Oddly enough, most of the editors liked the story, but none of them were quite sure what it was. One or two objected to its implied political content. It was great to place it with two good writers and good editors.

There are quite a few unanswered questions in the story (if they were all answered, it would be a novel, not a short story) and it might amuse you to consider the implications of those unanswered questions. You will undoubtedly come up with a different set of conclusions than I have.

In my own writing (and in reading the works of others) I value highly something I call consistency of vision—in other words, a story that does not deviate from its own rules (one excellent example of this is George MacDonald Fraser's Flashman novels). In that respect, I'm very pleased with the way the "Butterfly" turned out.

ALLIES

Something was out there.

Chris Tuttle shifted the patrol gun, forcing it tight to the shoulder, feeling the bite of the metal through the heavy surface uniform. It was hard, reassuring.

Overhead two of the rumpled moons shed their wan light on the vast emptiness of Scranton's Marsh. Stiff reeds rattled in the lonely wind, their endless tattoo restlessly beating out the long hours, their sound spreading like gossip.

But something was out there. Beyond the reeds, something moved, making silence where there should have been sound. It moved, vast and unseen over the sodden waste, pulling mystery with it.

Now Chris had the gun at the ready, wishing Sidney or Robin, someone else from the station had also stood watch. Chris had often stood watch alone, since Gabe died. But this time, there should have been someone else, so that there would not be this terrible silence, this strangeness that filled Scranton's Marsh. Chris would never have felt the thing moving, had another person been in the shelter, someone to talk to, someone familiar.

Something moved nearer.

It was not just for Gabe that Chris was nervous, it was because of Dana and Evelyn. Chris remembered the way they looked, lying together, their uniforms slimed by the Marsh, his face smoothed in death, and hers with a half smile that haunted Chris now, out here alone at the edge of the Marsh.

But Chris was not alone. There was something else. Involuntarily Chris slid further back in the patrol shelter, making a futile gesture to shut away the images of Evelyn and Dana, and their deaths.

Nearby the reeds were still, and the hushed winds failed. A shadow touched the pale tracks of the moons.

Chris Tuttle hated to be touched. The nearness of another person brought a deep kind of panic which had been with Chris since childhood. People, nearness, touching, small places, all of them caused fear. Now something, perhaps the something that had killed Evelyn and Dana, was coming nearer, nearer.

If it came closer, they would touch.

The bright flame of the patrol gun lanced into the dusk, making stark shadows among the reeds, making the oily water sleek, clothlike, unreal. The light was protection; it would fend off whatever was coming. It would hold the ghosts at bay.

Nothing showed in the glare. The Marsh lay unnaturally still as the light of the patrol gun faded and its efficient crackle died. There was no echo.

Breathing harder now, Chris waited, hugging the patrol gun as if its metal was proof against the thing coming nearer. The gun was light and strength and power. As long as Chris touched the gun, nothing else would have to be touched. Nothing. No . . . thing.

The feeling, the sensing, the sureness of something coming grew stronger, and Chris's eyes widened in terror. It was nearer. It was there. It would reach out, invisible, and they would touch . . .

And then it was gone. Scranton's Marsh rippled and clattered in the night wind and the potato-shaped moons blundered along the sky.

In the watch shelter Chris felt tightened muscles relax, fingers falling away from the patrol gun of their own volition. Stifled laughter loosened them still more until the whole episode seemed foolish, nothing more than the result of being in the shelter too long, of thinking too much about Dana and Evelyn. It was always hard on a station when part of its staff died, particularly when the death was sudden, terrible. Gabe had died gently, letting go of life as easily as water slid away on the night tides.

That was it, Chris was sure. It was the long hours of patrol, and the deaths. Evelyn, tall, blond, with eyes bright, never far away from the cool, dark Dana. A man and a woman, not yet thirty, either of them, and they were dead.

"I must be getting squirmy. It's the strain," Chris said aloud, and ignored the hollow sound the words made in the shelter. It was the shelter that had caused the feeling, and the memory of Dana and Evelyn. Not Gabe. Chris had got over that months ago.

There was nothing moving on Scranton's Marsh.

Later, when Jecks came for the next watch, Chris almost mentioned the strange moment as a casual warning, in case Jecks, too, found the shelter disturbing, filled with memories; then, embarrassed by the weakness this showed, decided not to. There was no reason to give another member of the Squad a case of the spooks.

"Anything happening?" Jecks asked in a raspy, bored voice, knowing that nothing ever happened on Halverson's Stopover except when one of the Squad died.

"No. Nothing."

Jecks chuckled. "Sure, what else?" and took over the patrol gun, laconically waving Chris away, uncaring.

"What else?" Chris said in agreement. Dreary planets like this one were of use only to the Rare Resources Board, and then at some distant date, far in the future. In the meantime, Chris reflected on the long walk back to the squad station, they were being paid generously to keep an eye on it, and a few dozen other planets like it. All because the R.R.B. had the uncomfortable suspicion that somewhere, sometime, they might run into outside opposition that would want the place for themselves.

Opposition? Chris knew better. The hours of tedium, the long hours of staring into nothing until you conjured visions to offset the unending sameness. Only imagination born of boredom would flourish on Scranton's Marsh. Or Tidwell Marsh. Or the Shallow Sea. Or Halverson's Slough. There was nothing to do but watch the place. Or you could die. Evelyn had died. And Dana. And, oh, God, Gabe.

Chris glanced once more at the boggy waste before going into the squad station, and back into a world of color and light.

They sat apart from each other, like slow private snails on different leaves of a plant. Between them the shiny walls were bright with the warm colors of home: here orange, there marigold, with panels of lime and olive to separate them. The room was large, light and airy. It was filled with all sorts of recreational equipment. The Squad hated it.

Chris had discarded the outer layer of the surface uniform and left it for the jeeves to clean. Regulations required that all Squad members remove their inner suit lining while in the station, but no one ever did, and the R.R.B. did not complain.

They sat alone in the dull green coverings—it was all part of the routine, part of being a staffer with the Squad, part of the life they shared on Halverson's Stopover. Chris, like all the others, had been living this way for so long that the routine was automatic.

"Busy day?" Jes Northrup asked derisively as Chris came into the bright, sterile rec room.

"Same as always." Chris had come to ignore the constant jibes Jes offered. There was no way to respond that did not bring more scorn, and Chris had learned that the truth was as acceptable to Jes as any other answer.

"Just right for you, then. No tax on the brain."

On the other side of the room, Tracy Lexington cracked out a laugh. There was anger in the sound: Tracy had been set to retire in a year, but now faced departure on the next R.R.B. supply ship, after three years as station chief.

Jes turned. "Heard from the Bureau?" The question was poisonous. "What was their excuse? Or did they bother to give you one? Maybe they hold you responsible for Evelyn and Dana dying."

Like Chris, Tracy had learned to tell the truth to Jes. "I heard from Tenning on Markley Four. The R.R.B. is pulling the same thing there. You get fired six months before they retire you. They aren't out any money that way, and you have no claim against them."

"Think what you've got to look forward to, Chris," Jes said with satisfaction. "You retire in eight months, right? In two, look for the axe."

Chris often wondered why it had to be Jes, why of all the Squad staffers since Gabe's death Jes was the one, sharp words and all, who was part of those lonely dreams. Privately Chris admitted that it might be self-protection, for as long as Jes was involved elsewhere, there was no chance for Chris. And even if this were not the case, Jes's merciless tongue would excoriate love from their talk—Jes's tongue and the memory of Gabe.

"What about the axe, Chris? You ready for it?" Jes had come up slyly.

Chris nodded without answering, then took a much-used viewer and found a spot on the wall away from Jes and Tracy.

"That won't make us go away," Jes mocked, and Chris felt the power of his presence. Jes filled a room, was a palpable thing in the air. "It's coming, Chris, and you're going down with the rest of us, fired, broke, and on the beach."

Chris couldn't resist saying, "So yours came today in the mail. Sorry to hear it, Jes."

For a moment the rec room was silent. Then Jes rose as if each bone were made of china; fragile, brittle, too precious to be clothed in flesh, and the aura of presence shrunk. "That thing in the Marsh. I hope it gets you."

Surprised, Chris looked up, but saw only Jes's back. "Jes?" Chris half-rose to follow, then stopped, feeling too naked under Tracy's keen, inquisitive gaze.

"The thing in the Marsh?"

"That's just Jes. It doesn't mean anything," Chris said, wishing that Jes had not been so acute. "I guess I'm not over Evelyn and Dana, that's all." The thing, whatever it was, had been a private matter. Jes should have no part in it. Nor should Tracy.

"Something bothering you, Chris?" Tracy asked, not letting go, one eyebrow raised in punctuation.

"Um?" It was too late to hide a case of nerves. "A little. I'm getting jumpy is all. Like I said, Evelyn and Dana, they haven't been dead long, and before they died, she told me a lot of things—I liked her better than the other women at this station, and I miss her. I miss him, too, because of her."

"Do you?" Tracy Lexington hardly moved.

"And then the shelter. Sometimes the shelter gets to me, you know? It's too much the same out there: you start seeing things, after a while."

"I know what you mean," Tracy said, no longer truly interested. "I thought I saw an orchard out there one time. An orchard, blooming in the middle of Scranton's Marsh."

A buzzer sounded in the mess, and the sound rattled around the rec room like a marble. Chris welcomed it as a distraction.

"You coming?" Tracy said perfunctorily before leaving.

"In a bit. I'm not hungry."

"Suit yourself."

When Tracy had gone, Chris let a frown appear. What was happening here? Did the others see things as well? Tracy said there'd been an orchard, but that was not the same thing as the moving silence that had crowded Chris in the shelter. An orchard was part of a memory, a toy to help pass the dull hours spent in solitude. Could the silence be that, only that?

But Jes had implied something more. Jes spoke as if there were a preying thing that would lure Chris out into the sucking darkness of the Marsh . . .

The sound of the second buzzer broke through Chris's thoughts. The pierre would stop serving food in ten minutes. There would be nothing to eat after that for at least six hours.

Putting all the disturbing thoughts aside, Chris went in to supper and, sniffing the meal that waited, wished that the old model pierre was still in operation. This new one was much faster, but the food tasted terrible.

No one paid much attention to the change of watch. Squad members came and went without supervision. Mostly they were loners, willing to do the boring job, and asking little or no assistance, preferring the solitude and privacy of the Squad to the incredible crowding of the usual habitable planets.

So it was hardly strange when Lee Jecks did not show up to relieve Chris's watch the next day. Lee was fairly responsible, but schedules were not too rigid.

Chris waited, frowning a little, thinking that Jecks would not be too long. But the minutes stretched on and no one came.

The Marsh shivered under a cold wind and the reeds scraped each other and clattered as if they, too, felt cold.

Finally Chris called that station. "Tuttle here. Where's Jecks?"

"This is Tracy, Chris. What do you mean, where's Jecks?"

"I'm still at the watch shelter, Jecks was supposed to relieve me almost fifteen minutes ago. What happened?"

There was a pause before Tracy said, "I haven't seen Jecks since yesterday. Just before the change of watch. Here in the rec room. Jecks was going out to the shelter."

Chris felt that coldness which had nothing to do with the wind or the Marsh. "Since then? What about the rec room now? What about the mess?"

"Jecks isn't in the rec room; didn't use it much." Already Chris could tell Tracy thought of Jecks in the past tense. "I'll order a search. Maybe Jecks got sick, or hurt."

Or *dead,* Chris thought, but said dryly, "Sure. In the meantime, who's going to take over my watch?"

Again Tracy hesitated. "Can you keep on there for a little longer?" Then, hurrying to explain, "Look, we can check out the station in half an hour. I'll try to send someone out to you, but it'll take a little time. I'll get back to you." The connection was broken, leaving Chris alone with the Marsh.

The wind picked up, as if acknowledging its victory. The reeds got louder, almost angry, their clickings turning to a persistent buzz, like derisive applause. Out there the water stood in brackish pools, the surface wrinkling, hidden eyes narrowing into sinister smiles, their malicious green depths lost in the movement of the water.

"Shit," Chris said, feeling the danger of the place. At times like this the Marsh was almost human, almost alive, with a feeling like hatred.

Then there came a silence that did not stop the wind, but rode with it across the Marsh. It was huge, powerful . . .

Sentient.

Something was out there.

The hostility of the thing was almost cloying, like a terrible embrace. It reached out for Chris and Chris watched, fascinated as the soundlessness spread. The reeds still rattled—Chris could see them tapping on themselves and one another—but the sound did not reach to the watch shelter. It was swallowed, absorbed, as if it had never happened.

The nearness of the thing was suffocating, suffocating.

"It's my imagination," Chris said aloud, hoping it were so. "I am alone here: there is nothing on the Marsh."

A soft rumble, like laughter or thunder shook the air. Chris gripped the gun tightly and wished that someone would call or come.

Along the edge of the Marsh there was a glow in the sky, at the limit of the stagnent water there was the promise of dawn. Only one moon rode in the night and it paled with the advancing light. Scranton's Marsh shone in the early dawn, the wind once again quickening. Where the light touched there was noise, the familiar rustle and rattle of the reeds, the gentle sucking of the water. But in the green shadows the silence lingered, promising, waiting.

Even as Chris watched, the shadows were banished, the world grew suddenly brighter as the distant pale star that was Halverson's Sun poked itself like a finger over the edge of the Marsh. The night fled in long tattered shadows before it.

"Tuttle!" The communicator snapped on, very loud.

Wincing, Chris answered. "Here. What about Jecks? What about my relief?"

"We're going to have to extend the search beyond the station. There's no sign of Jecks in the station; there hasn't been since watch yesterday."

"Have you asked Jes Northrup?" Chris wished the words unsaid, wished that Jes did not have the power to touch other lives, to touch Chris's own life.

"Jes doesn't know anything. We're breaking out the prowlers now and setting them to hunt."

"Good idea," Chris said, fighting back new fright. They had lost two already. Of the twelve women and eleven men who staffed the station, the squad could not afford to lose another one.

"We're sending Jean DeEtoil out there now. You can come back in."

"All right." Chris felt the relief like a cold shower. It would be good to get out of the shelter and back to the station. Chris knew now that too long in the shelter and your mind played tricks on you, you started to see things, remembering things, people, fearing things . . .

The Marsh was brightening now, long slender lines of shadow marking the path of the sun. The water made even the shadows bright, casting the rays into pools, seeking out the hidden world below the Marsh in the shallow green depths which the light made deep. Motes hung over the water, shining like tiny halos, making the water glisten. The world was toy-bright, attractive, touchable. It called, and the call was pleasant, promising.

"Tuttle!"

Chris did not hear the cry from behind. The Marsh was too important. There was something out there, after all, that had to be checked; something that *was not* too far away, not dangerously far away; Chris knew it would be an easy thing to check, a problem simply solved. The water was shallow here, safely shallow.

"Don't." DeEtoil's arm shot out, pulling Chris back from the soft, oozing edge of the Marsh. "You know better than that, Tuttle."

Chris leaned dizzily against the rim of the shelter, suddenly breathing very hard. "Sorry. I don't know what happened. I thought I saw something. I was going to check it out." It was not true. Chris could not remember leaving the shelter.

"Check it out? There's nothing you want out there," DeEtoil said, with a gesture toward the Marsh, as if wishing it away from them. "It's horrible, this place. Isn't it?"

"Yes," Chris answered uncertainly. Yes, of course it was horrible. It had taken Dana and Evelyn. But for that moment it had been incredibly beautiful, like a jewel lit from within. And Chris knew now that just below the surface rare beauty indeed lay hidden. Under the horror there was a loveliness that ached to be seen. "I better go in now."

DeEtoil didn't argue. "Watch out for the prowlers. They're all over the place. Tracy put them out ten minutes ago. They're on close pattern search. You could run into one."

"They haven't found Jecks." It wasn't a question.

"Be careful," DeEtoil said, taking over the shelter.

Jecks was found lying in the shallows, headgear off, gloves torn. Under the mud Jecks's face smiled tranquilly, shining a little with the swamp phosphorescence.

"How long?" Tracy asked Lou Wellington.

"It's hard to say. I'll have to do an examination first. Maybe a day." Wellington glanced uncomfortably at the others standing uneasily on the boggy hillocks. "You'll have to bring the body back. We can't leave it out here."

"Tracy, this happened to Dana and Evelyn," Robin Clay said, voicing what the others thought.

"We don't know that yet," Tracy snapped.

"It'll kill us all."

Tracy looked at the Squad staffers. "You don't know that. Now, who was sleeping with Jecks?"

There was a pause, then Jes Northrup surprised them all but Chris by saying, "I was. Off and on. It wasn't a regular thing."

"Do you want to make the arrangements?" Tracy asked gently. "You have the right, Jes."

Jes looked down at the body as if it were an alien and repulsive life form. "I don't know. It's not like Lee anymore. Lee's gone. Being nice to that thing there won't change it."

Tracy looked over the others. "Who then? Merriwell? Oxford? Who?"

Chris said, "I will," and wondered why. Was it for Jes? Or for Lee Jecks because Jecks's watch had come after his own?

"Tuttle?" Tracy was surprised.

"I'll do it." There. The words were firmer. Chris looked at Wellington for instructions, bending to lift the body.

"Not over the shoulder. Get someone to help you. Leland," Wellington rapped out the order, "give Tuttle a hand there. You take the feet."

Sandy Leland swallowed uncomfortably. "Uh, Lou . . . Do I have to?"

Wellington glared. Leland was young, and unused to Squad work. "You're going to have to do it sometime. You might as well start now."

Between them Leland and Chris slung what was left of Lee Jecks, carrying it with careful detachment back to the station. Along the way, Chris felt the heaviness of the corpse; the weight was not figured in pounds alone.

"Why'd you volunteer? Did you like Lee?" Sandy Leland asked as they picked their way along the edge of the Marsh.

"I don't know. No, I didn't like Lee at all. Lee was a rat, an animal that gnaws. But it's a lousy way to die, out here all alone. Dana and Evelyn . . . they died out here . . ."

"Did you see the face? It doesn't look like . . . you know . . . like it was very bad. I don't think Lee suffered, do you?"

"I saw the face," Chris said, and would have said more but thought better of it. Leland was still very young, and might not understand.

Lou Wellington looked awkward, standing there in front of the Squad in the absurd brightness of the rec room. There was a tightness about the mouth that made Wellington look uncharacteristically grim. "May I have quiet, please." When there was no lull in the conversation, Wellington spoke louder. "Quiet! Please!"

This time the words took effect. The drone of conversation faltered and came to a ragged stop. Almost two dozen anxious eyes turned to the raised platform in the expectant hush.

"All right. I've done the workup on Jecks. First, let me assure you there was no sign of violence. It was not murder." Wellington paused to let that sink in.

"What about Evelyn and Dana? Did they die the same way?"

Wellington scowled and told the truth. "Yes. They died the same way."

Chris wanted to shout "Why?" but did not.

Wellington coughed, and went on. "I'm speculating, of course, but there's reason to think we might have a clue to the deaths. As most of us know, the Bureau has a new policy of firing Squad staffers six months before they are to retire. Now, a staffer leaving the Squad at thirty has a right to expect some money from the Bureau, but this new policy has eliminated that right. On the other hand, those of you who have actually read your contract know that if you die on Squad assignment, your heirs must receive double your retirement benefit for a period not to exceed fifty years. Dana and Evelyn were both twenty-nine, and would have been fired soon. Lee Jecks was twenty-eight. All but four of the men and three of the women at this station are over twenty-five."

"Are you saying this was suicide?" Jes Northrup jeered.

"I say it's a possibility," Lou Wellington admitted. "Not many of us can afford to go home and start over at thirty."

"People don't die, don't kill themselves for a few extra bucks for the family. They die for revenge, maybe, but not for the money. It isn't worth it."

"Do you know something you aren't telling us, Jes? Did Lee Jecks tell you about this?" Tracy Lexington spoke rapidly, almost too rapidly.

"I'm not going to help you kiss the Bureau's ass," Jes said languidly. "When they really investigate the deaths here, then talk to me."

Taking a deep breath, Lou Wellington went on. "In Jecks's quarters we found notice of firing. There is reason to believe that Jecks might have suicided. Or perhaps just given up. Rather than be stranded out here in the pioneering belt, Lee Jecks decided to die." Wellington waited, expecting further challenges.

"Lou," Sandy Leland spoke up. "Jecks was smiling. I remember. It was the happiest smile I've ever seen."

Wellington nodded. "I know. It probably happened as a result of suffocation. Jecks was in the mud, not in water, and died of suffocation, not drowning. Sometimes suffocation does strange things. Jecks might have had a hallucination then. There's no way to be sure, but a hallucination would account for the smile. It's the same case with Dana and Evelyn."

Chris listened, not believing. Jecks had not died feeling the joy of a beautiful vision in place of fear, Jecks had died because the thing in the Marsh had wanted it that way. Jecks had gone willingly, and had become part of the thing.

"Is there any objection to the report being submitted in this form? Accidental death? A misadventure?" Tracy asked for the sake of ritual.

No one would object, not in a matter of this nature. "Very well, then. This report will be faxed to Dutton at planet control immediately. Relevant additions, alterations and observations may be appended to the fax." That was all there was to it. One more casualty out in the middle of nowhere, one more Squad staffer dead for no reason.

"Tracy." Chris had not meant to speak. "I think we should request an investigation. Dutton can send a crew over. Three deaths in ten days is too much. We could all die out here . . ."

"Investigation? Things aren't that bad, Tuttle. There's no call for it yet." Tracy could not meet Chris's eyes. "Investigations are very expensive, Chris."

"Maybe so. But the peculiar circumstances . . . The way Jecks died . . . And Evelyn and Dana . . ." It had seemed to be a good idea when Chris first thought of it, but saying the words made the whole proposal sound foolish. "Never mind," Chris mumbled. "It really doesn't merit that kind of attention, I guess. Investigations are only for important matters, like stealing from the R.R.B."

Tracy looked upset, but went on smoothly, "If anyone else here feels that a formal investigation is in order . . . ? No? Then this report is adopted by this R.R.B. Squad and will be filed in form."

"What made you say a fool thing like that, Tuttle?" Tracy wanted to know later that day.

"I don't know. Sometimes the Marsh gets spooky and then maybe one of us will go crazy. I just thought something like that might have happened to Jecks, that there might be something about the Marsh we don't know. Maybe the Marsh gas gives hallucinations sometimes, or maybe there's some kind of real life out there. It's not impossible." Bright blue eyes met Tracy's cold gray ones.

"I'm going to let Sidney take your watch with you for a while, Chris," Tracy said measuredly. "You're pretty spooked yourself. You could use the company." There was something in Tracy's manner that brooked no opposition.

"All right," Chris said slowly. "But you better put doubles on all the watches, at least for a while."

"You tell me why?" This was Tracy's last indulgence. Chris sensed it, and said, "If I can get spooked after twelve years out here with the Squad, then so can the younger ones, and a lot worse because they are newer to this. Better give it some thought. One death is just bad luck,

Tracy, but three is something else. If we have any more, the Bureau will start asking questions, even if you don't request it."

Tracy nodded once. "You're right. Double watches. You're with Sidney."

Chris did not particularly like the ebullient Sidney Peterson, but accepted the assignment without protest. Tracy would not listen if Chris balked now. "Sidney it is, then. Now, what about communication with the station? Do we leave the shelter channel open?"

Tracy said coolly, "I don't think that will be necessary. This isn't a first order emergency, Tuttle. No R.R.B. property's been damaged. There's no reason for me to authorize such a procedure."

Tracy had been pushed too far, Chris realized. "You're the boss, Tracy. It's your decision." And for the first time, Chris wished it were not so.

Sidney Peterson was the sort who filled up places—a large, enthusiastic puppy, big-footed, good-willed and clumsy. In the cramped shelter Chris found it hard to take.

"Do you know what we're guarding? I mean, what's so precious out there? What's the Marsh got?" Sidney rumbled, moving restlessly in the confines of the shelter. "What does the Bureau want out here? I asked once, but they wouldn't say a word about it . . ."

"That's the Bureau's business," Chris said automatically, hoping that the last hour of watch would go quickly.

"You'd think they'd let us know what we're taking care of. You'd think they'd want us to know so we'd do a better job. Wouldn't you? I mean, if I were in charge here, I would want everyone to know. I'd make sure they took an interest, and had all the information they needed."

"We can't talk about what we don't know about, Sid." In the last month or so, Chris had seen the wisdom of the Bureau policy that kept the rare resources a secret. With termination coming up, and no pension, Chris knew that there would be offers from other people interested in the secrets of the R.R.B. that would get fabulous prices. And Chris, after working for the R.R.B. for fourteen years, had nothing to sell.

"But it's silly of them to think we would talk about our jobs. I mean, who would we talk to? And besides, the Squad isn't like that." Sidney laid an anxious hand on Chris's shoulder. "Tuttle? You mad or something?"

Flinching at the touch, Chris stepped farther back into the shelter. "That's not our business, Peterson, You haven't been here long enough to understand. You will, some day."

"I've been here three years. I've been on station assignment almost five years now." This was a point of pride with Sidney, who was only twenty-three.

"You wait until you're ready to retire and they send you notice. No more pension, no more pay and no place to go. Wait until you're twenty-nine and see if that's the way you still feel about the Squad and the Bureau." Chris wished the words unsaid, seeing the alarm on Sidney's face, the eager smile hanging distortedly on that fresh young face.

"Then it's happened to you, too. Lee Jecks saw it, and the others, and that's why . . ." Sidney broke off awkwardly. "I don't blame you for being upset, Tuttle. It's a bad thing to do, this firing. But when we were in training, we were assured that all deserving staffers would be looked after. If they don't give you the pension, you can always apply for hazard pay. That'll give you some money. The thing is, the Bureau's making a mistake about us. They've probably got their records confused again. That happens, you know. You wait a year or so, you'll find out this was all a mistake and your pension will come through like that."

"Peterson, do you mind if we don't talk about it?" Chris had the watch gun now and was holding it between them.

"Oh. Oh, sorry, Tuttle. I forget Jecks was a friend of yours. So was Dana . . . or was it Evelyn? Lovers get upset when things like this happen, don't they? I read Lou Wellington's evaluation . . ."

"Jecks and I were never lovers." No, Jecks had been Northrup's lover, and Chris could not forget that. "But we were stuck on this damn mudball for seven years. That's a long time, Peterson." Chris turned away, hoping to end their conversation.

"That's too bad, you know? It hurts when the Squad gets reduced, like with Dana and Evelyn. I mean, any way is bad, but somehow, suicide, that's a lot worse. It reflects on the Squad staffers, you know? You think the Bureau would do something about it . . ."

"Peterson," Chris said shortly, "shut up."

Chris did not go to the rec room that day. Four hours of Sidney had taken away any desire to see other squad staffers. Instead Chris stayed alone in the tape room, going over viewzines that were years old. Chris had reached the reports of the three-year-old Pan-African Boycott when Tracy knocked at the door.

"Come," Chris said automatically, not turning from the screen.

"Oh, it's you, Tuttle. Have you seen Pat Felton? Or Robin Clay?"

"At the shelter when Felton and Clay relieved us. Why?"

"Nothing. I'll ask Oxford."

"Terry hasn't been in all afternoon."

"Terry Oxford is in the mess room right now." There was a hesitancy about Tracy, who lingered a moment longer than necessary. Chris looked up. "Is there trouble, Tracy?"

"Oh, I don't think so," Tracy forced a smile. "You know Felton and Clay. They probably wandered off for an hour or so. They're both interested in plants. Sometimes they get carried away. That's probably what happened. Jes Northrup saw them earlier outside the shelter." From the sound of it, Tracy needed to be reassured.

"Well, give it an hour, and if Felton and Clay haven't shown up by then, I'll take Terry Oxford and we'll go looking." Chris did not want to go with Oxford. For Chris felt a sickening certainty that they would find Felton and Clay as they had found Jecks, as they had found Evelyn and Dana.

"That's good of you, Tuttle. I'll let you know if we need you." With those words Tracy was gone, leaving Chris to stare unseeing at the tapes of the Pan-African Boycott.

The prowler went ahead of them, marking out the safe ground leaving a trail of flares that would guide them back to the station, or, if they failed, bring others to them.

"Pat and Robin didn't usually go this far," Terry Oxford said uneasily, eyeing Chris as they followed the prowler. "There's plenty of strange plants near the station. Most of the time they kept close in."

"I know. But maybe they weren't looking for plants." Chris knew what Pat and Robin had sought, what had called, lured, tempted Pat and Robin out into the Marsh. The silence was heavy, like a lingering afterscent. Through it Chris could sense the thing that rose in the silence, beckoning.

"But what else would bring them out all this way?" Oxford slid on a hillock, cursing softly as Chris reached out a steadying hand.

"What got Pat and Robin out here isn't important." At least, it wasn't important to Chris, who knew they would not find Pat and

Robin now, not alive. They were already too late. Whatever it was in the Marsh had done it again. And two more Squad staffers were lost to it.

"You don't think . . . Dana and Evelyn came out this way . . ." Terry Oxford looked sick behind the face protector.

Ahead the prowler stopped, signaling a dead end. Beyond the busy machine the ground was unsafe.

"Maybe they didn't go this way. Though Jes said . . ." Terry began tentatively.

"Then whose tracks are we following?" Chris broke free of Terry and scrambled along the hillocks to the prowler. Beyond, the ground sank into slick pools. In the fading light the whole Marsh was a monochrome of tarnished silver. Even the occasional humps of rock, tufted with reeds, shone the same dull color, dark in the shadows, bright to whiteness where the light struck. The reeds clacked nervously to one another.

"We should get back," Terry said urgently. "We'll need more prowlers. And more staffers."

Chris motioned for silence. There was something, part of the hillock several yards beyond. Its silvery color was like the rest, but it was not silver from the sun. Even at a distance, the surface uniform was unmistakable. "I don't think we need look any further, Oxford. Pat's out there, and Robin. Look. See that mound?"

"What mound?"

"There. Two beyond this."

Terry peered with shaded eyes into the glare. "That's just a rock. Like the other rocks."

"No." Chris took the communicator off its belt catch. "Station? This is Tuttle. We've got Felton and Clay in sight. Better tell Wellington to be ready. There's work to do."

"Dead?" The voice was Tracy's, tight with strain.

"Yes. Like Lee Jecks and Dana and Evelyn. Dead." There was nothing more Chris could say.

Lou Wellington's brows were worried over tired green eyes. "I don't understand it. Tracy, I don't. This is just like Jecks and Dana and Evelyn. Suffocation. No sign of struggle or violence. What made them do it?"

"Felton and Clay?"

"Felton and Clay and Jecks and Dana and Evelyn. All of them. Any of them."

"I don't know. Jecks was fired. So were Dana and Evelyn. But Felton had two years to go. Clay had four." Tracy stared gloomily at the service records of the staffers. "No hint there. They had good records, good health, families on Earth or pioneering. Clay had two lovers once, but the arrangement was amiable. Felton won out. There's no reason for Pat or Robin to have died."

"There was no reason for Lee or Dana or Evelyn to die, either. But they're dead." With slightly shaking hands Wellington covered the bodies on the surgical table. "Damnit, there's something wrong at this station. If you don't know it, Tracy, I do. Order an investigation. Call Dutton. We have to have help here before we lose another one."

"Do you think we will have more?" Tracy looked at Lou Wellington, some of the steel returning, saying, "If you think we will, tell me now. I'll have to break it to Dutton carefully. The Bureau isn't going to like this."

Chris had been sitting with Terry Oxford, listening. "I'll warn Dutton, if you like," Chris said softly. "I brought it up first. I'll stick my neck out now, if that's what has to be done to bring help." Inwardly, Chris wanted Tracy to do the job, but feared that it would seem too irrational to insist. And someone had to convince Dutton of the urgency; Chris was not sure that Tracy would, or even wanted to.

"If I need help, I'll ask for it," Tracy said sharply. "It's my risk, Tuttle. This is my station."

Chris stared down at the shapes under the sheets. "Then you should have taken it before now. There may be others, Lexington. And we might be too late. Dutton will have to believe we're in trouble, believe it enough to ignore all the Bureau's red tape. It might be hard to show a real emergency, one that Dutton would understand."

"Are you through, Tuttle? I said I would handle it. That should be enough." Tracy's eyes held no touch of sympathy now.

"All right. I'll leave it to you. But do it, will you, Tracy, before there's another death? We've lost five, five staffers. That's too many."

"It's not your worry."

"You don't know that," Chris shot back, giving in to anger. "You don't stand watch out there in the shelter. You haven't felt the silence that comes through the Marsh, that calls out to you. It's like a living thing, that silence, and it pulls you to it . . . I remember what it felt like, the times it's happened to me. And I know it's what happened to them."

"When it happened to you? Why the hell didn't you say something then?" The suspicion in Tracy's voice was blatant. "If you're making this up, Tuttle, or trying for an effect . . ."

"When have I made things up, Tracy? Especially about standing watch? You know I don't do that." Chris turned helplessly to Wellington. "You're the medic here, Lou. You've seen my psych profile. You know that I don't imagine things. It's there in my record. You've seen it." The frightened, anxious words spilled out and Chris did not stop them. Somehow, somehow Tracy had to be made to realize that they were all in danger. "You can check me again, right now, if you think I'm making this up. Use the stress machine or anything else you want."

Wellington turned to Tracy. "Tuttle's right. There's no history of hysterics or grandstanding in any staffer's medical records, and you know it. Chris is telling you the truth."

"And you say you've felt this thing?" Tracy asked, skeptical but withholding judgment.

"Once very strong. A couple of other times, a touch. It's not like what you might imagine. Tracy, it's like a cloud—a clear cloud with all the force in the world in it. It draws you to it . . ." Chris could not touch the bodies on the table. "Look what it's done already. And think about Jecks and Dana and Evelyn."

Tracy nodded decisively. "I'll talk to Dutton. Today."

With a grunt Meredith Dutton put down the last of the reports from the station. "Right. You've had some peculiar happenings here. But I don't see what the investigation team can do about it. Five deaths, that's bad. Looks like your people are getting sloppy."

Tracy kept a rigid self-control. "My staffers are getting killed. You heard what Tuttle there had to say. You know that something is going wrong. It's your responsibility to investigate."

"We'll see what the Bureau has to say." Dutton looked longingly at the empty cup on the desk. "You wouldn't have any more tea, would you? We've been out of it at central and we won't be getting more for another two months. The requisition didn't get filed."

"If you hear me out, Leland will bring you your tea," Tracy bargained, casting an anxious look at Chris and Sandy.

Dutton sighed. "Very well. But I'm warning you, Lexington, you have not given me enough information to recommend anything to the Bureau, except perhaps your replacement. They're going to look into their firing records and come to the conclusion that you have a lot of malcontents here waiting for the axe."

"Pat Felton wasn't old enough for the axe and neither was Robin Clay. Jecks had been fired, but so has Tuttle over there, and Northrup. We're all in the same fix, Dutton. But we aren't all dead yet."

"But a story like this—'Something in the Marsh' . . . it's ridiculous, Lexington. You can't blame me for questioning it. Now, if there had been love trouble, hell, we all have love trouble on these stations, it's expected. But this business about some force out there lurking and leading your staffers into the Marsh. Come off it, Lexington. That's crazy."

Tracy said through clenched teeth, "I admit it sounds far-fetched. I didn't buy it myself when Tuttle first told me about the thing. But Northrup has felt it, too, and Northrup doesn't invent things, either."

"At least nothing that would interest you," Jes Northup said acidly.

Dutton ignored Northrup, gesturing to Chris. "You. Tuttle. Come here."

Chris rose slowly. The room felt enormous for the ten steps it took to get to Dutton's desk. "Inspector Dutton?"

"Lexington says you brought this Marsh thing up. Suppose you tell me what it is, and what it's doing out there?"

Once again Chris described the sensation of silence and the menace it brought. "It's got to be stopped, Inspector. If it can reach us here, it can reach other stations. It's learning all the time."

"And we don't want it to get the edge on us," Jes sneered.

How Chris wanted to hate Jes for that cynicism, to deny the attraction that was as compelling as the thing in the Marsh. "Not now, Jes."

Ignoring this, Meredith Dutton remarked, "You're still alive, Tuttle. The others are dead. How do you account for that. Does the Marsh have a soft spot for you or what?"

Chris hesitated, looking covertly at Jes, then said, "I'm a tangiphobe. I hate being touched. I think that thing has to touch you to work. I think that's how it makes people go into the Marsh. It fascinates them, and then it touches them."

Dutton gazed steadily at Chris, an unreadable expression masking any thoughts; then suddenly Dutton laughed. "Well, that's one explanation, and it's original. A tangiphobe. Well, why not."

"Do you think I'm lying?" Chris asked with dangerous quiet.

"Let's say I don't think you know the whole truth." It was plainly a dismissal, for Dutton turned back to Tracy. "See here, Lexington. I am putting your station on partial alert, with a patch through to central open all the time. If you run into any trouble, I want you to buzz us immediately, and we'll authorize an inspecting team at once. Personally, I think this is nothing more than a contagious dose of the spooks, with some of your staffers panicking and going off into the Marsh. But for the time being, I'll give you the benefit of the doubt. If you can't come up with any solid evidence in, say, ten days, I'll call off the alert and we'll get back to business as usual."

"By solid evidence, you mean another corpse." Tracy was openly angry now. "If enough of our staffers die, you'll take this station seriously; that's what you're saying."

Dutton started to say "Of course not," but was cut short by Jes Northrup. "I know people like you, Inspector. You get the whip hand, and that makes the rest of us peons. Oh, you'll show your ass and pull your forelock quick enough for the Bureau, but we get the boot here. Anything the Bureau says is great and dead staffers are an inconvenience, a blot on your record. I get it. I get it." With those bitter words Jes Northrup left the room.

"Is Northrup always like that?" Dutton asked genially. "Sounds like you've got a morale problem at this station. You said Jecks and Northrup were lovers."

"Jes is always like that, lovers or no lovers," Tracy said.

"Charming. Well, you appear to be able to handle that. I'm looking forward to your report. Say day after tomorrow for final filing." Dutton gave Chris a broad wink. "If you run into any more bogies out there, make a note. See if you can get it to stick around long enough to answer some questions." When Tracy and Chris were silent, Dutton supplied the polite laughter. "You staffers in these watch stations: you lose your perspective. Damn shame."

"Chris." Jes Northrup had waited in the hall after Tracy and Dutton had left.

The few seconds Chris hesitated made Jes smile. "That's right. You can't quite walk away from me, can you?"

Fighting an inner panic, Chris thought wildly, trying to think how Jes could know. Or perhaps Jes's malicious tongue had instinctively found the one weak spot in Chris's armor. "What is it?"

"You've been close to that thing a couple times now, and you're still alive. I was just wondering why. I wouldn't have picked you for the survival type." This was said with an unpleasant smile.

"Maybe I'm immune. Maybe I'm lucky."

"I'd say lucky," Jes decided. "You sure as hell aren't immune."

"Stop it."

"I wonder," said Jes speculatively, nastily, "I wonder if you'd say that if we were the same sex?"

Chris moved back as if slapped.

Laughing now, Jes said, "So that's not it either. We've got a fucking romantic staffing the Squad. Oh, pardon me. Not fucking. You don't do that, do you?" adding maliciously, "No fucking since Gabe."

"I don't have to listen . . ." Chris yearned to find the word that would hurt Jes. "You're as bad as that thing. You're as poisonous . . ."

Jes's laughter deepened, not sounding like laughter anymore.

Chris stared, and when the sound did not stop, fled.

"Wellington wants me in half an hour," Sid announced to Chris two hours into their watch. "Can you manage, or should I send someone out to you? I mean, if you're feeling jumpy, it would be easy to get someone. But we're short-handed."

"Who's available?" Chris asked, glad to turn away from the Marsh.

"Jes. Maybe Leslie in an hour or so. But Jes is willing."

"Never mind. I'll take the last alone. It's only ninety minutes. I can hack that." Ninety minutes, with room in the shelter, with space enough to breathe without Sidney's enthusiasm spilling over, taking up the shelter, taking up space and thought and air.

"I hate to go off and leave you out here. Tracy was pretty firm about doubles on watch, you know. It's only reasonable, to take this precaution now, when you think what's been going on. The Bureau doesn't require us to take unnecessary risks . . . You could insist on a replacement for me, that's in the regulations." The concern in Sid's face was almost as amusing as the constant chatter was annoying.

"If there's any trouble, I'll take the blame." Chris looked past Sidney into the Marsh, now bright with a low haze hanging over it, shining with the green light of the water. "Look for yourself, Peterson. There's nothing out there, I'll be safe. You don't have to worry."

Sidney's pleasant, open face showed doubt, but nothing more was said. Changing the subject, Sidney said, "I hear Tracy's real mad at Inspector Dutton. You were there, weren't you? You think the inspector would have been more interested, wouldn't you? I mean, five staffers dead, that's a lot. The Bureau doesn't like its staffers to die."

Because then it has to pay double to the heirs, Chris thought, saying "I guess the Inspector figures this is the way to handle the problem: ignore it and it will go away. And no R.R.B. property has been damaged. Things would be different if the shelter were wrecked, wouldn't they?"

Nearby a few of the reeds clicked, a sound like clapping.

"You know, Pat and Robin's death bothered me a lot more than Lee's. I mean, it's not like I didn't know Jecks, or anything like that. It was that Pat and Robin were after three other deaths. Somehow, that made it worse, like we're being picked off one at a time."

"Or two at a time." Chris wanted to be alone, to be free from the constant run of words, from the encroaching friendliness.

"You and Terry Oxford found them, didn't you? That must have been really horrible. I don't think I could have done it. Even if you knew what to expect, well, you don't expect things like that, do you? But you thought they were dead, didn't you? You warned Tracy about it, I remember."

"Do you mind if we don't discuss it?" Chris asked gently.

"Oh. I'm sorry. I didn't think. I mean, it would be hard on you, remembering, I guess. Really, I didn't mean it, Chris." The urgency of the words brought Sidney closer to Chris. "And it's not like you have anybody. You don't, do you? That must make it worse. It's easier if you have a lover."

"Until you lose them," Chris said with deliberate cruelty. "Then it's much worse."

Stung, Sidney retreated. "You didn't have to say that."

When the wounded silence became unbearable, Chris said, "Look, why don't you leave a couple of minutes early and get over to Wellington on time. Who knows? You might have time enough to come back for the rest of the watch if you make it quick."

Sidney's irrepressible grin widened. "Hey, you know, that's a good idea. I think I'll do that, if you're sure it's okay with you, Chris. I mean, you're not doing this just to be nice, are you?"

"It's fine with me," Chris said, adding sarcastically, "I'm glad you thought of it."

"What? Oh." Sidney laughed. "Say, that's great. Really, that's a good joke. Me, think of it when you did. I mean, that's great."

Chris was ready to scream. "You can leave now, Sidney. It won't take you long." Chris thought with luck Wellington would keep Sidney all afternoon.

"You're right. I think I'll go around the back way. It's faster, you know? That way I don't have to go through the station and all."

"Good idea."

"Well, if you're sure you're safe, I mean, if you don't think you'll need me." Peterson put out one big hand which Chris managed to avoid without being too obvious. "Well, if you're sure, then I'm on my way." Sidney clambered out of the shelter and waved before disappearing among the tall reeds and hillocks.

When Sidney was safely out of earshot, Chris moved to the edge of the shelter. "All right. You're out there: where? The words came through clenched teeth, a muffled shout. "I know you're out there. You're waiting for another one of us to come to you. You're stalking us. Why?"

Far out in the Marsh the reeds rattled in derision. No wind touched them, yet they rattled while the water stood shiny as glass. Daylight had spread itself over the place like butter, making the Marsh shine like polished metal.

"Where are you?" You're out there. I know you are." Chris was outside the shelter now deliberately vulnerable. "Here I am. Try to get me." The challenge rang over the Marsh, unanswered. Chris waited, the watch gun leaning against the shelter. At the farthest edge of the Marsh there was a ripple of what might have been silence, mocking. After a while Chris went back into the shelter, slumping against the turtleshell wall, at once relieved and disappointed. It would have been easy now, for Chris was ready and would fight it. But it had not come.

"Peterson?" Wellington's voice crackled from the wall speaker.

"Not here, Lou," Chris said.

"That you, Tuttle?" Wellington sounded worried. "When did Peterson leave?"

"A while ago. Sidney was going around the back way; probably went straight to your lab." Tension was draining from Chris, being replaced with a watery fatigue. Thank goodness there was less than an hour left of watch.

"I'm in my lab now. There's no sign of Peterson."

"Try the rec room. Could be Sidney came in that way, after all."

"I've just been there." Wellington said the next words as if each had a noxious taste. "Jes Northup thought it was funny, losing Peterson."

Chris was ready to protest the idea, then remembered the lip of silence on the far side of the Marsh. "Shit. Oh, shit."

"I'll get Tracy to send out a search party," Wellington said, breaking the connection.

Scranton's Marsh shimmered as the wind went over it. Then it was still again, even the reeds were hushed. The still water was ice-bright, slick, its perfect stillness impenetrable.

Chris glared at it through slitted eyes. "It isn't fair," Chris said softly, forced by the reflected light to turn away. "I was ready. I could have fought you. It isn't fair."

Search parties and prowlers hunted for two days, but there was no trace of Sidney Peterson. Scranton's Marsh remained shiny and still.

"Dutton can object, the Bureau can raise hell, but I want an investigation team here. We've done all we can. Without their equipment we'll never find Peterson." Tracy flung a breath support unit across the rec room. "That's all there was, that unit. Why do they take them off?" Tracy asked the ceiling. "Out there, with that damn drifting gas, why do they take off their breathers? Why?"

Lou Wellington sank tiredly onto a chair. "They all have. Dana, Evelyn, Lee, Pat, Robin, and now Sidney. It's the same. You can't suffocate properly with a breather on. You can't drown, either." Absently Wellington reached out, fingering the breather. "No damage. No gas. It wasn't pulled off, it was taken off. Willingly. They knew the dangers. They knew them and they took the breathers off. I've warned them about the gases here. I've warned them repeatedly."

"Dutton will see that as proof of suicide. They knew about the gas, they understood the risk, and they died," Tracy said glumly. "No other explanation makes sense."

Jes Northrup interrupted, "Unless one of us is a maniac, and is getting jollies out of killing us."

"Shut up, Jes," Tracy ordered, but without emotion.

"Take Chris Tuttle," Jes went on, paying Tracy no heed. "Chris could be doing it. It was Chris, wasn't it, who brought the whole thing up? Maybe this is all a clever cover for murder. We know Chris hasn't got a lover, and that's not normal. Maybe this is revenge for being alone? Hum?"

"You mentioned the thing, too, before I ever did. And maybe you're getting even with someone," Chris said petulantly, wishing that Jes had not spoken.

"Then maybe I'm a murderer. You'd like that, Chris. So would the rest of you. You'd love to put the blame on me, not on the Bureau where it belongs. They don't even trust us enough to tell us what we're guarding. What is the gas out there? You can't tell me we're guarding methane, because I won't believe it. It's the Bureau's fault the staffers are dead."

"Look, Jes, you know there's nothing we can do about the Bureau. We've got to look after our own."

Jes's face turned white with rage. "You're all snot-licking cowards. You want the Bureau to run roughshod over you. You're all bashful virgins like Tuttle, waiting around for your unicorn. You accept whatever drek is handed to you. And you think because we get to screw in our spare time that everything is okay." Jes turned on Chris. "You! You should know better. At least you aren't playing that game. But no, you're as bad as they are. Well, Gabe died seven years ago, so what are you waiting for?"

No one else had ever mentioned Chris's one lover. Gabe had been the first victim of Halverson's Stopover, when the breathers were optional. Gabe had been caught by a gas cloud without protection, and had died weeks later, skin and lungs rotted.

"You'd better leave," Tracy said quietly. "Now."

When Jes was gone Wellington started to apologize, but Chris interrupted. "About the murder part, that's what we're all thinking, at least part of the time. We can't help it. I know I can't help it. It's frustrating, dealing with something you can't see or touch or locate. So it's easier to look for the nearest thing . . . One of us."

Wellington nodded. "I know. I wish it weren't so. And about Gabe."

"Never mind about Gabe. Gabe's been dead a long time. And it wasn't this that did it."

"Maybe not, but whatever it is, it's as bad. Dutton's got to know about Peterson now," Tracy went on, heading for the door. "Maybe this time they'll listen to me at central. I wish to hell Gee Andrews hadn't retired last year. Andrews listened when you talked."

Chris turned to Wellington when Tracy had gone. "What do you think, Lou? Do you think Dutton will believe any of us?"

"Do you want an honest answer?" Wellington asked.

"Of course. What else is there?"

"I think Dutton figures us for psychos."

For a moment Chris was still. "Would it help to bring up Gabe?"

"Not with Dutton." Though Wellington was no older than Chris, there was age in the words that followed. "Dutton's figured it out. And that's that. No matter how many of us die." Wellington turned suddenly, grabbed the breather and threw it across the room.

Chris remembered the expression on the Investigator's face, the frank incredulity of Dutton's remarks. "We don't matter, Wellington. The deaths don't prove anything."

Wellington nodded. "Deaths never do."

"Dutton's people will be here tomorrow," Tracy announced to the Squad that night. "They're sending a full investigation team down. It'll be crowded, but we can handle that with a little planning."

"What about the shelter? Are we still going to use it?" Sandy Leland sounded frightened, as if the shelter shared in the responsibility for the death of each Squad staffer.

"Not if you don't want to. Standing watch will be voluntary." How Tracy hated saying that. It was a contradiction of the whole philosophy of the Squad, but it had to be done. There was no choice now. "Those of you who do not wish to stand watch, report to me and appropriate arrangements will be made."

"But they can die as easily in here as out there," Jes remarked to no one in particular.

"So we might as well all stand watch," Chris countered. "I'm going to." There was no need to tell the others that the challenge had failed, that the thing in the Marsh had not answered Chris when called outright.

"Who're you doubling with?" Terry Oxford asked.

"I don't need a double. If that thing can separate us out there, there's no sense in doubles." Chris's raised hand forestalled objections. "It just increases the chance of more of us getting it."

Tracy gestured for quiet. "We'll assign doubles to those who want doubles. That should settle that."

"You're all bloody fools," Jes said dispassionately. "As if any of this made a difference."

"Much more out of you, Northrup, and you'll find yourself at central until you have to leave."

When the whispers died down, Tracy went on. "We'll be expected to give the Investigation Team our full co-operation. I know you'll want to do that, and you'll make yourselves available to the team if they request it."

Chris felt a quiet elation. This time the thing would not have to choose between the doubles. This time Chris would meet the thing alone and would understand it.

"You're as bad as the rest of them," Jes murmured to Chris before leaving the room.

The shelter was dark, no moon being in position to give it its wan light. In the night Scranton's Marsh was restless, shifting its weight like a child jogging from one leg to the other. The reeds made sporadic noises, like social small talk, sending out ripples as they moved in the wind.

Chris sat alone in the shelter, waiting. If the thing were coming, it would find Chris and no one else. Watch had been lengthened to six hours because most of the Squad was waiting for the investigating team, and did not want to venture out until they knew they would be guarded. In six hours, Chris would learn a lot.

But the hours went over slowly and Chris was almost asleep when the silence began, hovering at the far side of the Marsh, out of reach, tantalizing. With a shake of the head, Chris was awake, watching anxiously for the approach of the thing.

Even though the movement, the spreading silence, had become familiar, its terror had not lessened. It was too vast, too present to be invisible, and yet only the reeds marked its progress.

The reeds near the shelter clacked in a gust of wind, and were quiet.

Chris forced sleep back, and made sure the breather was securely fastened in its helmet clips. "What are you? What do you want?"

The silence seemed to change shape, but kept its distance.

"What are you?" Chris demanded, louder, climbing out of the shelter. "Why are you here? Why are you hunting us?"

From the distances more vast than the wide Marsh, an answer touched Chris's mind, like a voice lost and unused. *I am not hunting you. It is you that hunt me.*

Around Chris the night trembled, as if a sigh had echoed there.

"You're crazy," Chris started to protest, then stopped. "Hunting you? Guarding you? Are you what the R.R.B. wants? How do we hunt you?"

That is meaningless to me. You have pursued me, your kind. I have tried to ally with one of you.

"That's how you killed them," Chris said, thinking of the others following the thoughts farther and farther into the Marsh, sure that they had come on the one thing that made Halverson's Planet valuable. "You led them out and you killed them." No wonder they had smiled, no wonder they had gone easily, thinking they had at last done something of worth.

No. I am allied with one. The others, they are gone now.

"Gone?" Chris said. "They're dead. Do you know what that means?"

The ally says that there is no harm in this death.

"Shit," Chris said. Who would be mad enough, stupid enough to . . .

This one is wrong?

Slowly the silence moved forward, menace increasing as it came, spreading over Scranton's Marsh like a shadow that was not a shadow. Chris watched it come, unflinching. They would touch, they would touch very soon, but Chris was no longer frightened. What was the touch of a shadow, the caress of silence? It would not be the touch of flesh, which wounds. No, this would be different. This would be alien, entirely different.

"Who is your ally?" Chris asked, realizing that the ally would be part of the shadow, its human component, its soul.

The silence spread out, chilling the Marsh, waiting expectantly a few yards beyond the shelter.

"Come nearer. I can't see you."

You are the hunter. You come to me.

Recklessly Chris grinned. "All right. I will." Slowly, deliberately, Chris stepped out into the bog of Scranton's Marsh, going to the thing that waited, going without fear.

The ally is satisfied. The thought licked at Chris's mind, and again Chris wondered who the ally was? Who would even want to take the Squad down to death, each one, until . . . "Jes."

Underfoot the ooze sucked and pulled, and where Chris stepped phosphorous lit the water so that the Marsh glowed emerald green. It was beautiful down in the water where the light lived. The thing beckoned, offering the beautiful silence of the green light.

Jes beckoned. Jes.

Now the silence engulfed Chris, stilling conflicts and quieting doubts. This was the easy way, the touch that Chris had dreamed of. It brought peace, where there was no worry about reasons and answers.

Then someone had clapped a breather into place over Chris's face, and there was grit in Chris's mouth from the mud.

Jes Northrup dragged Chris back toward the shelter, shouting for help from the others who watched from the edge of the Marsh.

The silence was gone. A cold wind snapped over Scranton's Marsh, making the reeds chatter like teeth.

Wellington pulled Chris from Jes's arms, instruments ready.

As Lou Wellington set to work, saying, "You're damn lucky," Jes stared enigmatically down at Chris. "I was looking for you."

"Lucky."

"If Jes hadn't seen that cloud coming, we might have lost you. Funny about those gas clouds. They're weird to see."

"Cloud?" Chris asked, bewildered. There had been no cloud, only the silence and the knowledge. The ally . . .

"Tracy thinks it was some kind of marsh gas, maybe like the gas that killed Gabe." Lou studied the monitor. "You had a hallucination. Jes came out when the cloud appeared. It's a good thing we checked."

Chris looked up sharply, seeing the cynical smile Jes wore, and the hard brightness in Jes's eyes. "Swamp gas." The tone was light. "Wouldn't you know it?"

"Are you sure?" Chris said, coughing. "Did you see it, Jes?"

"If it were anything else, Tuttle, you wouldn't have been so lucky," Jes said, and the warning was plain.

Chris sat up, panting, thinking of being fired at twenty-nine, of the long, poor years ahead, and realized that Jes had found the way to revenge the Bureau's callousness. It was a terrible solution, but before Jes was through, Chris knew that the Bureau would lose a lot of money.

"Dutton's asking the Bureau to keep me here on the research team for the investigation coming up," Jes added, smiling cruelly. "And you're fired, anyway, Tuttle."

Wellington looked uneasily at Jes, saying to Chris, "You know, Jes is right. Think of the power that force must have. You're very lucky."

So that was why Jes had relented: there was no need yet for another body. There had been deaths enough—R.R.B. would investigate. *Only* Jes would be left here, the ally. With careful consideration, Chris studied the sardonic lines of Jes's face, saying, "I guess you're right. I guess I am lucky. It would be foolish to ask why, wouldn't it, Jes?"

about "Allies"

This story was a challenge I set myself. I've always wondered if it was possible to write in English about characters of more than one sex in such a way that who was what was never revealed and was not, in and of itself, important to the story. I feel a guarded satisfaction in this novelette. True, some of the sentences are awkward, and once or twice it was very difficult to find a way to keep the dialogue moving.

Before Roy Torgeson bought "Allies" for his Zebra anthology *Chrysalis*, it had been rejected four times elsewhere. One of the rejects said that the premise was silly because Chris Tuttle was so obviously male. Another reject said that the premise was silly because Chris Tuttle was so obviously female. A third reject said that there wasn't enough real adventure.

Do I, in fact, know what sex Chris and the other characters are? Of course. Will I tell you? No.

DEAD IN IRONS

They all hated steerage, every steward in the *Babel Princess*. Mallory made that plain when he showed Shiller around the ship for the first time.

"Hell of a place," she agreed, looking at the narrow, dark corridors that connected the cold storage rooms.

Mallory chuckled, a sound of marbles falling on tin. "Worse'n that. Don't let 'em stick you back here, Shiller. They're gonna try, but don't you do it. You being the newest one, they think they can get away with it, making you do steerage. But this damn duty has to be shared." He cast a sideways look at Shiller. "Wranswell's the worst. You keep an eye out for him."

"It's like cold storage for food," Shiller said, peering through the viewplate at the honeycomb of quiet, frosted cocoons.

"Sure is," Mallory said, contempt darkening his voice.

"I wonder why they do it, considering the risks?" Shiller mused, not really talking to Mallory. "You couldn't pay me to do that."

A white grin split Mallory's black face. "Cause they're stinking poor and dumb. Remember that, Shiller; they're dumb."

Shiller turned her gaze once again to the figures stacked in the coffin-like tiers. "Poor bastards," she said before she moved away from the hatch that closed the steerage section away from the life of the rest of the ship.

"It's not that bad," Mallory said, running his eyes over the dials that monitored the steerage cargo. Some of the indicators were perilously low, but Mallory only grunted and shook his head. "Hell, Shiller, this way we don't have to feed 'em, except for that minimal support glop they get. We don't have a lot of crap to get rid of. We don't have to keep a shrink around for 'em the way we do for first class. We don't have to worry about space. It could be a lot worse. Imagine all of 'em running around loose down here."

"Yeah," Shiller nodded, following Mallory down the corridor to the drive shield. But she added one last question. "Why don't they buy into a generation ship instead of this? They're slow but they're safe."

Mallory shrugged. "Generation ships cost money; maybe they can't afford it. Maybe they figure that this way they'll be alive when they get where they going, *if* they get where they're going."

"If," Shiller repeated, frowning. "But what happens if we drop out wrong? Where would we be? What would we do with them?" She sounded upset, her face was blank but her dark eyes grew wide.

"Hasn't happened yet. Maybe it won't. It's only a seven percent chance, Shiller. That's not bad odds. Besides, we couldn't keep operating if we lost more'n that. Don't worry about it." He swung open the hatch to the small, low-ceilinged cubicle beside the core of the ship. "I'll show you what to look for if we get into trouble."

Although she had been to school and had been told these things before, Shiller followed him through the lock, turning to look one last troubled time at the hatch to the cold room.

"Shiller. Pay attention," Mallory's voice snapped at her. "I got to get back on deck watch."

"Yeah," she answered and stepped into the little room.

Wranswell posted the watches later in the day, and Shiller saw she had been assigned to steerage. Mallory's warning rang in her mind, but she shrugged it off. "Can't hurt to do it once," she said to the air as she thumb-printed the order.

"Don't let them get frisky," Wranswell said with ponderous humor. He loomed at the end of the corridor, filling it with his bulk. He was a gathering of bigness. His body, his head, his eyes, all were out-sized, massive, more like some mythic creature than chief steward of a cargo jump ship.

Inwardly Shiller shrank back from the man. Small and slight herself, she distrusted the big man. She knew that stewards rose in rank by their ability to control other stewards, and Wranswell's bulk clearly dominated the others.

"Got nothing to say? Well, that'll be good in steerage. All you got to do is sit there and wait for nothing to happen." He chortled his huge, rumbling chortle as he started down the corridor. "You haven't been to see me, Shiller," he complained as he grew nearer.

"I've been stowing my gear."

"Of course you have. It's a pity you didn't let me inspect it first. Now it's all over your cabin. And some of it got torn. You got to have tougher things, Shiller." He was close to her now. He leaned on the order board and smiled down at her. "You got to remember what my job is. And you're the new steward. I got to be sure of you, you know."

"My watch is about to begin," Shiller said in a small tight voice.

"Oh. Yes. It's too bad your cold gear got ripped. You'll get cold for those four hours." He grinned at the fear in her face. "I'd loan you some others, but it's against the rules. And you don't want me to break the rules, do you?"

Shiller said no, hating herself for fearing the big man, and for letting him see her fear. He was the sort who would turn it against her.

"Of course, Shiller. The rules shouldn't be broken. But I make the rules. They're my rules." He reached down and touched her arm. "I make 'em and I can break 'em. Because they're mine. Remember that, Shiller."

"I'll remember." Her fists were hard knots at her sides.

"Do you want me to break them for you? Hum?" His smile had no warmth, no humor. "What do you think, Shiller? What do you want me to do?"

She moved back from him. "I think a rule is a rule, Wranswell. I wouldn't want you to make an exception for a new steward like me." Then she turned and fled, followed by Wranswell's huge laughter.

Steerage was icy; the cold cut through Shiller's torn gear with an edge as keen and penetrating as steel. Her hands, inadequately protected by ripped gloves, were brittle and stiff, and her fingers moved slowly and clumsily as she adjusted the valves on the tiers.

The monitor showed that the indicators which had been near critical were now back within tolerable limits. The silent, cocoon-like figures stacked in the tiers drifted on in their sleep that was not sleep, their bodies damped with cold and drugs. One day they would be warm again, would breathe deeply the air of another planet, their hearts would beat a familiar seventy-two beats a minute. But at the moment, they were like so much meat stored for the butcher.

Shiller was horrified with herself as the thought rose unbidden in her mind. She had been determined to treat steerage passengers as the people they were, not as cold cargo. Yet in less than a day, she had found herself slipping, seeing steerage as meat only. She forced herself to pause as she worked, to talk to each of the passengers, to learn their names and destinations.

"How's it going?" Mallory's voice asked on the speaker.

"It's cold."

"Sure." He paused. "You're cold or it's cold?"

"Both," she said shortly, wishing she could ask him for help and knowing that she must not.

"You got your gear on, don't you?"

"Sure. But turns out some of it's ripped." She was too near telling him what Wranswell had done, and what he had said.

"Don't you know enough not to go in there in ripped gear?"

"It's all the gear I have," she said. The cold had gathered on her face and made it hard to talk.

"Ripped gear? Where'd you buy crap like that?"

"It got ripped after I came aboard." She thought it was safe to say that much, that Mallory would understand and hold his peace.

"Wranswell?" said the voice from the speaker.

"I'm not accusing anyone of anything." Her hands were so cold they felt hot. Carefully she rubbed them together and waited to hear what more Mallory had to say.

"I'll talk to you later." The speaker clicked once and was dead.

Shiller sat looking at the monitors, feeling the cold seeping into her body. It was too cold and too long. She knew that her hands would need treatment when she got off watch. It would go on her report, and she would be docked for improper maintenance of her gear. Bitterly she realized that Wranswell had engineered things very well. All he had to do was be sure that her gear was faulty, and he would be able to order her to do anything. She would have no choice but to obey, or the company would leave her stranded on some two-bit agricultural planet. It had happened before, she thought. Wranswell was too good at his game to be a novice player. Shuddering, she forced her attention on the tiers.

"You're the new one." The steward who confronted Shiller was an older woman, one whose face was hardened with her job and made tight with worry. "I heard we'd got you."

Shiller felt the hostility of the other steward engulf her, hot, a vitriolic pulse. "I'm sorry," she faltered. "I haven't learned who everyone is yet."

"No. Only the one that counts." The woman barred her way, one muscular arm across the door.

"Look," Shiller said, tired of riddles and anger, "my name is Shiller. I only came aboard last night, I don't know the ropes around here. If I've done something wrong, I wish you'd tell me, then I won't have to do it again."

"Shiller," the other said, looking her over measuringly. "Wranswell told me about you. You're the reason he's kicking me out." She waited to see what effect this announcement would have.

"No," said Shiller, closing her eyes, feeling the bile touch the back of her mouth. She dreaded what Wranswell had planned, and now she had made an enemy of his former mate. "I didn't do anything. I don't want him."

The laughter was unpleasant. "You're not serious," the other said, stating a fact. "On these tubs, you take everything you can get, and if you can get the chief steward, don't you tell me you'd refuse."

"I don't want Wranswell," Shiller repeated, very tired now, her hands beginning to ache now that they were warm again.

"Sure. Sure, Shiller." The woman leaned toward her, one hand balling into a fist, her face distorted with rage.

"Dandridge!" Wranswell's voice echoed down the hall, and in a moment he appeared, his big body moving effortlessly, swiftly to stop the woman's hands as she rushed Shiller.

"Oh, no, Wranswell," she cried out, turning to see his fist as it smashed the side of her face. Clutching at the sudden well of blood, she sank to her knees, a soft moan escaping her before she began to sob.

"Looks like you need someone to take care of you, Shiller," Wranswell said, ignoring Dandridge on the floor.

"Not you, Wranswell." Shiller had begun to back up, feeling her face go ashen under Wranswell's mocking eyes. "Not after what you did to Dandridge."

The woman on the floor was bleeding freely, her hands leaking red around the fingers. Her breath was choked now, and when she coughed there was blood on her lips.

"Dandridge is nothing," Wranswell said.

"She was your mate," Shiller said tensely, still hoping to break away from him, from the bloody woman on the floor.

"Was, Shiller. Not now. Now you're here and I got plans for you."

Shiller shook her head, sensing the hurt he would give her if he could.

"No? There's a lot of time you can spend in steerage. Hours and hours, Shiller. In torn gear. Think about it."

In spite of herself, she said, "Mallory said that watch was shared."

"Mallory ain't chief steward. I am. You'll do all the steerage watches I say you will. That could be quite a lot. Until you get sensible, Shiller."

Dandridge stumbled to her feet and, hiding her face, pushed down the hall toward the medic room. Shiller watched her go, her hands leaving red marks where they touched the wall.

"Think about what I said, Shiller." For a moment Wranswell studied her with arrogant calm, then he turned and followed Dandridge to the medic room.

The skin on her left hand was unhealthily mottled. Shiller studied it under her bunk light, feeling a worry that was not reflected in her face. Four days of steerage watch had brought her to this. She flexed her fingers uncertainly and found that even a simple movement hurt and left her hand weak and trembling. Taking the packet of ointment Mallory had left for her, she smeared it over the livid spot. The pain eased.

Out in the hall she could hear Dandridge talking to Briggs. Shiller knew what Dandridge was saying, that she was angry, taking vengeance where she could, the hurt and damage done to her much worse than the ruin of her face. Leaning back, Shiller tried to shut out the words, the spite that came through palpably.

A warning buzzer sounded the change of watch. Hearing it, Shiller felt a surge of rebellion, but she was too tired to ride it through. With tired acceptance she rose and pulled on her cold gear, checking all the temporary seals with more hope than trust. It would be a little better, but there was no way they could keep the cold out entirely, there was no way they could save her from the ache and the numbness.

Mallory's friendly face appeared around the frame of her door. "Ready?" he asked brightly.

"I guess."

"I'll walk you down." He waited in the door, his hands blocking the passage and the cruel words Dandridge spewed out at Briggs.

"Thanks," Shiller said, summoning the ghost of a smile. She had not smiled often since coming to the *Babel Princess*. Draping her headgear over her arm she joined Mallory in the narrow corridor.

"Too bad Wranswell's being shitty about steerage," Mallory was saying loudly enough for Dandridge and Briggs to hear them. He was still in his first-class uniform: tight breeches, loose shirt, half jacket and jaunty cuffed blue boots. Shiller looked at him with envy, her body made shapeless and clumsy in the cold gear. Mallory gave her clothes one uncertain look, then went on, "Say, Shiller, it's none of my business, but why fight it?"

"Fight what?" she asked, wishing he had not spoken.

"Wranswell. He's not interested in Dandridge anymore. You could be his mate. It's obvious he wants you."

"You're right, it's none of your business."

Mallory did not pay any attention to this. "What he's trying to do is wear you down, Shiller. He can do it."

"We're not out here all the time. Sometime we have to drop out and come into port. When we do, there's company officials . . ."

"Be reasonable, Shiller," Mallory said patiently. "We're in port maybe one day in twenty, then we're gone again. You can't begin to get to one of the officials of the Babel line. That takes weeks."

"Then I'd transfer to another ship." She was speaking recklessly and she knew it. If Mallory decided to, he could tell Wranswell, and then there would be no escape for her.

"Don't kid yourself. Shiller. It's no different on the other ships. We run by our own law out here. And if we break the rules now and then, who's going to come after us. And how?" He smiled at her, his dark eyes showing a gentle concern. "This is our universe. And Wranswell runs it."

"I'll think of something," Shiller said, not to Mallory. "I won't be his mate. I can't stand him." She turned, suddenly afraid. "Mallory, don't tell him I said that. Please."

He made a dismissing gesture, hands wide. "You don't want me to know, don't tell me. I probably won't tell Wranswell. But he's a tough man. Maybe I'll have to." He shrugged fatalistically.

"But Mallory . . . You wouldn't tell him." She felt suddenly desperate. Under the heavy wrap of her gear she felt a cold hard lump gather under her ribs.

Seeing her panic he said, "No, of course not, Shiller."

They were almost at the cold room. Shiller pulled her headgear off her arm and began to secure it. Her gloves made her hands awkward, and in a moment she asked Mallory to do it for her.

"Sure, glad to," he said, pulling the gear into place and sealing it. "Keep what I said in mind," he told her as they reached steerage. With a cuff on her arm for luck, he opened the hatch.

Shiller hesitated inside the hatch, dreading the four hours to come. She was still close enough to hear Wranswell stop Mallory outside.

"Well, Mallory, how did it go?" asked the hated voice.

"Well, I talked to her," Mallory said, hedging.

"Any headway?"

"Not so far." There was contrition in his tone, and embarrassment.

"Keep trying, Mallory. Or you can do your watches in there."

Mallory laughed uneasily. "You don't have to worry about that. You won't get me in there for anything." He paused. "I can talk to her again in the morning, when she's had some rest. Maybe she'll think it over while she's standing watch."

"I hope so, for your sake."

"It's gonna take time, Wranswell. The thing is, you got her real scared."

"That," Wranswell said, "is the general idea."

"You rotten traitor!" Shiller shouted when Mallory appeared in her door the next morning. "You can fucking well bet I thought about it!"

"Thought about what?" Mallory asked warily.

"You know. I heard you talking to Wranswell. I heard what you said, Mallory."

Mallory hesitated, indecisive. His face was a mixture of aggravation and loss. "Then you know how things stand," he said at last.

Shiller swung off her bunk. "No, I do not know how things stand. I thought I did, but obviously I was wrong." She found suddenly that it was hard to speak, and the difficulty was only partly due to the cold in steerage.

"Ah, Shiller." If he meant to be conciliatory, he failed.

"Don't you talk that way to me. Why did you do it, Mallory? I thought you gave a damn. I thought you were my friend."

"I am your friend," he said, speaking with a caution he might have used with a child. "Why else would I do this?"

"To save your hide, that's why."

"Look, Shiller, I told you the day you came aboard to be careful of

Wranswell. He's the boss here. Why didn't you listen to me then. You dumb, or something?"

"I didn't think you meant this," she shot back at him finding a strength in her that she did not know she had. "You never said a damn thing about what Wranswell wants, or what he's like. You never told me he'd want this of me." There was a burning behind her eyes and Shiller was shocked to realize that she was on the verge of tears.

"I figured you knew. What else would it be?"

"You were very careful about that, Mallory. You warned me to watch out for Wranswell. You said that when you showed me around the ship. But that wasn't what you meant, was it? And you didn't come out and tell me what I had to deal with. And you didn't tell me you were following Wranswell's orders."

Mallory was getting angry. "Who the hell else's orders would I follow? This is Wranswell's world, and he makes the decisions. More'n that, he's the one who makes sure things get done. You can't fight that, Shiller. And I can't fight it either."

"That's shit," she spat at him.

"Fuck you, Shiller." He turned away from the door, then looked back. "You keep this up, you're gonna be as dead as the stuff outside this ship. Wranswell ain't gonna wait forever. You gotta give in sometime."

Shiller grabbed her cold gear and hurled it at Mallory.

"You're as dumb as steerage. You belong there!" Casting the heavy gear aside, Mallory stormed off, his steps sounding like explosions along the corridor.

As Shiller listened to the sounds die away, she felt part of herself die with them. Mallory was right, and Wranswell waited inexorably for her, to possess her and break her. She did not recognize the terrible grating sounds as her own sobs.

By the time the *Babel Princess* dropped out for its first stop, Shiller had got used to the steerage routine. She figured out the colonists bound for Grady's Hole and prepared them for shipping to the surface. It was a long tedious job, but now she welcomed it, for at least in steerage she was safe from Wranswell.

"It's okay, Harper," she said to one of the cocoons, addressing it by the name stenciled across it. "You're gonna like Grady's Hole. It's sunny and warm, and the soil is good. The Babel line has an outpost there already, so you know you won't starve." She hooked the support tubes into his shipping capsule, noticing as she did that the color of the fluid was wrong. Quickly she checked the feeders to see if she had confused the line, but no, it was the correct one. And the solution that should have been mulberry was a pale pink.

Cautiously she tapped the feeder, drawing out a sample of the fluid for later examination. "Hope you're okay, Harper," she said to the co-coon. "Don't want you to get down there and find out they can't thaw you out." She put the sample into one of her capacious pockets and moved on to the next tier.

"Crawleigh, Matson, Ewings and Marmer," she read from her list, as if calling role. "You're the last of the lot. The consignment says four-teen, and you make it fourteen." She moved the tiers into position for capsule loading, making a final check of the list.

When she was finished she stamped the invoices and relayed them up to the bridge for verification. In her pocket there were now four samples, the other three drawn from Marmer, Ewings and from one of the earlier capsules which she had gone back to check after seeing Harper's feeder.

The invoices came back with the Babel seal and the captain's sigil on them. Shiller took them and put each in the capsule it belonged to. Then she sealed the capsules one after the other, checking each seal in the manner prescribed.

"Shiller." The voice on the speaker was Briggs. "I got something you have to ship down with the capsules."

"What?" she asked, not caring.

"Something important."

"It's against regulations," she said, speaking by rote. She no longer trusted anyone on the ship. "Sorry."

"Wranswell said to tell you that he'd count it as a favor. He said he might find some other work for you to do if you can get this stuff down for him."

"What is it?" She found that to her disgust, she was interested. She hesitated on the seals of the capsule.

"It goes with Baily. You seal it up yet?" Briggs sounded urgent, as if he too had some consideration riding on her agreement.

"Not yet," she admitted. She hesitated, thinking. If it were found out that she had added something not on the invoice, she could be stranded out on some distant planet where she could be a common laborer or a prostitute. But if she failed to do this for Wranswell, her life would continue to be a nightmare.

"Hurry up," Briggs prodded. "I got it right here. It's small. Wranswell really wants it, Shiller."

"Okay," she said. She went to the hatch and held out her gloved hand. To her surprise the thing Briggs dropped into it was only a small dark vial, weighing no more than a couple of ounces. "Is this all?" she asked, turning the thing over in her gloved hand.

"That's it. And remember, it has to go in Baily," Briggs said, sounding relieved.

"You can tell Wranswell it's done," she said and closed the hatch.

But she wondered idly what it was Wranswell was smuggling—for surely he was smuggling—that was so small and so precious.

"I haven't thanked you yet for that service you did me," Wranswell said to Shiller as they sat in the mess. "You're coming around. Perhaps all the way?"

Shiller did not even look up from her plate.

"You might be interested to learn what I am up to. No? Not the least curiosity?"

"No."

"No? But do you really have so little concern for your fate? You, Shiller?"

"I'm not interested, Wranswell," she said, and knew she was lying.

"But you might be arrested for this. Don't you want to know what the charge will be?" Wranswell was being funny again. His deep rumbling laughter filled the mess room. "We could all be arrested for this, certainly. But then, to arrest us, they would have to catch us. Out here." A few of the other stewards took up his laugh.

Shiller bit her lip and remained silent.

"Here we are, engaged in secret smuggling. Babel policy would condemn us all and most of you know nothing about it." He looked contemptuously over his underlings. "How many of you are like Shiller here, and don't want to know?"

"It's steerage," said Dandridge from across the room. "Wranswell smuggles the bodies. He waters down the feeders so the cargo is just getting cold and drugs; it makes 'em hard to thaw out that way. He ships along the feeder solution so his bunch in customs on the ground can keep 'em going until they can sell the cargo to slavers." Her voice was loud in a room suddenly still.

"Dandridge, is, of course, right," Wranswell allowed, spreading his huge hands on the table. "She is also very foolish. But then, I don't imagine anyone heard her very well."

Conversation erupted in the mess, the eleven stewards trying to shut out the accusation that would condemn them all.

Under the racket, Wranswell said to Shiller, "I would put it differently, but essentially Dandridge is right. From time to time I'll expect a little help from you. In exchange, you may be allowed to stand something other than steerage watches. Is your first-class uniform clean?"

"And if I don't cooperate?" In spite of herself, she knew she was striking a bargain with Wranswell, giving her consent to his terrible scheme. She had heard enough about the slavers to make her shudder, for they were far worse than anything Wranswell could hope to be.

"I think you will. In the next few days you might have a few words with Dandridge about it. She can tell you what to expect."

"Why Dandridge? What should I ask her?"

"Shiller, you will know when the time is right." He turned away from her then and spoke softly to Mallory.

Dandridge's body was stiff by the time Shiller found it. She had been struck many times, and even the ugly lividity of death could not disguise the large bruises on her arms and back. She lay now crammed between two rows of tiers at the back of steerage, her dead eyes blackened, horrified. She had not died easily.

"Briggs, you and Carstairs get in here," Shiller said to the speaker. She was feeling curiously lightheaded, as if Dandridge's death had spared her.

"Want some company, Shiller?" Briggs asked with an audacity he had learned from Wranswell. "Come outside here."

"I've got company. Dandridge's body's in here. You gonna come in and get it out or do I call the bridge?" It was a bluff: Shiller knew she could never call the bridge and risk the ostracism it would bring, or maybe an end like Dandridge's.

"You don't have to do that," Briggs said quickly. "You said Dandridge's body?"

"Yes. She's dead. Somebody killed her. You better tell Wranswell. He might be anxious about her." Shiller heard Briggs whisper to someone, then he said, "It'll take a couple of minutes. We'll get her out."

It was longer than that when they at last came through the hatch, shapeless in their cold gear, a stretcher slung between them. Shiller saw that the other steward was Mallory, and that he was calm.

"She's at the back under tier number five. You won't be able to lay her flat; she's got stiff."

When they got to the place, Briggs stopped, his eyes widening behind his mask. "Come on, Briggs," Mallory said. "We gotta get'er out of here. Wranswell's waiting."

Briggs pulled himself together, grabbing the out-thrust elbows. "Look at her. She sure got hit," Briggs said. Mallory only grunted.

They wrestled the body onto the stretcher and lashed it down as best they could. Then, without a word to Shiller, they left steerage, carrying their grim trophy between them.

Shiller watched them go, remembering what Wranswell had said. The warning was plain. If she talked, she, too, would be killed. If she did not cooperate with Wranswell's smuggling, she would find herself beaten and frozen at the back of steerage.

"It's too bad that we'd already gone hyper when this happened," Wranswell announced to the stewards. "If we were still in port we could report this to the Babel home office and they could investigate. But since we've gone hyper and we aren't due to touch port for another fifteen days, even preserving the body might be difficult."

Gathering her anger and her courage, Shiller said, "Why not put her in steerage? She'll keep in there."

Wranswell chuckled at the idea. "Well, it's a novel approach," he said as he loomed over her. "But it's not practical. We'll put her in one of the spare capsules and ship her off."

Briggs had got noticeably paler. "Off where?" he demanded. "Out there? We don't even know where that is. We won't know where she's gone."

From his side of the room Mallory gave Briggs an impatient sign. "Don't worry about it, Briggs. It's better this way. More'n that, there won't be any hassle at the other end of the line. Nobody'll investigate and we'll all be safe. Captain'll file a report and that'll be the end of it."

"Mallory's right, you know." Wranswell agreed. "Much less trouble for everyone. Believe me, the Babel line doesn't like these occurrences any better than we do. We'll prepare her for burial and send her off tomorrow."

When the others got up to leave, he motioned Shiller to stay behind. "I trust your talk was constructive? I know these one-sided conversations can be trying, but I'm sure she had some information for you." He reached out one hand and tugged at Shiller's hair. "Be reasonable, Shiller. You won't get anywhere if you antagonize me."

"I got the message. Can I go now?" She refused to look at Wranswell, at his bloated, smiling face and his eyes that raked her body like nails.

"Not quite yet. I want to explain about the next drop out. On Archer Station, the next port, we play the game a little differently."

"I hear you," Shiller said, wishing she could scream.

"There, one capsule more or less makes little difference to my agent's clients. And I find it hard to justify keeping a steward on who is only good for steerage work. Unless I find out you're more versatile, there might be an extra capsule. Archer Station deals with Ranyion slavers. I understand they're most unpleasant."

Shiller felt her teeth grind as she held her mouth shut. There was little she could say now. Archer Station was two weeks away, and they would be her last two weeks of freedom.

In the end they had to break Dandridge's bones to fit her into the capsule. But at last her stiff, distorted body was closed away, sealed for a journey into nothing that would lead nowhere. The stewards gathered at the lock, as Wranswell had ordered.

Briggs arrived last, looking haggard. He watched Mallory through exhausted eyes, fingering a lean statue which he clutched to his chest. Mallory deliberately ignored him, turning away when Briggs started his way.

Wranswell, his big body looking out of place in his first-class uniform, arrived to deliver his eulogy before sending the capsule on its way. He wore a secret smile that grated on Shiller's nerves. Wranswell was obviously satisfied.

"For our comrade who has died in the line of duty," Wranswell began the traditional benediction as the rest of the stewards shifted on their feet and felt awkward, "we praise her now for all she accomplished while she worked among us and did her tasks. . . ."

Before Wranswell could continue, Briggs shouted out, "You killed her!" and he lunged at Mallory, the statue he had been holding at the ready. "I loved her and you killed her!"

Mallory shouted and leaped aside, bringing his arm down on Briggs' back. Briggs staggered under the blow, but turned, his face filled with loathing. "You're Wranswell's errand boy. He gave her to you and when she wouldn't take you, you killed her!" He sloughed around on Wranswell. "You're as bad a slaver as the ones you sell to."

This time it was Wranswell who hit him, sinking his balled-up fists deep into Briggs's gut. Retching, Briggs fell to his knees. Beside him the little black statue lay broken. "You can hit me till I'm dead. It doesn't change anything. You still killed her."

"When you're finished, Briggs, we'll get on with this ceremony." Wranswell turned to Mallory. "You're okay?"

"Sure. Briggs's just upset. He don't know what he's saying. Why, when this is all over, he's gonna forget all about it." Mallory was straightening his uniform as he spoke, adjusting it with strangely finicky gestures.

Briggs looked up. His face was ashen and his voice hoarse, but there was no mistaking his words. "You hear me, Wranswell. So long as Dandridge is out there, we're gonna stay hyper, too."

"Go away, Briggs. If you can't conduct yourself right, go away." Then Wranswell turned from him, ignoring him now. He began the ceremony once more in impressive sonorous tones. No one but Wranswell spoke.

Above decks the captain played back Wranswell's report, shaking his head, not caring about what went on below decks. He heard the thing out, then connected it to his log, giving his formal acceptance to the report. It was too bad that the steward had died. They would have to lay over a couple extra days at Archer Station while a new one was sent.

It was several hours later when there was the first indication that something was wrong. The *Babel Princess* gave a lurch, like a boat riding over choppy water. But in hyper there were no waves, and there was no reason for the ship to lurch. Alarms began to sound all over the ship.

Shiller tumbled out of the bunk, still half-asleep, knowing that something had wakened her. The shrilling of the alarm broke through and she began to dress automatically. The cold of steerage was still on her and she trembled as she pulled herself into her clothes.

The alarms grew louder. Down the corridor there were other stewards stumbling about, shouting to each other.

Suddenly the ship's master address system came on. "This is the captain. This is the captain," the system announced. "We have encountered unfamiliar turbulence. For that reason we are going to drop out and see if there is any reason for it. I apologize in advance to our passengers for this inconvenience. I ask your indulgence while we complete this maneuver. The stewards are standing by to take care of you should you experience any discomfort. We will drop out in ten minutes. For that reason, please remain in your quarters. If you need assistance, buzz for a steward. Thank you."

Mallory pounded on Shiller's door. "Get your ass above decks, Shiller. First-class uniform so the tourists can throw up on somebody neat and clean."

"Shut up," she answered.

"The passengers are waiting," he said in a brusk voice.

Sarcastically she asked, "And are you looking after steerage? I thought that regulations required that steerage be manned during every drop out and every pass to hyper. Don't tell me you're going in there, Mallory."

"Not me, but you are," Mallory said, taking cruel delight in this change of orders. "You can take care of the cargo in steerage. You been doing it so long, you're real good at it. Maybe you can snuggle up to 'em and keep 'em warm." He laughed in imitation of Wranswell, then hurried down the hall.

Slowly Shiller changed into her cold gear, a deep worry settling over her with gloom. Unlike the others, she suspected that Briggs was behind the trouble. And when the others discovered it, what would happen to him? Mutiny brought with it an automatic death sentence. Shiller had seen a formal execution once, and it had not been pretty. To watch poor, crazy Briggs die that way . . .

"Hurry up, Shiller," Langly shouted from down the hall. "Time's short! Three minutes!"

"Coming," she answered, and went out into the corridor still pulling on her gloves. When the one-minute warning sounded she began to run.

The drop out did not work. The drive whined, the ship bucked and slid like a frightened horse, the shield room grew unbearably hot, the core reached its danger point, but they failed to drop out.

There was a wait then, while the core cooled down, and then they tried once more. Above decks the tourists in first class watched each other uneasily, not willing to admit that their pleasure jaunt could end this way. The stewards kept to their assigned posts, not daring to show the panic they felt. For if the tourists did not know they were in trouble, the stewards did.

The fear did not touch steerage. Shiller braced the cocoons, strapping the tiers to their stanchions on the walls. She steadied herself between them and stoically rode out the first attempt to drop, and the second. She knew a morose satisfaction: if they were stranded in hyper, she would be free of Wranswell, free of Mallory. She glanced around the familiar bleakness of steerage, thinking of the names stenciled on the cocoons with a certain affection, as she might have thought of plants.

"Don't let this worry you, Ander," she said to the nearest one. "This doesn't matter. If we don't get where you're going, you'll never know about it anyway." Idly she wondered if Ander were male or female. There was nothing on the invoice that mentioned sex. Was Ander a great strapping lad with huge shoulders and hands the size of dinner plates? Was she a strong farm woman who could carry a sheep slung over her shoulders? Was he a short ferocious man with bright eyes and boundless energy? Did she work handily, driving her small frame to greatest feats . . . ?

She tightened the cocoon in place and moved on to the next one.

This was Taslit, bound for Dreuten's Spot, an out-of-the-way agricultural planet, the last on their outward run. "Taslit, never mind," she spoke gently, easing the cocoon more firmly into place. "Two to one Wranswell would have sold you to some slaver anyway. You won't have lost anything this way."

Then the alarm sounded once more and another futile attempt to drop out began. As the heat mounted in the core, steerage began to warm up, the temperature rising almost five degrees. Shiller watched with concern as more and more indicators moved into the critical zones. If they kept this up long it would kill her cargo. She couldn't let that happen.

She went like a drunken man across steerage, reaching for the speaker button as she was thrown against the wall. She grabbed for a brace and held on as the *Babel Princess* sunfished about her. At last the attempt was broken off, the core stopped its maddened hum and the ship righted itself in the vastness of hyper.

Again the speaker came to life. "This is the captain speaking. This is the captain speaking." There was silence following that announcement.

"We appear to be having some difficulty returning to normal space. As it will take time to effect the necessary repairs, we will continue our journey in hyper until we can drop out without endangering the ship or her passengers . . ."

Shiller stared at the speaker, incredulous. "We're never gonna drop out; you know that," she told it, shaking her head.

"We may be delayed in arriving at Archer's Station . . ."

"We sure will. Forever."

"But the Babel Company will gladly refund part of your fare to compensate for this delay. I trust we will proceed without incident."

When the sound died away, Shiller sank onto the monitor bench. She wondered if the others in the seven percent who never came out of hyper did this, lied to the passengers and to themselves, pretending that everything was all right, promising an end to the voyage they would never live to see.

Shiller started to laugh. In the eerie cold the walls echoed her laughter, making it louder.

Wranswell was left to deal with Briggs; the captain had decided that it was a matter for the chief steward because Briggs was a steward. Wranswell had smiled, accepted the responsibility and sought out Mallory. Together they decided what had to be done.

They attached burners to Briggs' hands and feet and lit them. Then they locked him in steerage, alone with the cocoons. Wranswell and Mallory took turns at the hatch window, watching him as he died. They watched for a long time.

And when at last they dragged the body out, it had burned-off hands and feet, leaving charred, bleeding stumps on a corpse rimed with frost, seered with cold, the skin mottled blue where it was not black.

On Wranswell's orders it was left in the corridor for a day, a silent ghastly reminder of Wranswell's power. Then it was loaded into a capsule and sent out to join Dandridge in the lost places.

There had been trouble above decks. Rations had been shortened again and a fight had broken out, the stronger taking what little food there was from the weak. Now that most of them knew there would be no escape from hyper they cared less what became of one another. There had been several injuries and medicine was running as short as food.

"Look," said Mallory to a general meeting of the stewards, "we can take the ones that are worst hurt and we can stick 'em in cocoons and hook 'em up like the rest of steerage. We won't have to feed 'em, they won't get any worse, and if we ever get out of this, they'll be alive. They'll be grateful."

"And if we don't get out of this?" Shiller asked, the fear of Mallory all but gone. She had not bothered to change out of her cold gear.

"Then it won't matter, Shiller," Wranswell said from the head of the table. He had lost weight and his flesh hung in folds about him like a garment that no longer fit.

"Then who's supposed to look after 'em?" Shiller went on, seeing with contempt that the other stewards did not challenge him.

"You are."

"What? No more flattering offers?" She barked out a laugh, and found that it no longer hurt to laugh, or to die.

Stung, Wranswell retorted, "I've made other arrangements. You lose, Shiller. Too bad." His greedy eyes fastened on the slender grace of Langly, and the boy pouted in response.

"Lucky you," Shiller said before she walked out.

She woke to the smell of cooking meat. She sat up slowly, for hunger had made her faint. The light over her bunk was off but she did not bother to turn it on; she knew it was dead. More awake, she sniffed again. Yes, it was meat, fresh meat broiling. She felt her way to the door and pulled it open.

"Hey, Shiller, come on down and have some breakfast," Langly called when he caught sight of her. His bony face was wreathed in smiles and grease.

Shiller shook her head as if to clear it. "Where'd that come from?"

"It was Mallory's idea." He turned into the mess to answer a question, then said to her, "You're entitled to two pounds of meat a day so long as you're working."

"What'd you do, kill someone?" she asked without thinking.

Langly's answering giggle told her what she did not know.

"Oh, shit," she cried, ducking back into her room and pulling on her cold gear as fast as she could. It was a slow business in the dark, and she had to pause often to regain her strength. When she was done she stumbled down the corridor, oblivious to the mocking words that Langly sent with her.

When she pulled open the hatch, she knew.

The tiers had been raided, the cocoons pulled apart and the bodies harvested for the stewards. Here and there a few of the cocoons remained intact, awaiting the time when the others would be hungry again. Some held the injured passengers, their new seals not quite dry.

Shiller stood in the door, swaying on her feet. That they had done this to her steerage, that they had damaged her cargo . . . She moved into the cold room, unbelieving. Ander was gone. So was Taslit. And Ettinger. And Swansleigh. Nathan. Cort. Fairchild. Vaudillion. Desperately she searched the tiers for the cocoons and found them empty. Gone, gone, gone . . . She thought of Wranswell, his sagging face full of meat, smiling, gesturing as he ate, his thick hands caressing Langly and his dinner alternately.

Vomit spewed from her before she could stop it, and she sank to her knees until there was nothing left for her to cast up.

"There she is." Mallory's soft words reached across steerage to Shiller as she lay exhausted on the floor.

"Good work," Wranswell said, a contented grin spreading over his shiny face. "I was afraid we'd lost her."

Shiller turned her head slowly, filth and ice clinging to her face. Dully she watched as the two men came nearer.

"Hello, Shiller," Mallory beamed down at her. "We've been looking for you." He was much closer now. He put his boot on the side of her face and pushed.

Shiller gasped and was silent.

"Come now, Shiller. You aren't going to spoil this for us, are you?" Wranswell leaned down next to her. "Let me hear you, Shiller. It's much quicker if you do." He sank his hands in her hair and pulled sharply back. Shiller left blood and skin on Mallory's boot.

Mallory was good at his job. Each time a fist or a boot struck her, Shiller remembered the way Dandridge had looked when she found her. Now she knew how it had happened. She tried to let go, to ride with the punishment and the pain, but she knew that she fought back. In some remote part of her mind she knew that she struck at Mallory, trying desperately to stop him, to give him back hurt for hurt. Once she had the satisfaction of connecting with his eye, and as he beat her into unconsciousness, she could see the slow drip of blood down his face, and she was satisfied.

When she woke it was warm. Her cocoon had thawed around her and the room reeked of putrefaction. Of the few remaining bodies in steerage, only she was alive. Numbly she felt for the feeder lines and found none. They must not have had time to attach them.

Carefully she eased herself off the tier, her hands shaking when she tried to close them around the lip of the tier.

Then she heard the sound. "Wranswell? Wranswell? Where are you?"

The voice was Mallory's, but so changed. Now it was a quavering thread, coming on uneven breaths like an old man's.

"Wranswell?"

Shiller listened for the answer, hardly daring to breathe. She did not want to be discovered, not by Mallory, not by Wranswell. She was not alive for that. Discovering that she was trembling, she willed herself to relax.

"I know you're down here," Mallory went on, his voice reverberating in the still corridors. "I'm hungry, Wranswell."

At the words Shiller felt her own hunger rage in her with fangs as sharp and demanding as some beast's. She knew that her trembling weakness was from hunger, that her bony hands were the face of hunger.

Something stumbled near the shield room. Then lumbering footsteps came down the hall, wallowing, blundering into the walls, no longer careful or cautious, wanting only escape.

Now Shiller understood, and it was what she had feared. It was the hunt. The last hunt. She lay back on the tier, very still, hearing her heart very loud in the stinking room.

There was a scuffle now, flesh meeting flesh, and a mingled panting of voices, senseless sounds that neither Mallory nor Wranswell knew they made.

Then came the heavy, final sound, as though something large and moist had burst.

"Got you. Got you," Mallory chanted in ragged victory. He was not good to hear. "Got you. Got you. Got you, Wranswell." His high crowing made the hackles on Shiller's neck rise.

Now the sounds were different, a chopping and tearing as Mallory set about his grizzly work.

This was her chance then. Her hunger was gone and her mind had become clear as her terror dissolved. After this, there could be no more terror, no more fear.

Carefully, very carefully, Shiller eased herself off the tier. Slowly, so slowly, she slid across the room, no longer seeing the slime that oozed underfoot, or seeing the things that rotted on the other tiers, or the wreckage in steerage. That was over and done. That she could not change. There was only one thing now that she wanted, one last act she could perform.

She reached the monitor bench, raising the lid so that it made no sound.

In the hall Mallory began to sing.

Then Shiller had it, the long wedged blade that opened the capsules. Its edge shone purposefully. It had been designed to cut through seventeen inches of steel without slowing down.

Ander was dead, and Taslit. Dandridge, Briggs. Langly, too, she supposed. Wranswell. Cort. Ettinger. Harper. All of them.

The *Babel Princess* was dead, lost in uncharted darkness, derelict, drifting on unknown tides, its last energies draining into emptiness.

She was dead, too.

Shiller fondled the blade with care, testing the edge against her thumb, sucking the blood, tasting the salt. Weak as she was, she would not fail.

In the corridor Mallory was almost finished.

And in steerage, on the other side of the hatch, Shiller was waiting.

about "Dead in Irons"

This story was written for Jack Dann's and George Zebrowski's Harper and Row anthology, *Faster than Light,* in which all stories had to have some aspect of faster-than-light travel function as an important and integral part of the work.

Leaving aside the question of whether or not FTL travel is possible (and I remind you to read some of the various "proofs" that rail travel and air travel are impossible before making up your mind), one of the hazards of such travel has always seemed to me that you might get stuck doing it. And then what?

The answer to that question, at least one of the answers, was this story.

SWAN SONG

By the lake the air was still, but its biting cold felt greater there than anywhere else at Eric Shreck's arctic Canadian retreat. Even now, in June, the piercing chill was inescapable and made all sport unthinkable.

Eric himself didn't seem to mind. Fishing held few attractions for him, unless it was fishing for information, which was why he was enjoying his walk with his guest, Tapio Nälkaniemi. The Finnish engineer had recently resigned from a rival firm and it was very much in Shreck's interest to woo the man into his company. For that reason, he didn't begrudge the afternoon it took to draw out the taciturn Finn.

"You still don't understand, Shreck. I left Nord-Fission because of the arms trade division. It was taking over the whole company, and the electric power division was only an afterthought, a kind of nod to the critics of the corporation." The intensity of Tapio's feeling was reflected in his growing willingness to speak. "If you will forgive me, Shreck Production and Design does not take time to do that. You ignore your critics. Even those who say we could yet destroy ourselves through you and your company."

"Because we manufacture arms and fissionables?" Eric favored Tapio with his most charming smile, a smile of such openness, such sincerity that experienced diplomats had believed it. The engineer didn't have a chance.

Nälkaniemi's slanted eyes were a slate blue and he gave his host a steady look along with his uncompromising nod. "Yes. Your company has one use and one use only: you make war."

"Never." Eric showed Tapio a face rendered blank by shock.

"You supply arms, bombs, planes, guns, ammunition, and now

fissionables. Armed conflict keeps you warm, secure, happy. This lodge of yours"—he gestured toward the splendidly rustic façade of Black Lake Lodge, a building large enough to house twelve guests and four full-time servants in considerable comfort—"it was raised by misery and is maintained by suffering."

"Come, don't be melodramatic. You're much too severe. I admit that Shreck makes arms. And sells them to whoever wants to buy. It's no secret. You forget the advances we've made in textiles, in metallurgy, in construction, in telemetry, and in communications. And our endowments to universities all over the Free World run into eight figures every year."

"Your profits exceed that by a few decimal points," Nälkaniemi reminded him dryly. "I think that what I am trying to tell you, Shreck, is that I won't work for you."

"Not even in our Space Sciences division? I need a man like you, Tapio. We've been limping along because I can't find a man of vision to take over the whole thing and keep our projects going."

Far out on the silent, dark lake, something vast seemed to move, though no wind touched it and the trees on the far bank were still.

"You've got three countries interested in spy satellites. I learned from Albert Weister before he killed himself last year that you've agreed to sell."

Wisely, Eric made no attempt to deny it. "It's true, of course." He forestalled Nälkaniemi's objections with a raised hand. "But what else can I do? There's no one who will pay for the moon miners we have on the development boards, and I can't justify that kind of expense to the stockholders if there isn't some interest in taking the project further. The satellites will pay for the miners, and research for . . ." He stopped, realizing that Nälkaniemi wasn't listening. "Tapio . . . ?"

The Finn shook his head and wrenched his gaze away from the black surface of the lake. "I'm sorry, Shreck. What were you saying? Your moon miners?"

"We have a program that could put telemetrically controlled mining machines on the moon in five years if there were a way to get the company behind the project. But to do that I'd have to convince the Board of Directors that we'll eventually realize a profit. The satellites give me bargaining power." He paused, waiting for some kind of response from Nälkaniemi.

Although the lake was sheltered, having both mountains and a stand of hardy trees behind it, it shimmered, and the silent wind made a sound, incredibly distant, pure as grief.

"I understand the need for profit," Nälkaniemi said after a moment. He was frowning and the expression seemed to have nothing to do with his earlier objections. His eyes were distant. "I don't begrudge Shreck Production and Design its profits, only the way those profits are achieved."

"Then don't refuse my offer out of hand. You'd like the work, Tapio. It's right in your field. With you in charge, the Space Sciences division could pay off in a big way, and those are profits you can approve of. I know you're the man to do it. You may not know it, but you have quite a reputation." Shreck was as anxious to hire Nälkaniemi for this reputation as for his formidable engineering skill. With the adverse publicity Shreck Production and Design had had recently, he badly needed a pacifist with the company.

"My reputation is overrated," Nälkaniemi said and turned once again to look at the lake. "Do you know Finnish mythology?" he asked after a moment.

"No." And he was determined not to be sidetracked into so useless a discussion. "I've heard a little about the project you were working on at Nord-Fission. Think what you could do with that shuttle plan, using my company's resources. I'd like to see us branch along those lines. I'm certain there's a market developing there. The big thing with space technology is the recycle problem. From what I understand, you had that almost licked. If we have units we can use more than once, and from our own launching ports, we'd take the lead in the field ahead of everyone, including the Russians and the Americans. And if we build the launching ports for the buyers, we have ready-made bases for future developments. Imagine a standardized launcher used internationally."

"Like Phillips tape cassettes? It's tempting," Nälkaniemi admitted. "A space shuttle is the answer, that's obvious. Otherwise, waste makes the whole thing impractical and irresponsible."

Eric was so pleased with himself that he wanted to shout. But he merely held out his square, well-manicured hand. "Then we're agreed? You can take whatever time you need to come to your decision, say, sixty days." He would notify his arms division tomorrow, he promised himself. A standard launcher could be used for many more things than satellites. "We'll talk then. And in the meantime, we might as well go back to the lodge. It's clouding over, and you can imagine how cold it gets here once the sun's down."

It was Tapio's turn to laugh. "Yes. I come from a little town in the north of Finland. Every year we celebrate the Midnight Sun with bonfires and feasting. It's very old, coming from a long time before we were forced to turn Christian." He saw Shreck raise his brows and added, "We came to it late, you know. Through the influence of the Swedes, mostly. But there are old ways still." He gave the lake a quick, uneasy glance. "Do you ever hunt here?"

"Hunt?" Shreck asked, politely incredulous. "I'm afraid I don't go in for blood sports. And it's probably just as well. I haven't seen so much as a duck on the lake in the six years I've owned the lodge."

If he thought this would reassure Nälkaniemi he was mistaken. "And no fish either?"

"I don't fish. I don't remember that any of my guests have had very good luck, but most of them go to the river three miles from here. They say it's better sport. Most of my guests like a challenge."

"And the Indians? Do they hunt or fish here?" He was worried, and his wide, normally impassive face showed lines and grooves that were rarely so apparent.

"There are very few Indians around here. They were wiped out almost a century ago. There was a measles epidemic, and they died by the hundreds. No one has settled here since. Most of the big reservations are to the south, and the Eskimos stay away from this area." His voice was level, and nothing but the brightening of his eyes betrayed his excitement. "They are superstitious about death."

For a last time Tapio Nälkaniemi turned his back on the lake. "You're right, Shreck. It's cold here."

"And my cook is preparing Beef Wellington tonight," Shreck said, to speed their progress toward Black Lake Lodge.

Their snifters had been refilled twice and the fire had burned down to warm coals. The library at Black Lake Lodge was certainly one of the most pleasant rooms in the building. The walls were lined with glossy walnut shelves, filled with fine books in beautiful condition. Every subject was represented. The curious guest could read excellent translations of the commentaries of Julius Caesar in Russian, English, German, and French, or, for the more scholarly, there were editions in the original Latin. There were novels in eleven languages, ranging from great classics to the current fad in hard pornography. There were books filled with reproductions of great art. There were copies of technical journals all neatly bound and cross-referenced in the card catalogue that stood in a fine walnut case to the left of the fireplace.

The windows were covered with long, respectably aged velvet draperies, so the haunting cry of the wind was muffled and only occasionally managed to intrude a finger of cold at the wide door which led to the terrace.

"Midsummer like this," Eric Shreck said as he lit his second cigar of the evening, "it doesn't really get very dark. You'd probably be able to read good dark print if you were outside. But it's warmer in here and easier to read, too."

On the other side of the wide marble hearth, Tapio Nälkaniemi looked up from the journal he had been reading and reached for the crystal snifter on the table by the overstuffed leather chair he had taken a few hours before. "What did you say?"

"I said that it doesn't get dark out," Shreck repeated, keeping his affable smile firmly fixed over his teeth.

Tapio Nälkaniemi shrugged. "You forget that I've seen this for most of my life. Finland is quite far north." He closed the journal and gave his attention to his host. "Did you read that paper of Stenholm's? He's incredible."

Shreck nodded. "I was talking last week to Martindale and Ostaggio about him. They're tied down with a new project in Houston, you know. But they've got some very interesting ideas, and they have some very bright young men working for them. One in particular Martindale mentioned—a Mexican, name of Celo. Have you heard of him?"

"No, I don't think so."

"You will, if Martindale's any judge." Shreck was always searching for young scientists and engineers to bring into his company. He did not tell Tapio that he had given Martindale a handsome present in acknowledgment of the recommendation on Celo.

"Martindale's very lucky," Tapio said as he gave the matter some thought. "I wish I had his resources, and Ostaggio to be my co-ordinator. Those two are doing incredible things in space sciences. But Houston is one of the best places in the world for that."

"You know Martindale personally?" There was nothing in Shreck's records that indicated the two men had ever met.

"We've corresponded. But when he accepted that military contract for space fortresses, we became . . . alienated."

"But the American space program might have died without it. Be practical, Tapio. If a couple of fortresses is what it takes to keep men in space, then Martindale's willing to design fortresses and battleships so that he can also have his exploratory craft and observatory. And who knows? It might be necessary to have those fortresses in the future, if laser technology continues to develop its potential."

Some of the Finn's geniality faded. "And that would hurt your organization, wouldn't it? I've talked to Rosenstein about his work. I know a little about that laser cannon you've got on the drawing boards."

Eric gestured with his cigar. "Having it on the drawing boards doesn't mean it will ever be used. You know that."

"Like your lunar miners, perhaps?" The question came quickly, but Eric was not off his guard.

"That's another matter entirely. Mining is a business that shows a profit. To develop the laser, we'd need to be a good deal closer to global war than we are."

"But you'd like that, wouldn't you?" He downed the rest of his brandy in one gulp. "You'd like to see the world at war again."

"No one wants the world at war," Eric said smoothly. "But as long as everyone keeps preparing for it, I can't see why I should refuse to make a profit from it."

"And promote it?" Tapio demanded.

"Oh, come now." He offered his guest more brandy.

At first Tapio refused, but this was for form's sake, and he allowed himself to take another generous splash in the bottom of his snifter.

There was a strange sound then, almost like the cry of wild geese, though it was the wrong season for them to be flying.

"The wind does strange things, sometimes," Shreck laughed, but his laughter was stilled by the horrified expression on his guest's face.

"Jumalaa!" the Finn swore, and drank all the brandy he had just accepted. His skin was blotchy and it was a moment before he was able to speak. "I'm sorry, Shreck. I don't know why I let it bother me." He gave a tight, embarrassed sound that was supposed to have been a chuckle. "I guess the old superstitions are harder to get rid of than we like to think."

"Superstitions?" Eric graciously refilled Tapio's snifter, giving him a rather larger portion than before.

"Oh, it's foolishness," he said through fear-whitened lips.

"Foolishness? To make you start that way?" Shreck leaned back in the huge victorian chair he had long since designated his own. "Tell me about it."

"There's nothing to tell."

Shreck put all of his charm to work. "This afternoon you said very much the same thing out by the lake. What is it? I've always been fascinated by legends. And I don't know very much about your Finnish mythology. It's like the other Scandinavian myths, isn't it?" This was a deliberate goad and it got the anticipated results.

"Finns aren't Scandinavians. We don't even have the same language. Finnish comes from the Finno-Ugric group, and the Teutonic languages are Indo-European, like Russian and Latin and Greek and Armenian. We're different from them. Our language, our racial background, our myths." He was grateful for the brandy now.

"I didn't know that," Shreck lied, and put the brandy bottle on the table beside Tapio. "I've always found Finnish bewildering, but I've never thought that much about it. I've had a certain amount of trouble with other languages, such as Jugoslavian, for instance."

"Jugoslavian is Indo-European," Tapio said, dismissing it.

"Well, I'm not too good at languages. I can manage French and German and make myself understood in Italian and Spanish, but that's about it." He didn't add that he spoke Russian fluently and had a nodding acquaintance with Arabic. He found it useful to conceal his knowledge.

"Finn isn't like most languages. Suomilainen like me has enough trouble keeping the ties going, and language is one way."

"Suomilainen?" Shreck repeated awkwardly.

"It means Finn in Finnish. The country is Suomi. Accent is on the first syllable. Always." He sipped at the brandy and stared into the fire. "Your lake," he said musingly after a while.

"Yes? What is it about my lake that bothers you?" He put out his cigar and sat back contentedly.

"In Finnish mythology, there's a lake, Tuonela. It has a Swan floating on it."

Shreck nodded encouragement. "Isn't that the one that Sibelius wrote the music about?" He knew it was and didn't wait for an answer. "I've always liked that piece. But it seems terribly somber for a beautiful swan. I try to picture it, white, pristine, floating alone, watching its reflection. I reminds me a little of a ballet."

Tapio shook his head. "No. It's not like that. The Swan is black. It's huge: more than twice the height of a man. And it sings forever. Tuonela is the Lake of the Dead. The Swan is its guardian."

Now Shreck's smile was uncertain. "A guardian for the dead?" He watched as Tapio poured himself another tot of brandy with a decidedly unsteady hand. He mentally reviewed the dossier he had on Nälkaniemi and recalled that there was some question of a drinking problem. He decided to see what would happen if the Finn became very drunk. It was better to find out now than six months or a year from now, when Tapio would be very much involved in Shreck projects. "Do the dead need a guardian?"

"No. No. You don't understand. It's the dead who protect us. Tuonela is for us, the living, the earthly, the mortal. It keeps away Hiisi."

"What's that? Are you saying that there's some sort of hostile extraterrestrial in your mythology?"

"Not that way." He tossed off the brandy, then leaned forward with the particular intensity of drunkenness. "They're something like demons, the Hiiet."

"Hiiet?" Shreck was sorry he'd let the conversation take this turn because it might be hours before Tapio was in any condition to talk about business. Eric wanted to catch him off guard so that he could learn how best to attract Nälkaniemi to his company. If Shreck Production and Design was to have the first lunar rocket launching base, he needed Nälkaniemi. He stifled his boredom and decided to let the Finn maunder on about demons and get it out of his system.

"Hiiet, the plural of Hiisi." He spoke the words with ill-concealed dread. "They're destructive forces, wholly evil creatures that bring about war, domination, catastrophy, disruption, upheaval, revolution, disaster. They loathe humanity and are anxious to see us in ruins, to be like them. And the only things that stand between us and them are Tuonela and the Swan. It's human death, human mortality the Swan protects, not decay. Don't you see? Without Tuonela . . ."

The sound came again and this time the snifter fell from Nälkaniemi's fingers. Glass spattered over the marble hearth and lay like diamonds on the three-hundred-year-old oriental carpet.

Shreck uttered a terse obscenity, then swiftly assumed a more friendly air, helping Tapio to his feet. "No, never mind. It was an accident. I'll have one of the staff clean it up. By tomorrow you won't even know it happened."

Nälkaniemi shook his head emphatically. "I shouldn't have had so much. I didn't think I had . . ." His slurred words trailed off and he looked about in confusion. "And telling you about Tuonela. You'd like it, wouldn't you, if Hiisi was turned loose. You'd be richer than you are now."

"Tapio," Shreck said with a hint of urbane laughter, "I already pay outrageous taxes in eleven countries. If I were richer, it would make no difference to me." He put out his arm to steady the Finn.

The arm was refused. "Then it must be power. With you supplying arms, you could run the world. If things got bad enough, you would be godlike, deciding what nations would survive, and on what terms." He stopped suddenly, then lurched toward the door. "I didn't mean that . . . I thought . . . you're playing with so much . . . desolation. . . ." The door closed on this, leaving Eric Shreck standing in front of the fire, his glossy shoes marred by drops of brandy.

For some time he stood still, looking down at the broken snifter, but not seeing it. He considered what his guest had told him. Hiisi, hiiet. Demons bringing destruction and war. Malevolent forces on the other side of death, with only the lake between them and a vulnerable humanity. Then he laughed once, unpleasantly, and rang for a servant.

Frost covered the ground like a sugar coating, rendering the morning fantastically bright, fantastically distorted. In the long slanting rays of the sun, boulders became gigantic jewels; the railings around the terrace of Black Lake Lodge glittered like diamond necklaces. Only the lake was still, dark, unfathomable, taking none of the light from the morning. No ripples disturbed its surface; and in the distance the row of tall pines that rose in the protecting bend of the mountains framed the far shore like silent mourners.

Tapio Nälkaniemi was a little pale but otherwise showed none of the signs that might be expected from one who had passed such a night as he had. He was dressed in heavy, warm clothing, but he held two suitcases in his hands, and the fur hood that framed his face was part of a handsome overcoat that was designed for cities, not the Canadian wilderness.

"I'm sorry you feel you have to leave, Tapio. I was hoping we could talk again today. I have a lot of things to tell you."

"That's what I am afraid of." Tapio's tone was almost apologetic. "After last night, I found myself thinking about how fragile the world is. I'd forgotten about Hiisi. Perhaps it's foolish of me, and childish, but I can't let myself be party to war, not even in the very minor way you ask." His slanted eyes met Shreck's for one long moment. "I know you don't agree with me, but you weren't raised with the specter of Hiiet and the Swan. I know I couldn't accept your offer, not even for the opportunity of heading up your Space Sciences division. So I won't waste your time any more, Shreck. Thank you for ordering the car for me. And thank you for the weekend and the brandy. I wish you well. I appreciate what you've done."

Eric Shreck was politely incredulous. "Do you mean that you really believe all that about Tuonela and Hiiet? I would have thought you'd outgrown that."

The barb did not have the effect Shreck had anticipated. Tapio smiled diffidently. "So did I. Apparently I was wrong. And if there are truly no Hiiet, I still don't want to help us get any closer to what they represent."

Now the laugh Eric gave was the sort most adults reserve for annoying children. "Well, if you insist. I'll let you know if I ever see a gigantic swan. Black, wasn't it?" He stepped back, indicating that the farewells were over.

"Yes. Well, good-by, Shreck." Nälkaniemi offered his hand; and when Shreck didn't take it, he turned away and trod down the frosty steps to the jeep waiting to take him the one hundred thirty miles to the nearest airstrip. By evening he would be in Montreal.

Shreck watched until the jeep was gone, and then, instead of going back into the lodge, he walked toward the dark vastness of Black Lake.

He stood on the shore, feeling the cold, listening to the wind that moaned but never stirred the surface of the water. As he often did, he sensed that something vast moved on the far shore, something that could not be seen against the dark bulk of the trees. He watched as the sun at last rose high enough to touch the water, and noticed, as he had once or twice before, that the water never gleamed or shone in the sunlight. All that happened was that its depths took on a kind of baleful glow. Still, no ripples dimpled the surface, winking back the brightness of the sun.

As he watched, Shreck smiled ironically, wondering if Nälkaniemi would attribute the glow to the dead or to the Hiiet waiting to bring disaster on humanity. He listened but could not hear the eerie cry in the wind that had so disturbed the Finn only last night. He decided that it must have come around to a different quarter, and now there was just that low, familiar sound, like undistinguishable voices heard at a distance.

Somewhat more than an hour later, he walked back to the lodge. The frost had faded and the world was quite ordinary again. If there were forces in this part of Canada, they were hidden.

As he climbed the steps, his secretary came out to meet him. This colorless man had shown himself time and time again to be utterly devoted to Shreck and to Shreck Production and Design. His face, normally wholly without expression, now had an animation about it that might have been anxiety and might have been triumph. "There's a call in from our Greek representative. He's on Cyprus. It's very urgent, he says."

Shreck nodded in grim satisfaction. "Very good, Talbot. Is he optimistic?"

"He says that he had had offers today from Turkey, from Greece, and from Algiers for certain—ehr—products. Immediate delivery is desired."

"Immediate? I'll take care of it."

Talbot very nearly bowed. "I suggest the library phone. It has a scrambler. May I do anything while you're on the phone?"

Shreck hardly paused to give the order. "Yes. Drain the lake."

about "Swan Song"

My grandfather, whose name was Matti Kokonmaa until he became a naturalized citizen of the U.S.A., was the first person to tell me about Finnish mythology. His own attitude toward these myths was quite ambivalent because he was anxious to leave behind what he considered to be the backward superstition of his home country. He was a man of very few words, and so much of what I learned from him was spread over several years, until he died when I was seven.

As I recall, the first time he told me about the Swan, I was about four, and I found the idea fascinating. Since I had been listening to symphonic music before then, I quickly made the connection with Sibelius' tone poem, and while I was working on the story itself, I had *Swan* and the other Tuonela tone poems on the turntable, Kamu conducting the Helsinki orchestra.

For once the names of the characters are somewhat significant. Nälkaniemi means, roughly, starving village, and Shreck is a variant on the German word for terror. Make of it what you will.

THE FELLINI BEGGAR

Deftly he turned the page with his hooked toes, hardly pausing in his reading as his foot passed over the score.

How misassembled he was with his huge puppet's head and barrel chest haphazardly joined to spindly legs and topped with short, gnarled arms which ended in twiglike fingers.

He sat in his hovel with the open score at his feet, flapping his arms to the music he heard in his head. Occasionally he would sing in a pure and vibrant tenor that rang through the ramshackle hut to echo over the wasted land beside the depot.

Guarnelli had picked his way over the lacing rails to this place beyond the sidings, and now he stood in disbelief as the beggar filled the day with his singing.

"*Non piangere, Liu,*" he sang, his voice strangely sweet for its dark spinto sound. The knobby face the music came from was smoothed by the plaintive aria. "*Dolce mia fanciulla mascolta: il tuo signore.*" He skillfully lengthened his phrases. "*Questo . . . questo . . .*" His light, restrained poignancy, his elegant musicianship made Guarnelli's brusque professional heart ache. *Chiede colui che non sorride più, che non sorride più!*"

Guarnelli could not see the movements of the beggar's hands, but he waited for the closing chords of the aria to sound in his mind before he stepped forward.

"Ah, signore," Guarnelli began. His hands were wet.

The beggar turned and saw him, a lean young man in a new suit of the most fashionable Milanese turquoise and Paris cut, adorned with a camera and a notebook that seemed talismans against the heavy pall of haze and smog that had become the Roman sky. "Yes?" he asked.

They looked at each other for a moment, the beggar holding his place in the score with his feet. Then Guarnelli banged his hands together. "Bravo!" he cried frantically. "Bravo! Bravo!"

"A million thanks," said the beggar.

They regarded each other again.

"I am Vincento Guarnelli," he said. "I work for an American magazine. The best." He went on after a moment. "We want to ask you some questions about the film you were in." It was almost a statement, but not quite.

"Come in," said the beggar.

As he crossed the threshold, Guarnelli saw the books. One wall of the bare, cramped room was neatly shelved and filled with books. Guarnelli hesitated in his surprise. Books were rare even in great houses, but here, a miracle. And Guarnelli did not believe in miracles.

"Oh, those are my scores; my one excess," the beggar explained. Guarnelli accepted this without comment. He took in the careful neatness of the shack: the few pieces of furniture were sturdy and clean, the windows decently shuttered. One of three windows framed an ancient, long-handled pump.

With an effective twist of his foot, the beggar closed the score and stepped back. "Sit down, signore," he said, motioning to one chair—the only chair.

Involuntarily, Guarnelli paused and thoughts flickered at the edge of his mind. "You are the one who made the film, aren't you? I have not made a mistake?"

"You are correct. I am. Prego," and he again motioned to the chair.

"You see, it is ten years since he died. We want to do a memorial retrospective, a sort of review of his work. . . . A tribute, you might say, one that would remind the world how great an artist—"

"I know what retrospective means."

"Ah. Ah, yes." Guarnelli cackled nervously, caught off balance. "Yes, I suppose you do. Now. . . ." He settled back into the chair as far as its uncompromising frame would allow. "We want to know about the film you were in. What your work was like, how you remember him, that sort of thing."

The beggar sighed. "That was a long time ago. Fourteen, fifteen years at least. It seems longer." His head was highlighted by the slanting sunlight, making the odd protuberances more prominent. The wisps of hair surrounded it with a glossy, gauzy web. But Guarnelli tried not to look. It was not good to see such things.

Seeing his discomfort, the beggar smiled. Its warmth was out of place in the bulbous face. "Do not be embarrassed. I am used to being stared at, you know. It is my occupation."

"I am sorry," said Guarnelli, who had to say something.

"It is how I make my living. I understand. You need not fear me." With a listing nod he dismissed the subject.

Guarnelli was not satisfied. "Does it not pain you to be so? Are you not enraged at the injustice? But for this"—he wagged his hand at the beggar's hulk—"you might have been another Bjoerling, another Domingo or Pavarotti, another Tauber—"

"I might have been deaf."

Guarnelli tried to fill the awkward silence that followed by lighting a cigarette, knowing that the beggar would realize his importance if he could afford to smoke casually. He selected the cigarette carefully from his engraved, gold-plated case, tamped it precisely, lit it with a flourish, inhaled and exhaled with studied ease, as if he smoked every day. The focus was back with him now. Then he remembered to add the final touch. "Would you like one?" he offered.

"The air itself is harm enough. It was kind of you to think of it, though."

Guiltily, Guarnelli finished the cigarette as quickly as he could without appearing to rush. When he ground the butt on the rough planking, he noticed that the ash was the one spot that was not swept and scrubbed. What must it be like for him, thought Guarnelli, to be that way and scrub floors?

"What do you want to ask me?" The beggar had seated himself on the other side of the room on his sleeping pallet. The score lay open on the pillow beside him, one stubby finger caressing the page.

And Guarnelli felt in control again. This was the world as Guarnelli understood it. He took his notebook from his outer pocket, opened it, making a show of selecting a page, heading it, describing the interview, knowing that, in fact, a tiny recorder would take down the entire conversation. He wished he had had it on earlier, for he had not anticipated the beauty of the beggar's voice. "Yes, yes," he remarked to himself. "This will do." He looked up, brisk, very professional, expectant. "First, we would like to know something about you. Background material, as it were."

Was there faint mockery in his eyes as he answered? "Very well, Signore Guarnelli who works for American magazines, I will tell you. I was born in Siena, thirty-four years ago. My father was an engineer working for the Russians there. My mother had been a few seasons at La Scala before she married. My father," the beggar said with a slight laugh, "had great moustaches. He was very proud of them."

Guarnelli knew it was time to respond. Like the beggar's father who had prided himself on his moustaches, he prided himself on his sense of rhythm in interviews. "I see," he said.

"For a time they hoped I would go to the Academia Santa Cicelia. I had shown an early gift for music and I think they hoped that no one would notice how . . . different . . . I was." For a moment he lingered with the memory, then: "Is that what you are interested in, signore? Is that background?"

"Yes. Yes. Exactly. If you would not feel too upset about telling me these things. . . ." And he probably would not use any of the material in the story in any case. "If you would? . . . A few more words, perhaps? . . ." It helped to have the subject talk about himself. It made for a better presentation later on. "This is not easy for you, I am sure." Sympathy helped as well.

"Not at all." The beggar looked at him in some surprise. "It is a pleasure to remember such things. After all, my parents were kind and indulgent. They tried to find help for me long after all the others had given up. They cared for me, even though they did not understand why I could not be what they had hoped I might become. There should have been a transformation for them, a new child. They had enough faith for it, in the face of all truth."

The drowsy September wind stirred the ashes by the chair, winding them on an invisible finger. The beggar shifted his weight to his elbow.

"Go on," urged Guarnelli.

"If you wish. I realized before they did, or perhaps before they were willing to realize, that I would never be able to live in their neat, ordered world, where you, too, live, signore. Oh, they would have kept me with them until they died if I had let them. How unfair it would have been to them, to use their love in such a dreadful way. Unfair to them, and unfair to me."

Guarnelli raised an inquisitive eyebrow.

"But surely you see what I mean. You are a man of some insight, are you not?"

Guarnelli could not understand at all, but he said, "Yes. Of course. But that you were willing to make such a sacrifice . . . though you were right."

The beggar shrugged. "As to that, who knows? Yes, when I realized that their love was wrapping more and more tightly around my body, trying to make a shield for me, I had to leave them. They would have bound me hand and foot with their love, had I let them."

Guarnelli had not intended to record any of his reactions, so he was startled when he found himself writing his impressions as the beggar spoke. The thought of a special human interest article ripened in him and he felt his eyes grow large. They would give him credit. He would earn his rightful recognition at last. He would be famous.

"When I was fifteen I ran away. I came to Rome and soon found that as a beggar I could do very well for myself. Ever since medicine improved most deformities with artificial this and rebuilt that, there has been a great opportunity for those like me. We are suddenly very much in demand."

"Why didn't you sing?" The choice seemed so obvious that Guarnelli was amazed that the beggar had not thought of it for himself. The fame he would have enjoyed, the attention, the respect. . . .

"I do not mind being a beggar, for there are uses for us and we are a tradition in Rome. Had I sung, I would have been a freak. How could I do that to a voice such as mine?"

Guarnelli glanced about the hut, at the neat poverty of it, at the wall of scores.

"You see, I pay no rent here," he said, following Guarnelli's unspoken comment. "I can sing when I wish without attracting undue notice. I have a privacy that only the very rich can enjoy in Rome. And here, the cats do not stare, and they treat me well as long as I feed them and speak softly."

Absently, Guarnelli lit another cigarette, realizing that he would not be able to buy more for a month. He accepted this philosophically, tucking the empty case into his pocket without the strain he had shown before. "Now, about the film," he prodded.

This time the beggar laughed outright. "What a film it was. He had already outdone Petronius, and himself, so this film had to do more. The bizarre, the grotesque. . . . I remember the director coming up beside me as I stood in the Vatican ruins. He gave me a piece of plaster, saying that he thought we were over *The Last Judgment* of Michelangelo, there with the saved and the damned. The Forum Museum was still being built, so the tourists came to the rubble to see where St. Peter's had been. It was a good place for me. They seemed to think of me as a living relic and would reward me handsomely, particularly the priests. I do not go there now."

"That was where you met the director?"

"Yes. As I said, he came to me and we spoke. I was much younger then." For just an instant his eyes were clouded over, as if he were shutting out the picture, as if the memory pained him. "He told me about the film later, and the offer he made me was one I hardly believed but could never turn down." He shook his head. "No. I could not, even today." He turned to Guarnelli apologetically. "Pardon, signore. I did not realize how much I had forgotten."

Guarnelli gestured neutrally, wishing he could dig deeper into the particular meeting.

"When I went to his studio, I did not think he truly wanted to have me in his film, but I went out of curiosity. For I did not want to let the opportunity pass me by. As I said, I was much younger then."

Guarnelli was scribbling furiously now, trying to describe the nuances of the beggar's voice, the suggestion in his words. "What happened when you arrived at the studio? What sort of reception did he give you?"

"Oh, he was quite cordial, even expansive. He thanked me for coming and he told me what he was planning, what he wished to do and what he was prepared to pay me for my part in it. I think he sensed everything about me when we stood together in the wreckage of the Vatican. I don't know how he could have known about me otherwise, but he surely did. He knew what to offer." Although the words were bitter, there was no anger in him. Time had washed that away.

This was the part Guarnelli was after; this was what the American magazine would wish to buy. If he could get the whole story behind the people in that last, agonizing film, he would have the issue practically to himself. His eyes brightened as with a fever. "Yes. Go on. What arrangements did you make? What sort of money did you agree on?"

"Money?"

"How much did he pay you?"

Disgust showed in the beggar's face. "I have never taken money for anything but begging."

"But surely he paid you." Guarnelli knew no one would have been beaten and assaulted as the beggar had been without payment, and very high payment at that. It was ridiculous to think otherwise.

"He paid me very well." With those few words the beggar stepped back from Guarnelli. His manner became as it had been at first. Some part of him had retreated and was beyond the reporter's reach. But as Guarnelli felt contact slipping, he fought to regain it. He asked, "What was it? What did he give you to make you do that? Did you beg for your acting?"

"I am not an actor," said the beggar.

Guarnelli had to admit that was true. "Yes," he said impatiently, his hands rising with his emotion, "I realize that. But he had to give you compensation for being in his film. That's the law."

The beggar nodded but said nothing.

Guarnelli tried another tack. "Even small parts have their worth. Especially in his films, particularly in that film. It was full of small parts that made the whole piece worthwhile. The critics all agreed on that," he said emphatically, remembering how little else they had agreed on. "You do understand, don't you? It's that part of the film that gives a better point of view, a better overall impression, a better . . ."

"Perspective?" suggested the beggar.

"Yes. Yes, of course. Now, I know that you must have been worth a lot to him because only you could have played that part. You are the only one. You know that," he ended awkwardly, hating to allude to the beggar's ugly body.

"Possibly," the beggar murmured.

Incautiously, Guarnelli continued. "He was able to pay a great deal. We researched it thoroughly. I know some of those actors in small parts got rich from that film. Even if you took no money, he must have given you something. That was the way he worked. He gave the prostitute with the odd breasts a car, designed for her alone. The German who bought it paid her four million old deutsche marks for it. That was after those cars were outlawed." He did not add that he had got the idea for the retrospective as he listened to a worn-out whore reminisce about her custom-made car.

The beggar moved his hands and rested them on the score. His thumb rubbed at the binding.

"Did he give you the scores? You said yourself they were your one indulgence. He had access to things no one else had. Did he indulge you?"

"I said excess," he corrected gently.

"Did he give you these?" Guarnelli demanded.

There was a long silence. The distant hum of the city came through the windows like the droning of insects. Finally, the beggar sighed deeply. "Just one," he said at last.

Guarnelli looked up sharply, alert. "Which one?"

Again it took the beggar some little time to answer, as if saying the words robbed him. "Puccini's own *Turandot*."

Guarnelli stopped writing. "In manuscript?"

The beggar held up the score lovingly and returned it to the pillow.

"A regular score?" He looked at the beggar to be certain it was no joke. Then he closed his notebook deliberately.

"I wanted it, you see," the beggar remarked diffidently.

"But why? Of all things, why that?"

For the second time that day the beggar spoke openly. "When I was still young, in Siena, my mother took me to Milano to hear it with the New Zealander Te Kanawa and Domingo. Mackerras was conducting. Cabelle was Liu, I remember. She was a little past her best voice then, and tremendously fat, but her high pianissimo was still magnificent. She kept her flexibility, too, and had it till the last. . . . But I did not hear her perform in person again."

"But why *Turandot*?" As he asked, Guarnelli thought he knew the answer. That contrived ending, so unlike the rest of Puccini; that unbelievably happy ending of redeeming love, the Unknown Prince winning at last his unattainable Princess by the ardor of his passion.

"After I heard it, I knew I had to have it. To see how Puccini did it. It was his last opera, you know." He stared out the window. "Didn't you ever wonder what it would have been like if Puccini had lived just one month longer? Just long enough to finish it?"

"But *Turandot*," scoffed Guarnelli. "You could have gone to the library, the university, or bought it. You didn't need him to give it to you for your part in the film."

"Didn't I?" With the hint of a smile that closed him off again, the beggar shrugged. "You may be right."

"That whole sequence in Jerusalem wouldn't have worked without you," Guarnelli accused him.

"He paid me what I wanted. It was worth it to me."

A great irritation took hold of Guarnelli. He slapped his pen closed and slipped it into the pocket of his long vest. Then he stuffed the notebook into an outer pocket, thumbing the off button on his concealed tape recorder as he rose.

"Thank you for your time. I'll let you know how much of this material we use in the article so you can get a copy if you wish." His recitation sounded as much like formula as it was.

"It isn't necessary."

Guarnelli scuffed at the two dead cigarettes by the chair, finding them too much like maggots. "Is there anything you want to add?" he asked perfunctorily.

The beggar shook his head. His face had become a mask, an ugly mask from the vaults of a medieval cathedral. Guarnelli did not want to look at him any longer, for the deformities were suddenly frightening.

"Then I'll be leaving." He turned toward the door. Just as he was about to leave, he turned back. "You could have asked for more. He would have given it to you. He would have given you anything. He had to use you. You could have had anything you wanted. Do you understand that?"

"But I got what I wanted."

"An opera with a stupid fairy-tale ending. Not even complete. You are a fool." With an abrupt movement, Guarnelli left the hut. An unidentified anger raged in him as he stalked back across the tracks. Once he turned to look back and saw that the beggar was standing in the door watching him. At that, the professional in him took charge of his commercial soul and Guarnelli fumbled with his camera, thinking this might save his day, the shot of the beggar in the open door, a silhouette that should not be.

But by the time he had the camera ready the beggar had turned back into his hut, had closed the door, and was gone. Guarnelli cursed and continued across the tracks toward Rome.

He had watched Guarnelli depart with mixed feelings. But he had told the truth, that the reporter did not hear it was not his concern. He went to his pallet and picked up the score, setting it open at his feet as he began once more to sing and conduct. After a while it grew dark and he was forced to light his lantern and continue by its soft gold light.

At the end of the score many of the printed pages were missing and in their place were some fifty manuscript pages written in a wandering, shaky hand, a dying hand. The vocal line was plainly indicated although the text beneath was barely legible. The orchestration was sketched in, thematic lines, a few dominant chords, bass dissonance, no more.

42 With great care the beggar adjusted the light so that it fell brightly

on the page. He hummed experimentally the first few orchestral notes which began the hand-written pages, beginning to move his hands as the sound leaped in his mind. He added the harmony as it was needed, familiarity making his reading fluent.

Occasionally he sang.

The despair and rage in "La Mia Regal Danata!" he could sing only in part, as it was a bass aria. It was a pity, too, for no one else would ever sing it.

For Guarnelli had been wrong about the plot, although he remembered the opera he knew correctly, and those pathetically few pages that lived in the ruddy light were all that would ever prove him wrong.

The beggar thought of Guarnelli as he began the last scene.

The Unknown Prince, who had committed himself to love his cold Princess, his fire in ice, crying out in his love to her. . . . The crowd awaiting her command, eager brutality hidden beneath the formal pageantry. Now the Princess beckons to the Prince, pronouncing his name, and the Prince runs forward, up the stairs to the Imperial Throne to embrace her and claim the prize of her love. The entranced crowd repeats his soaring theme, rising upward with the Prince.

In triumph the Prince, Calaf, seizes her in his arms, exalting in the conquest of the unconquerable Turandot. Then he staggers back. And the crowd breaks off in a gasp. An exquisite dagger protrudes from his heart. As he falls on the stairs to die at her feet, he demands, "Why?" The victorious Princess Turandot repeats her refrain to death, the death she has promised him and he has desired from the first, the final answer to her three riddles.

The orchestral finale faded out after two spidery bars.

The beggar stared down at the page where the signature, "Puccini," now faded, was still visible, and the date, November, 1924.

For those few pages he had been beaten, had been nearly torn apart by a mob driven to near frenzy by the director's genius.

He sighed a little. Love and death, hope and despair, trust and betrayal. It was all there in the music, so much clearer than the noise outside filtering in from the ruin that was Rome.

With infinite tenderness he caressed the last page of the score.

Then, gently, he closed it.

about "The Fellini Beggar"

Late in November of 1924, Giacomo Puccini died of complications following an operation for cancer of the throat. Puccini was not young; he had been diabetic for more than twenty years. His last few letters indicated that he knew he did not have long to live. He left his last opera, *Turandot*, unfinished. Two years later, the work was premiered under Toscanini, and at its first performance, the opera was stopped at the place where Puccini had stopped. The rest of the opera, which was finished by Franco Alfano, was not performed that night.

Since then there have been many tantalizing questions about what was in the last manuscript pages (and reports indicate that there were anything from thirty to eighty-five pages for the end of the opera). The way the work stands now, it is, in terms of its musical structure, leading toward the end in this story, not the end that Alfano wrote.

I love Fellini films. You may argue that some or all of them are flawed. It may be, but that is not important. His ability to merge the real and unreal is his special gift, and it makes him something unique in films. (For example, does Giulietta really have very weird neighbors in *Juliet of the Spirits*, or do they only seem that way to her?)

It was my hope to write this story so that it had some of the same feeling as a Fellini film. You alone know if it does.

Of all my short fiction to date, this is my favorite.

Once was a place called Eden
  supposed to have existed around Lebanon.
Nobody knows for sure
  but that's what the experts think.
So you and me'll go off
  and laugh under the apple trees—
No use us spoiling
  their fun.

                                        Chelsea Quinn Yarbro